DOUBLE TAKE

HANK HAMMOND P.I. CASE #1

FEATURING LORI REED

J.P. DAVID

Also by J.P. David
Mind Game

DOUBLE TAKE

This is a book of fiction. Names, characters, places, and incidents either are the product of the author's imagination or are used fictitiously, and any resemblance to actual persons, living or dead, businesses, companies, events, or locales is entirely coincidental.

While the author has made every effort to provide accurate telephone numbers and Internet addresses at the time of publication, neither the publisher nor the author assumes any responsibility for errors, or for changes that occur after publication. Further, the publisher does not have any control over and does not assume any responsibility for author or third-party websites or their content.

CAVEAT

I have taken great pains to be certain that all descriptions of the cities, businesses, neighborhoods, and characters in **DOUBLE TAKE** are totally factual and absolutely accurate. I have done this by making up all of the cities, businesses, neighborhoods and characters.

For those subjects that are not totally of my imagination, I have endeavored to be meticulously accurate. There are, however, some exceptions. The most egregious of these has to do with pizza and a stun gun. You'll recognize it when you get to that point in the novel. I considered deleting this particular scene to ensure absolute authenticity, but my alter ego convinced me otherwise stating that it added a certain jauntiness to the passage. Come to think of it, any other inaccuracies that the reader may note are most certainly not the result of my ignorance, but further evidence of my alter ego convincing me that more jauntiness was in order.

J.P. David

ONE

"Hank, you've got a *very important message*." Lori spoke the words I'd learned to dread. Ever since I'd started sub-leasing my closet-sized office from Barry Green, lawyer extraordinaire, Lori has greeted me with these words—accompanied by a smile that reminds me of the line about the difference between people laughing with you and at you. The only problem is that with Lori, I'm not sure which it is. I'm hoping she's just teasing me, but the fact is that I don't much like being teased.

Lori is Green's office manager, and my arrangement with him is that she will take messages for me and do light typing. Up to now, my *very important messages* have consisted mostly of solicitations from MCI, AT&T and Sprint; various carpet cleaning companies; and a local firm that specializes in purifying drinking water and treating septic tanks—hopefully not in the same process.

I waved at her, shut the front door behind me and walked across the tiled floor toward her substantial U-shaped desk which strikes me as more of a command-post than a desk, what with its computer, monitor, laser printer, scanner, fax machine, typewriter, multi-line phone/answering machine, and microwave oven lined up efficiently within her reach. Today, something about Lori looked different, but I couldn't quite put my finger on it.

"Don't you want your very important message?" she said, her eyebrows arched.

"Sure," I said reluctantly, bracing for the punch-line.

1

"A guy named Armando called. Said it was about your murder investigation. Said he has the information you need."

I stopped in my tracks. "Armando? He called? How long ago?" The words exploded from my mouth. I took a deep breath and concentrated on calming myself down. No reason to appear anxious . . . or desperate.

"It's been about twenty minutes." She riffled through the stack of pink message papers until she found the only one with my name on it. "At exactly 11:18. See?" She handed me the note with a flourish.

I read her perfect penmanship beneath the *While You Were Out* heading. Sure enough, Armando had gotten back to me much faster than I'd anticipated. Actually, I hadn't thought that he'd get back to me at all. "What's his phone number?" I asked.

Lori flashed that familiar smirk. "You're the detective, you tell me."

That was what had been different about Lori. She hadn't been smirking when she'd told me about my very important message. Now she looked more like the Lori I'd come to know during the past two months. She folded her hands neatly in the precise center of her aggravatingly well-organized desk and replaced her smirk with a look of interest. "Well. Are you going to tell me about it?" she asked.

"About what?"

"The case. You finally have a case. Isn't that exciting? And it's a murder case at that. This is a very big deal, Hank. When did it happen? Who's the victim? Who's the killer? Who hired you? Who's Armando?" She rattled off the questions like a machine-gunner . . . or a skilled touch-typist.

"Yes, I have a case," I said matter-of-factly. "The details are confidential at this point. All I can tell you is that there is a victim and there is a killer—"

She rolled her eyes ceiling-ward. "Well, *duh*,"

I inhaled deeply, tucked my thumbs into the waistband of my Dockers and pulled them up over where my paunch had been just a moment earlier, then I exhaled uncomfortably. I didn't want to tell Lori any details of the case—not because I didn't trust her, but because I didn't actually know any details of the case. The truth was that I didn't even know if there was a case, let alone any details. But one thing I did know was that I'd do just about anything to avoid that smirk of hers. "Sorry Lori, it's confidential. I'd like to tell you, but this is like an attorney-client privilege sort of thing. I'm sure you understand. After all, Green has to keep some of what he does confidential too."

"Not with me, he doesn't," she snapped. "In addition to being his office manager, I'm his confidential secretary. I suppose that in a sense I'm yours too, now that you finally have something that requires some secretarying. Now, Hank, *please* tell me about this murder case. I'm dying to know."

I paused for a moment, stalling as I thought up a new excuse. "That's just it Lori. You could die if you knew what I know. You're better off this way. You've got to trust me."

She slumped in her chair like a kid who had just been told to finish her lima beans before she could be excused from the table. "But—"

"It's for your own good," I said paternally, turned and walked into my office, closing the door behind me. I could hear a muttered "It's for your own good, my ass!" emanating from behind my door, followed by "What a chauvinist!"

"Hey, I was shot at this morning," I protested through the door.

"Sure Hank, and I was piloting the space shuttle."

My name is Hank Hammond and up until two months ago I was the security manager for the Weisbach-Lander's department store here in Kingston Beach, just north of San Diego. I started working there as a part-time stocker about fifteen years ago, in 1974, when I was going to junior college. I figured I'd work there until I got my AA, then I'd quit and go find a real job. It didn't quite work out that way. After about a year as a stocker, the personnel department offered me a full-time job in security. I was kind of bored in school—really only being there for football, and I hadn't made the team through no fault of my own—so I accepted the job and dropped my classes. Who needs to know about Shakespeare and Freud and all those other dead guys anyway? Or so I thought when I was nineteen. Besides, I'd kind of fantasized about being involved in investigatory work ever since I was ten and I watched Paul

Drake tracking down clues for Perry Mason every Thursday night. I'm not actually sure what qualified me to become one of Weisbach-Lander's security operatives, but I always suspected it had something to do with being six four and looking more than just a little rough around the edges.

I ended up making a career at W-L's, as everybody calls it, and I must have caught at least a thousand teen-aged girls shoplifting Monét charms, and probably a million guys stealing Levi's. Must've been a couple hundred employees I caught with their hands in the cookie jar . . . a twenty-dollar bill here, a customer's credit card number there. I apprehended Mrs. Kuebler, the attention-starved wife of the president of a local bank, at least fifteen times. She was a classic kleptomaniac and I personally thought she ought to be locked up until she could learn to control herself. Instead, her husband always came to her rescue. He finally just wrote a big check and gave it to Mr. Eaton, our nervous Nelly of a store manager, and told him to put it toward everything she shoplifted during the next five years. That was when I really became disgusted with my department store security work—the day Mr. Eaton told me not to bother with apprehending Mrs. Kuebler anymore . . . and Eaton picked up his new Lincoln Town Car.

Along the way, I'd managed to juggle my work schedule with night school and I'd earned a BA from San Diego State. I'd assumed that the degree would help my career, but I found that the corporate personnel department had long ago stereotyped me as a big, dumb jock and the corporate security department figured that only an egghead would waste time earning a degree.

Then, about three months ago I received my ticket out of W-L's. We had a special phone number at the store for employees to use when they wanted to leave an anonymous tip about a dishonest co-worker. Every day I'd go into my office and retrieve the messages and every day some wise guy would've left a message saying that Mr. Eaton had been spotted stuffing lacy lingerie into his pants. *Is it any wonder that I'd become sick-and-tired of my job?* Well, three months ago I received this message about some guys down in shipping who were sending cocaine out of our store via American Parcel Delivery. I did about twenty minutes worth of snooping around and then called APD with my findings. They conducted some sort of paper-trail investigation while I hid on the shipping dock inside a big corrugated carton, watching through peepholes at identical-twin-brothers-from-hell Ray and Roy Norville. It didn't surprise me in the least that the Norvilles were dirty, I'd suspected as much from the very first moment I'd laid eyes on them. In fact, I remember quite distinctly that I'd demanded they be fired on the day they'd first reported to work. But personnel was so gun shy about wrongful termination lawsuits that they weren't about to let a couple of dirtbags go just because I didn't like their looks. So the twins continued working at W-L's and they'd managed to set up a drug trafficking operation right on our very own shipping dock. Fortunately, with the help of the anonymous phone call, the investigators from APD, and my own surveillance work, we'd busted what turned out to be the biggest drug ring in Kingston Beach's history.

The bust up of drug traffickers made the front page of our local paper, complete with a picture of me standing next to all these corrugated cartons that were supposedly filled with cocaine but were actually just empty props made up for the photo. The best thing that happened though, was that I received a reward of ten thousand dollars from the police department as part of their *Nope On Dope* campaign. The Chief of Police could barely contain his contempt for a mere "security guard" as he handed me the check. I chalked it up to professional jealousy.

At first I didn't know what I'd do with all that money. I thought about putting a down payment on a condo, or buying a surround-sound stereo, or a big-screen TV. But the moment I figured out what to do with the money came about a week later when I was flopped out on the floor of my apartment watching a rerun of *Magnum PI*. Tom Selleck was running all over Hawaii trying to figure out who had killed the father of this incredibly gorgeous beauty contestant. It was so obvious to me who had killed her dad, but Magnum kept going about it all wrong. Finally I just yelled out to the TV that I ought to be doing the investigation instead of Tom Selleck. That was when it hit me—I should follow my childhood dream and become a PI.

The next day I handed my resignation to Mr. Eaton and deposited seven thousand dollars (I'd spent almost a third of my bonus on a very hot five hundred horsepower engine for my Vette which exploded within ten minutes after I fired it up and is now back in the shop awaiting parts), into a new account I established under the name of Hank Hammond Private Investigations.

That's how I got hooked up with Lori. I knew I'd have to market my services and I'd developed two parts to my marketing plan—one was to run some ads in the newspaper, touting myself as the man who'd busted an international drug ring; the other was to hook up with a lawyer. In business, they call it a strategic alliance. I called around to a couple dozen attorney's offices asking if they'd sublet office space in exchange for a discount on my investigative services. The only moderately receptive voice I encountered belonged to Lori Reed at the Law Offices of Barry Green. She called me back the next day with the terms of Green's offer—office space, message taking, and light typing for five hundred bucks a month, plus my portion of the phone bill, electricity, etc., etc. I accepted it with visions of becoming Paul Drake to his Perry Mason, not realizing that Green was a former CPA who'd only recently become a tax attorney.

That was two months ago, and up to today I haven't had one case . . . until this morning when I happened to be stopped in the world's tiniest rental car at the corner of Ocean and Swann.

TWO

I was waiting for the light to change—listening to some radio-shrink dispensing more bromides than a pharmacist—when I noticed the car ahead of me, one lane over. It was a faded green Fiat station wagon, at least I think it was green. I'm one of the twenty percent of the male population who can't see colors the way others do. It's not that I can't see colors—I can. It's just that I don't see them the way God and Ralph Lauren intended. I mistake blues for purples, browns for greens, and vice versa. It's a trait passed on by women and inherited by men, which Lori says goes a long way toward explaining why so many of us men dress with such questionable taste. I'm not certain if she includes me in that category—I've carefully written the color of each article of my clothing on pieces of duct tape and then stuck them inside my clothes—but I have the sneaking suspicion that she does.

What caught my attention about the station wagon wasn't its color, it was actually three things: First was the fact that it was a Fiat—most people around here wouldn't be caught dead in anything other than Japanese or German. Second was that the Fiat was actually running—and they aren't really known for being the most reliable cars in the world, hence all the tired old "Fix It Again Tony" jokes. Third was that when the light turned green, the car peeled away like a top-fuel dragster—and old Fiat station wagons are usually clogging up the roads like little Winnebagos.

In spite of accelerating away from Swann like Neil Armstrong to the moon, the Fiat's driver immediately became stuck behind some snow-birds in a slow-moving Chrysler. The Fiat rode on the LeBaron's tail for about a block, listing anxiously to the left then the right, its tenor horn blasting continuously. Just as I was about to pass the Fiat, the driver took a wild swing into my lane. I wrenched my steering wheel to the left and slammed on my brakes. The nose of my rented Geo Metro barely missed slamming into the Fiat as my tires streaked about a year's worth of tread onto the roadway and my safety belts cinched up around my forward floating torso. The latest issue of *Sports Illustrated* and my gym bag flew off the passenger's seat and slammed into the dashboard. The red "oil" light flashed momentarily on the instrument panel, punctuating the exact moment that my teeth bit through my lower lip.

Unlike far too many of this city's fine citizens, I didn't react by pulling alongside the Fiat, pointing a gun at the offending driver and threatening him . . . or worse. I couldn't—I don't actually own a gun. Not because I don't want to, but because Uncle Sam doesn't want me to. Technically, he doesn't want Hank Hamm*and*, an ex con with a social security number just one digit away from mine, to have a gun. But the government's computer can't figure out who is who, despite my many letters and phone calls of complaint. As a result, I'm probably the only PI in the world who is forbidden by law to carry a gun.

I followed the Fiat driver—curious to see what kind of a jerk he was, and definitely to give him a piece of my mind once I caught up to him. He turned right onto a side street, then left, then right again, driving deeper and deeper into the industrial section of town. As he passed an old brick factory building, he suddenly slammed on his brakes and swerved against the curb. I didn't have time to react and went wobbling by on the one-way street at about fifty miles-per-hour. At the next intersection, I turned right and circled around the block to where the Fiat had parked.

By the time I'd reached a point where I could see the Fiat again, a black Suburban 4X4 had pulled up alongside it, partially blocking the road. The driver of the Fiat hopped out of his car and opened its tailgate.

The driver of the Suburban climbed down out of his truck and did likewise. I pulled over to the side of the road and watched. The two men moved nervously and awkwardly, and weren't saying a word, exactly like shoplifters did at W-L's as they stuffed their bags full of goodies and headed for the nearest exit. Something was going down, I could feel it, and the investigator in me needed to know about it. I backed the Metro around the corner and parked it where it couldn't be spotted. I grabbed my gym bag from the floorboard, unzipped it, and rooted through the contents—the essentials were all there, including a ball-point pen, a small spiral-bound pad, a tiny camera, a cell phone (service disconnected), a lock-picking gun, a stun gun, a miniature 8X telescope, and a myriad of other toys I'd recently bought from a surveillance paraphernalia catalogue. I'd bought a lot of keen stuff from it as soon as I'd set up shop as a PI, that's one of the many reasons why I was running a little low on cash (and why the phone company had disconnected my cell phone).

Gym bag in hand, I slunk toward a Dumpster, keeping myself pressed up against the factory wall and crouching low—invisibility techniques I'd mastered among garment racks and shelving units in my department store days. Once I reached the Dumpster, I climbed up the metal ladder and peered over the stinking trash as the two men removed a large wooden crate from the car and placed it into the truck. Judging from the way the men struggled with the crate, I figured that it must have weighed a least a hundred pounds . . . probably more. Probably just about the weight of a dead body, I thought—and the crate was exactly big enough to hold one.

I unzipped my gym bag and raised the monocular to my eye—juggling it, the pen and spiral pad as I scribbled down the Fiat's license number—unfortunately, I couldn't quite see the one on the Suburban. Then I aimed the scope first at the driver of the Fiat and then at the man who'd arrived in the Suburban. The first man wore a pair of khakis and a white polo shirt. He was very tan and his blond hair was cut short and neat, reminding me of the countless young trainees who were always kissing up to Mr. Eaton. He looked to be just under six feet tall, and probably wore a size forty-two coat. The second man, twice the young man's age, was tall and rail-thin, had long gray-streaked hair pulled into a pony-tail, wore faded jeans and a cowboy shirt—don't ask me for the colors.

I only needed to move myself about six feet to the left to be able to get a clear view of the Suburban's license plate. I stuffed the telescope into the pocket of my Dockers, put my pen and pad in my mouth, pushed the handles of my gym bag up my wrist and onto my shoulder, and grabbed the top of the Dumpster. Then I carefully stepped off of the ladder and slid the toes of my Reeboks into a horizontal groove that encompassed the Dumpster. I eased my body to the left in cautious micro-steps until I could see the truck's plate, but I still couldn't make out the numbers. I let go of the top of the Dumpster with my right hand, still holding fast with my left, and reached down to my pocket for the telescope. *SLAM!* My left foot slipped out of the groove and crashed into the side of the Dumpster. The moment my foot slipped, I reached my right hand up and grabbed the rim of the Dumpster. As I caught my balance, I dropped my telescope and it clanged and banged its way to the ground.

In one remarkably efficient move, the man with the pony-tail spun around, reached beneath his pant cuff, pulled out a revolver, and aimed it directly at the Dumpster. I snapped my head down out of view. Three shots rang out and I heard the bullets *thwang* through the trash bin's walls. I scanned the surface to my right—one bullet hole was eighteen inches from my hip, another about five feet away. I heard a blood-curdling scream and looked up just in time to see an alley cat jumping out of the Dumpster. Two more shots rang out, followed by metallic pings and then a pair of voices.

"Put it away Al. It's just a cat."

"I hate cats."

"Put the gun away before someone sees you."

"Like who, another cat? Lemme at it!"

"I'm serious man. We've got to get out of here."

I raised my head up slowly and peered over the top of the Dumpster. The man with the pony-tail was returning the gun to his ankle-holster as the young man slammed the back of the Suburban shut. They hopped into the truck, fired up the engine, and chirped off about four feet of rubber on the asphalt as they accelerated away.

As I jumped down from my perch, I looked up at the Dumpster's holes. This time I saw where the third bullet had gone . . . about two inches below where my crotch had been. I made a mental note to start going to church again, ran back to my rental, jumped in, flipped the ignition key and waited for the tiny three-banger to start. At the count of ten the engine caught, sounding for all the world like a demonic popcorn popper. I eased the shifter into gear, taking off in vain after the Suburban that had already long since disappeared.

After fifteen pointless minutes of driving, I decided to do what any decent, law-abiding citizen would do. I pulled over to the nearest pay phone and reported what I'd seen. The woman on the phone displayed absolutely no interest in what I had to say, responding—with a very snide tone to her voice—that if it were a crime to carry a wooden crate in a vehicle, then the police department would be spending all of its time busting customers at The Home Depot. She also must have been a cat hater, because she didn't seem at all concerned that someone had shot at one. And she didn't believe for one minute that anyone had shot at me. The only moderately positive response I received was when she agreed to take down the Fiat's license number, saying that the police would tend to the vehicle if-and-when it became classified as abandoned. *Click*.

The woman's attitude really steamed me. I'd just seen a crime going down—I'd almost had my privates blown off for god's sake—and she wouldn't even relay what I'd told her to the cops at the nearest donut shop. Well, I'd show them! I squeezed back into the rental, pulled away from the curb, whipped the steering wheel around, and headed back to the Fiat for a look-see. After all, I didn't have anything particularly pressing on my agenda at the moment—in fact my entire calendar was distressingly empty.

What I wanted to discover was anything that would tell me about the Fiat's driver and former contents. What I actually saw was just an old car. I peeked through the windows. There were no clues on the cracked vinyl seats; nothing of interest resting on top of the dashboard, center console, or lying on the flat part behind the back seat. Nothing clipped to the sun visors. No decals on the windows or stickers on the bumpers. The doors were locked, as was the tailgate. I was just about to fold myself back into the Metro and drive off, when a light bulb came on over my head. I circled back and opened the Fiat's hood. *Jackpot!* Stuck right on top of the air cleaner was a maintenance sticker from a shop called Tony's Imported Car Service—maybe the old "fix it again Tony" joke about Fiats wasn't so tired after all.

That's where Armando came in. At the very instant that the police had hung up on me, I'd decided to show them a thing or two about how to conduct an investigation—after all I am a private investigator and I have the business cards to prove it. Maybe I could find out what these two guys were up to. Maybe it'd turn out to be a big case like the one I'd cracked back at W-L's. Maybe I could get a lot of publicity out of solving a major crime that the police department had ignored. That would do wonders for my business.

I drove to Tony's and met briefly with Armando, a mechanic with long, stringy black hair who looked all of eighteen years old and a hundred pounds . . . with much of his weight coming from an even coat of 10-30, visible on nearly every square inch of his skin. He told me that all their customer records were confidential. I gave him my tough-guy look, told him I was a PI and handed him my card.

"Wow, just like Barnaby Jones?" he asked, rubbing more grease across his chin as he scratched it.

"More like Paul Drake."

"Who?"

Armando was obviously way too young. "Like Magnum, only better lookin'" I said, sucking in my stomach.

He glanced back at the pink Metro I'd just pulled up in. I'd thought it was beige when I'd picked it up at the discount rental lot and had been properly mortified when Lori pointed out its true color.

"If you're like Magnum, how come you don't got a Ferrari?" Armando asked sarcastically.

"The Vette's in the shop," I said. He didn't seem the slightest bit impressed so I decided to use another approach. I told him about the big drug bust I'd just completed, manufacturing a few details to add a more cinematic quality to the story—a gun fight, a car chase, and a beautiful woman saved in just the nick of time. Well, it could have happened that way.

Armando's eyes opened big as hub caps. "Cool. This Fiat you're askin' about. Is it part of another big drug case?"

Then I went a little too far in my attempt to impress him. Don't ask me why, but I just found myself getting carried away about the possible contents of the crate. "Possible murder case," I said. At least I think I said "possible." Actually, I know I didn't say "possible."

Armando lowered his voice. "Maybe I can help you out, but I really can't talk now. I've got a Alfa Romeo over there I gotta fix." He pointed over to a sick looking coupe with its hood open like a seal's mouth at feeding time. "I gotta finish it 'fore Tony comes back and gets on my case. He'll be back any minute."

"Maybe I should be talking to him."

Armando shook his head so fast that his hair whipped at his neck. "No way. He wouldn't tell you nothin'. He's a real by-the-book kind of guy. You'd just be wastin' your time. Fact is, he'd probably kill me if he knew I was talkin' to you about one of his customers."

"In my business, kill is a very strong word," I reprimanded. "You shouldn't use it unless you mean it."

"I'm not kiddin' you. You better get out of here before he comes back, or I won't be able to tell you nothin'." Armando looked at my card, already covered with his Pennzoiled thumb prints. "I can reach you at this number?"

I continued playing my role. "I'm usually out on assignment. You know, stake-outs and the like. But one of my people will take your message and I can get back to you."

"Okay man. Maybe I'll talk to you later." He turned around to resume his work on the Alfa and I turned around and exhaled, letting my stomach return to its natural state.

"Barnaby Jones," I said to myself as I walked back to my micro-car. "Give me a break."

Now, sitting at my desk with the door to my office closed, I picked up the phone and called information to get the number for Tony's Imported Car Service. For an extra twenty-five cents, I was connected without even having to dial the number. On about the tenth ring, a male voice I recognized as Armando's answered.

"This is Hammond," I said. "You called me."

There was silence on the other end of the line.

"Armando, are you there?"

"Right, yeah, I'm here. It's hard to talk right now, Tony's just outside the door. But I got what you need."

"Okay, shoot." I uncapped a stick pen and pressed the ball tip against a note pad, ready to write.

"Shoot what?"

I rolled my eyes. "Tell me who owns the Fiat and where he lives."

"Can't tell you right now. Meet me on my lunch hour, 'cross the street from the shop.

"Why can't you just tell me the man's name and address over the phone?"

"'Cause I don't know it."

I threw my pen in the air and watched as it dropped to the linoleum and rolled under my desk. "I thought you told me you had the information I need."

"I do. I pulled his service file out of the file cabinet, stuffed it into my shirt, then walked out to my car and stuck it under the seat. I haven't even looked at it yet. Tony finds out I done this, he's gonna fire me for sure."

"Okay, I'll meet you."

"And bring some money."

I thought about my dwindling checking account. Between the office rent, my share of the utilities, phone hook-up, far too many goodies from the detective catalogue, plus my expenses just for living, I needed money to be coming in, not going out. "How much?" I asked through clenched teeth.

"A thousand bucks."

I held the receiver at arm's length and stared at it like it was a foreign object. "I'll give you a hundred," I finally said once my blood pressure had dropped.

"Cash money, no checks," Armando said.

"You don't trust me?"

"I don't trust nobody."

"All right, cash it is," I said as I mentally mapped my way from my office to an ATM and then to Tony's Imported Car Service.

"And make it five hundred or I won't show," Armando whispered.

I could hear a second voice over the line and figured that Tony must have entered the room. "Is that Tony?"

"Yes," Armando said, still whispering.

"Let me talk to him."

Armando suddenly found his voice: "What for?"

"I'm going to tell him what's under the seat of your car." I paused while Armando thought that one over. "Unless you agree to fifty dollars."

"You said a hundred a minute ago."

"That was before you started to piss me off."

"Give me a hundred."

"Fifty."

"I dunno."

"Here's your choice: We meet and I give you fifty bucks to see the file or I tell Tony you stole a customer's file. What'll it be?"

Silence on the other end of the line.

"Twenty-five bucks," I said. "In two more seconds it'll be twenty."

"Make it fifty," he whispered.

"Forty, or nothing. Okay?"

I waited while Armando said nothing. Finally he mouthed a weak "in ten minutes" and hung up the phone.

THREE

Tony's is on the other side of town from my office. In order to make it on time, I had to get a move on. I sprinted out my doorway and past Lori. She looked up from her command post with a puzzled expression on her face.

"I wish you'd tell me what's going on," she declared. Lori isn't the type who likes being out of the loop, so I decided to create one.

"Confidential documents," I said as I pulled open the front door. "My informant just got hold of several and I need to examine them quick before a certain someone finds out he has them." I slammed the door shut behind me, scrunched into the Metro and wobbled toward the closest ATM. Two minutes after inputting my PIN, I was heading toward my rendezvous with the mechanic—two, fresh twenty-dollar bills stuffed into the front pocket of my Dockers.

I rolled to a stop across the street from Tony's. The digital clock on the Metro's dash displayed that it was twelve thirty-five. My watch disagreed, putting the time at twelve twenty-eight. Either way, I was late in meeting Armando. He'd been pretty emphatic about my meeting him across the street from his work, so I sat in the pink-mobile and waited for twenty minutes. I figured that I'd missed him and I made a mental note to myself to always be in time for clandestine meetings.

Just as I fired up the Metro, a purple metal flake Honda Civic—with wheels and tires so low and wide that they made the car look like a gigantic skateboard—pulled up in front of me. As I cringed at what had been done to a perfectly good car, the driver hopped out, ran back to the Metro, opened the passenger's door and jumped in. Mental note number two: In the future, always keep my doors locked.

"Here it is," Armando said, unzipping his Budweiser jacket halfway and exposing a manila folder. "You got my money?" His breath reeked of beer and his skin smelled like stale Jade East.

I squirmed around in my seat as I extracted the bills. I handed them to him in a wad. He counted them, slowly and deliberately, before passing the file to me.

I paged through the work orders and invoices. The Fiat had been maintained by Tony's for several years. Owned by a Walter Tompkins. I jotted down the phone number and his address in the outrageously expensive suburb of La Camino.

"Come on, I don't have all day," Armando growled.

I continued thumbing through the contents. "What do you know about Tompkins?" I asked.

"He's old." Armando reached for the file and tried to tug it away from me.

I held it tight. "That's all you know about him, that he's old?"

The mechanic stuck out his lower lip and blew air between it and his upper one. I expected his breath to go right up his nostrils and then shoot out his mouth again in a kind of perpetual motion. Fortunately, I was wrong. "You want to know what he looks like?" he asked.

"For starters."

"He's not real tall, maybe five-four. Stoop shouldered. Kind of skinny. White hair, what's left of it anyway. But he's a feisty old bugger." Armando yanked on the folder again.

I tightened my grip and described the two men I'd seen earlier in the day. "You ever see anybody fitting those descriptions with Tompkins?"

"Nope." Another tug.

"You know what Tompkins does for a living?"

"Nope." Another harder tug.

"You got anything else you can tell me about him?"

"Nope." The hardest tug of all.

I quickly released the folder. Armando and the file slammed against the passenger's door panel. He straightened himself up, stuffed the file back into his jacket and unlatched the door. I turned the ignition key at the exact moment he hopped out of the car. He didn't close the door and when I backed up it swung fully open. I shifted into first and accelerated away as fast as the puny little car would go, expecting the door to slam itself shut. It didn't. A half-block away, I pulled to the curb, leaned across the minuscule interior, pulled the door closed, and began driving the ten miles to the La Camino district, home of the rich and pompous.

I couldn't miss Walter Tompkins's house, it was perched regally atop a knoll at the end of a palm-lined cul-de-sac. All of the homes on the street were grand and impressive, but Tompkins's was the one that would catch everybody's attention first. The lawn that sloped up from the sidewalk was perfectly manicured—not so much as one weed had dared to poke through the magnificent green carpet or climb into the colorful flower beds. Weeds, like discarded beer cans and Big Gulp cups, were obviously much more welcome in my neighborhood than in La Camino.

The circular driveway was bordered by bright, beautiful flowers—don't ask me what kind, I don't know. The two-story house appeared to be constructed of marble. There were ornate leaded-glass windows across the front, framed by slate blue shutters set behind ornate white columns. The massive front door was a deep red. If you're wondering how I can be so sure about these colors, I'll let you in on a little secret—sometimes I have to use logic. To my eyes, the shutters could be either blue or purple, so I have to ask myself what the chances are that someone would want purple shutters. Answer: zero chance. Ergo, the shutters are blue.

I parked on the street, directly in front of Tompkins's house and directly underneath a very large tree. If I were in my Vette, I'd never park under a tree for fear it would be attacked by a flock of birds with a bad case of the runs. With the Metro, I'd actually prefer a coat of bird crap to the embarrassingly pink paint.

I noted that Tompkins's driveway was empty, and wondered if he would be home. Only one way to find out, I thought as I climbed out of the bassinet-mobile and trudged up to the red door.

The doorbell rang in the classic manner that makes you want to say "Avon calling" as soon as you hear it. Shortly after the ring, the door opened and an athletic looking but very shapely woman in her twenties stared at me with the kind of big eyes usually found on bad paintings of waifs. She wore a nurse's uniform that she must have re-hemmed herself because the skirt wasn't much longer than a wash cloth. I could barely stop myself from eyeing her legs. From the expression on her face, I don't think she minded my reaction in the slightest.

"May I help you?" she said with a whispery voice that drew me closer to her like dirt to a vacuum cleaner.

I sucked in my gut. "I'm here to see Walter Tompkins." I found myself deliberately deepening my voice and immediately becoming embarrassed by my teenager-like posturing, but I certainly didn't stop.

"Is he expecting you?" she purred.

"I'm here about his car."

Her head cocked to the left. "You found it?"

I wanted to be the one to ask the questions, not her. "Is it missing?" I asked.

She gave me a disapproving look. "Wait right here." She pirouetted and whisked away from me with a mesmerizing wiggle. I've seen enough nature shows on *Wild Kingdom* to know that certain specific behaviors of one sex of a species are uncontrollably tantalizing to the opposite sex of the same species. I don't profess to understand why a female lizard finds the bloated throat of a male lizard to be exciting, and I don't think I'll ever know what could possibly be sexy about a rhinoceros in heat. I suppose that if some creature from another planet were observing me at this very moment, watching this woman's swaying hips and shapely legs, the creature wouldn't understand my fascination either.

I waited for her to reappear, disappointed when a small, hunched-over man with pale, age-speckled skin peeking through his wispy white hair hobbled to the door instead.

"You found what I'm looking for?" he said in a loud, scratchy voice. He leaned up to look at me through glasses thick as ice.

"I came to ask you some questions—"

"Why should you be asking me anything?" he snapped.

A good question, but I wasn't in an answering mood—especially when I didn't have any good answers for him.

"I asked if you found what I am looking for," the old man repeated.

"That depends."

His eyes scanned up and down my body, finally locking in on my face. "You some kind of charlatan?"

I started to laugh, but the old man's expression told me that he wasn't kidding. "No sir," I said with as respectful a tone as I could muster.

"'No sir' you didn't find what I'm looking for, or 'no sir' you're not a charlatan?"

"No sir, I'm not a charlatan."

"So you're not trying to get your hands in my wallet?"

"No sir—"

"Because I'll have none of that. Everything I've got, I earned. You can't just march up here and try to take it from me.

'I don't have any intention—"

"Just because I'm old doesn't mean that I'm some kind of fool. The brain doesn't cease to function the moment a body hits eighty, so if you've got it in your head that you can waltz up to my house with some cock-and-bull story so you can fleece me, you can just turn yourself around and prance back to that little gumdrop of a car you drove up here in."

"I—"

"If you really know where my grandson is, I need some tangible proof. Give me some facts to prove you're on the up-and-up. If not, then kindly escort yourself away from here."

"I never said anything about your grandson, sir. I came to talk to you about your car."

"My car?" He steadied himself on the door frame. "Describe it."

"A green Fiat wagon."

"False." He pointed up at my face with a gnarled finger. "Now *git!* You go back to wherever you came from and don't ever bother me again." He dropped down into his hunched-over position, slowly turned his back on me and shuffled away as he muttered to himself. He forgot to close the door.

I yelled after him. "You're telling me that you don't own a Fiat wagon with the license number 2NTV 266?"

He turned and raised his head. "I didn't say that, young man. What I said was that I don't own a green one. It's brown." He stared intently at me, moving his jaw back and forth. "Do I know you?" he asked as he stepped toward me and squinted through his lenses.

"I really—"

"Of course," he interrupted, a wave of recognition crossing his face. "You just wait right there on the porch. Don't go anywhere. Don't return to your gumdrop and don't follow me into my house. Just do as you're told." He swung the door shut so hard that the brass knocker slapped itself.

After ten minutes of waiting, I grew impatient. Just as I reached for the doorbell, the door opened just a crack. I heard the rustling of paper and then the door opened fully.

"Come on in Mr. Hammond," the old man said warmly. "Let's you and me get ourselves comfortable. You just come on in through the foyer and have a seat in the library. Any seat you want, nothing is too good for you. The green wing-back is the most comfortable, why don't you take it? I'll sit on the sofa. Come along."

Walter Tompkins motioned me into his mansion with an exaggeratedly gracious sweep of his right hand. The foyer was paneled in dark mahogany, the floor covered with marble and topped with an ornate oriental rug. In the center of the ceiling was a crystal chandelier the size of a disco-ball. If the chandelier hadn't been turned on, the foyer would've been pitch black the moment I closed the front door. The old man reached across me to lock the door, turned, and then led me into the library. It looked more like the lobby of an old fancy hotel than anything I'd ever seen in a house. A huge cobble-stone fireplace, flanked by built-in bookcases that were crammed with leather-bound volumes, anchored the center of the wall opposite the entry. A leaded-glass window faced the street, the beveled edges refracting the sunlight like a prism. Oil paintings of the countryside, ocean scenes, and mountain peaks covered the remaining walls. The furniture was old, expensive, and in impeccable condition. I sat in the wing-back chair as requested. Walter Tompkins sat on a twelve-foot long sofa, close up at the end next to me. He seemed even smaller as he sank into the deep cushion, reminding me of a little boy on a church pew—all that was needed to complete the picture was for him to begin swinging his feet back and forth.

"Now then," he said, leaning toward me with his elbow propping himself up on the armrest. "How are things over at Weisbach-Lander's?"

His question made me wonder which of us was the private detective. In under fifteen minutes, old Walter Tompkins knew far more about me than I did about him. "I'm sorry," I said. "I didn't think I'd mentioned anything about W-L's to you. Or my name for that matter."

He retrieved a newspaper clipping from his pocket and examined it through the lower portion of his eyeglasses, moving his arms back and forth until he could focus. "Didn't need to. Recognized you from the picture in this newspaper article. My wife Nettie, God rest her soul, worked as a saleswoman at Weisbach-Lander's in Kingston Beach for half her life. That's where we met, when she sold me this watch." He twisted his left wrist and aimed the watch face toward me.

"Nice," I said as I noted diamonds where my watch had black dots.

"Nice is what a puppy is. This is damned elegant."

"The damnedest," I said.

Walter smiled approvingly. "Nettie loved Weisbach-Lander's, it was just like a second family to her. That's why she didn't quit when she married me. Lord knows we didn't need the money. Now, Nettie wasn't much of a reader but she used to love it when I'd clip out any articles from the newspaper about her store." Walter stared up at the ceiling. "Remember when you had that water pipe burst on the second floor back in nineteen-and-fifty-eight?"

I sat with a blank look on my face.

"Of course not. How foolish of me. You were probably still in your short-pants back then. Well, Nettie was mighty upset that she was off work on that day and missed out on all the commotion. Nettie didn't like to be left out of anything. The next day, I saw an article in the paper all about the water soaking through hundreds of thousands of dollars worth of designer dresses. I cut the article out and gave it to her. She really appreciated it and I've been clipping out articles about Weisbach-Lander's ever since." He tapped the newspaper. "When I saw this one, I snipped it and saved it out of habit. Nettie's passed on, did I mention that?"

"Yes sir, you did."

He dropped his head and puckered his lips, then took a deep breath and continued. "When you showed up at the door, I knew I'd seen you someplace before. It just took a minute or so for it to register." He held up the clipping for me to see. There was my picture beneath the headline about the narcotics ring.

Mental note number three: Publicity photographs can be detrimental to undercover work.

Walter Tompkins seemed to be genuinely pleased to have someone to visit with, especially someone who'd been part of Nettie's "second family." As he talked, I could see him warming up every time he mentioned his wife. I pretended to remember her, even though I didn't have the vaguest idea who she was. That's the problem with security work—you focus all your attention on the bad apples, and miss out on knowing the good people. After a good thirty or forty minutes of listening to the old man, I knew quite a bit about Nettie and absolutely nothing about the Fiat wagon. I was about to shift the conversation over to the car when Walter—he insisted that I stop calling him Mr. Tompkins . . . made him feel too old—asked me about my work. The moment I told him that I'd become a private investigator, his eyes lit up, he clasped his hands together into a bony ball, and he leaned forward and whispered.

"This is my lucky day," he said. "I've got this problem and I haven't known what to do about it. Now it's all crystal clear. Do you believe in fate, young man?"

I nodded, although I'd just as soon put my trust in the Psychic Hot-Line.

"Well, so do I. And fate is what brought you and me together at this precise moment of time. I know it. I can feel it." He pushed himself up from the sofa and walked across the room toward the foyer. "You wait here a minute, I'll be right back."

While I waited, I walked over to a bookcase that held several wooden-framed photographs. There was one of a very young man and an equally young woman standing next to an antique car, of course the car had been new when the picture was taken. The man had one foot on the ground and the other on the car's running board. The woman stood next to him, her hands holding a bouquet of flowers. The two looked straight into the camera, eyes filled with happiness. The man was a young, vibrant version of Walter Tompkins; the woman had to be Nettie. The photo jogged my memory and now I could place her at W-L's. But whenever I'd seen her at the store, I'd just assumed that she'd always been elderly. I suppose people may begin reacting to me that same way . . . sooner than I'd like to think.

Walter's voice jolted me out of my thoughts. "Here, I brought you something to study up on."

I turned around and he handed me a leather covered box, about the size of a good dictionary. I snapped the brass latch and began opening it.

"Not now," Walter reprimanded. "Open it after you've left . . . after you've started on your case."

"My case?"

"I want to hire you. My grandson Richard is missing and up to now I haven't had the slightest idea what to do about it."

"Did you call the police?" I asked as I relatched the box and set it on the coffee table.

Walter steadied himself by holding onto the side of my wing-back chair as he shook his head. "Don't want them involved. Besides, what can they do about it? Richard is of age. If he wants to go off gallivanting all over the country-side, there's nothing the police can do to prevent it."

"How long has Richard been missing?"

"Three days. He borrowed my wagon on Friday and I thought he would be returning it to me the next day, but he never showed up."

"Has he called you?"

"No, so far I haven't heard so much as a peep from him."

"Has he done this before?"

Walter walked over to his spot on the sofa, sat down, took a deep breath, and rested for a few moments. Then he looked up at me and continued. "You have to understand. Richard isn't really a bad boy, but he had this habit of getting himself into trouble every now and again— back when he was young. He just didn't have the judgment to say no when he should have. I blame the hooligans he used to associate with for leading him into trouble."

"What kind of trouble?"

"Started with shoplifting. His so-called-friends called it a five finger discount. I call it taking without earning . . . stealing, plain-and-simple." Walter waved his hand around the library. "Everything you see here, everything you see in my house, I earned, dammit! You don't take things like this in life. You earn them."

I'd busted enough shoplifters to know that it sometimes led to bigger things, but just as often it didn't. Walter had said that Richard's problems had started with shoplifting, I wanted to know what they'd ended with . . . if they'd truly ended. "What else, besides the shoplifting?"

Walter sighed. "I don't want to talk about it. I thought it was all in the past. Now I just don't know. You'll find it all in that box."

"What about the people he used to hang out with? Do you know where they are now?"

"I don't have any idea and I don't care."

"Does he have any new friends who you're suspicious of?"

"Any new hooligans, is that what you're driving at?"

I nodded.

"I wouldn't really know about that. I try not to pry when Richard comes over. Did I tell you that he comes over once a week?"

"No sir."

"Well, he does. He's a good young man, at least he's good to his old grandfather. He may not be the quickest witted creature on God's green earth, but I can tell you something that makes up for that in my book . . . he loves his grand-father—"

"And his grandfather obviously loves him," I added.

"Well of course I do. Nettie and I, we loved that boy just like we loved his daddy. You know, when Nettie died, I had an emptiness inside me that I can't begin to describe. It's like half of me—no, pretty near all of me—had died along with her. Richard must've sensed that, because he did all he could to help fill that void. He'd come past the house at least every week, just to visit with me. He's a good boy, don't you know? Not smart, but good. Then when his father died, Richard moved in here with me. At first, I thought that the arrangement was just so that I could look after him, because that poor boy was simply lost."

I thought about my own father's death—I was just about Richard's age when Pop went. And even though he'd gone peacefully, I felt like a Buick had rammed me straight in the gut. I tried to imagine how Walter must have felt when Nettie died. I've been married twice, but both of my marriages started out hot and ended up cold. From the way Walter talked about Nettie, I could tell that they had accomplished something very special—they'd never let the warmth escape from their marriage.

"But the truth is," Walter continued, "that Richard looked after me just as much as I looked after him. You see, I took his father's death just as hard as Richard did—when Richard lost his father, I lost my only son. To this day, I can hardly bear to even say his name aloud. It simply hurts too much. A parent isn't supposed to bury his child." Walter eyes assumed a faraway look as the lights from the room sparkled on his tears.

I looked away to give Walter some privacy and snapped my mind from thoughts about love and pain. I forced myself to focus on the case at hand—specifically the man with the pony-tail who'd nearly turned me into a soprano.

"Have you ever seen Richard with a thin man who has a long, gray pony-tail?" I asked Walter after he'd taken a deep breath and dried his eyes.

Walter shook his head. "I told you, I don't know Richard's friends."

"And Richard, is he just a shade under six feet tall, with neatly trimmed blonde hair?"

Walter cocked his head and squinted at me. "No. He's a bit on the short side, like his daddy was. Tompkins family trait. Why, what are you driving at?"

I decided not to alarm the old man. Now that I knew that neither of the men with Walter's car were Richard, I certainly didn't want to tell the old man about the wooden crate. Walter might jump to the same conclusion I had—that his one-and-only grandson could be inside the crate, stiff as the surrounding boards. "Nothing," I said, deciding it best to not mention the gunshots either. I didn't want to ask my next question, but I knew that I had to. "What happened to Richard's dad?"

Walter looked me squarely in the eyes and spoke without emotion. "My son died a few years back. Automobile accident. Drove right off a steep cliff on Pacific Coast Highway and straight into the ocean."

"I'm sorry to hear that," I said while thinking that my words fell far short.

"Can't turn back time. What's done is done."

"And his mother?"

"Died when Richard was just three."

"I'm sorry," I said.

"Don't be. She was a tramp. My son never should have married her. But he never had much sense when it came to women. Come to think of it, Richard inherited that trait from his father. Neither of them would know a good woman if one came right up and bit them."

28

I amused myself for a moment by wondering how many good women actually introduced themselves by biting men, then went back to concentrating on my interview. "Any relatives that Richard might be visiting or might have contacted in the past few days?"

Walter reached into his shirt pocket and retrieved a fountain pen and a check. "No, he and I are the last of the Tompkinses. Now, I'm assuming that you'll start on this case right away. Am I correct?"

I wasn't through with my questions. "Did Richard say why he wanted to borrow your car?"

"I don't have any idea. I simply assumed that he was having trouble with that old jalopy of his. Now, you didn't answer my question young man. Are you going to take this case or not?"

I could tell Walter was becoming irritated with me, but I had more questions. "Do you know of anybody who would want to hurt your grandson?"

"No one."

"Please think, Mr. Tompkins. This could be important. Is there anyone—"

"I *did* think. Do you assume because a man is old that he can't think for himself? And, one other thing . . .the name is Walter, not mister. And I'll tell you something else; I'm getting sick and tired of these questions, and I know full well that this is important—otherwise I wouldn't be trying to hire you to find my grandson. Now, are you going to take the case or not?"

"Of course I will."

"What's your normal rate?" Walter asked with his pen poised on the check, ready to write.

I'd already figured what I'd charge my clients. I'd taken my annual salary from W-L's and divided it by fifty-two weeks. Then I took that number and divided it by five to give me my old daily rate. Then, so that I could recoup my overhead and hopefully enhance my lifestyle, I increased the daily rate by fifty percent and rounded it up. "Two hundred dollars a day," I said.

Walter looked up at me. "Nettie used to get a twenty percent discount at W-L's. Let me see now, twenty percent off of two hundred is forty dollars. I'll pay you one-sixty a day. Fair enough?"

It wasn't what I wanted, but it was better than nothing. And I figured that the case might end up being pretty easy since I already knew where Walter's car was and had seen the two men who were using it. "Plus expenses," I said.

"We'll see about that when the time comes." Walter wrote out the check. Once finished, he shook my hand and then passed the check to me. "I paid you for three days. That ought to do it. Don't you think?"

"I'll do my best, sir."

"*Walter*," he corrected.

"Walter," I said. "Do you happen to have a spare set of keys to your station wagon?"

"What for?"

"I'd like to be able to examine it thoroughly."

"You know where it is?"

I decided it would be better to impress him later, after I had supposedly just found his car. "I'm a detective, Walter. I can find anything." I looked carefully at the old man, he seemed to be fading. "You okay?"

His eyes narrowed into slits. "Don't ever ask me that. You get to be my age, that's all people ever ask you. It's like they're expecting me to die at any minute. Well, I'm sick, but I'm not *that* sick. Now, you go out and find my grandson. And make it snappy." Walter fished around in the front pocket of his slacks, retrieved what looked like a small remote control device and pressed a button. A few moments later, the strong young woman in the tantalizingly short uniform appeared in the doorway.

"Yes Walter," she said.

"Crystal, would you please fetch this gentleman a set of keys to my car."

"The Lincoln?"

"No, no, no, the wagon."

"Has he found it?"

Walter looked over at me, smiled and nodded. "He shall, of that I am most confident."

Crystal pivoted gracefully on her toes and walked away with the wiggle I'd been anticipating. When she was out of sight, Walter pressed his remote again. She returned immediately. "Yes?"

Walter looked up over his glasses. "Fetch the keys to Richard's apartment while you're at it. You needn't bother us when you've found them, just leave both sets of keys on the table next to the front door."

"He's going to find Richard too?"

"Of course he is. You don't think I'd hire a private eye just to find my car do you?"

Crystal nodded, turned again, and I was treated to another one of her hypnotic departures. Once she'd slithered out of visual range, I turned to Walter. "You have checked on his apartment haven't you?"

"What for?"

"To see if he's there."

"No, of course not. If Richard were home, he would have picked up the phone when I called him."

"You said that Richard used to live here with you. How long ago did he move into his own apartment?"

"It's been a bit more than a year. I thought it was time for him to stop taking care of his grandfather and time for him to be leading his own life. He balked at the idea at first, but he eventually agreed as long as I had someone here to care for me. I contacted some of those home health care services and they sent some nurses over for me to interview. I didn't like any of them. Then Richard found Crystal and I liked what I saw. She's been taking care of me ever since."

I felt like telling Walter that I liked what I saw too, but went on with my questions. "Where does Richard live?"

Walter suddenly seemed agitated and shot me a disapproving look. "That information is in the box. Now don't you be wasting time. You're on my nickel now, so I want you to find my grandson before he gets himself into some real trouble."

"But I need as much information—"

"It's all in here." Walter reached across the coffee table and tapped the leather box. "Where he lives, what kind of trouble he's been in, everything." He pushed it toward me.

I picked up the box and started to open the lid.

"Not now. Time's a'wasting. And I must get back to bed. I'm suddenly feeling very tired." Walter stood, slowly-and-feebly, and led me out of the library and through the foyer. As we approached the front door, he motioned me down to his level. I leaned my ear close to his mouth. "I don't want anything new to appear on Richard's criminal record," he said quietly. "Now promise me you won't get the police involved."

I thought about my nearly being killed while witnessing a probable crime, and the police department's feeble reaction when I reported it. "You don't need to worry about my contacting the police, Walter. This is *my* case."

"Thank you," he whispered as I picked up the two sets of keys that Crystal had left for me next to the door. I opened the leather box and tossed them in.

Just one more thing," Walter said as I stepped out onto the porch. "Is that store manager, Mr. Eaton still sneaking around with women's lingerie under his suits?"

"Huh?"

"Oh, it's just something that Nettie had told me. I thought that since you were the security manager over there for so long, you would've known about it."

"I'd heard stories," I said.

FOUR

I redlined that little three-banger straight out the cul-de-sac and toward the industrial section where this whole thing had started. I couldn't believe my luck so far. And the more I thought about it, the more I convinced myself that luck couldn't be the main ingredient here, it had to be skill . . . pure and simple. As I drove closer to where I knew the Fiat was parked, I outlined my day thus far with a sense of strong self-satisfaction: saw first perp in first vehicle, followed perp, watched perp rendezvous with second perp in second vehicle, observed perps move a body-sized crate from first vehicle to second vehicle, avoided bullets from second perp, tracked down owner of first vehicle, learned the name of probable victim and, most importantly, picked up a client who paid me up-front for my services. No question about it, I was hot.

I careened around the final corner, eager to reach my destination. When I pulled onto the street, I blinked my eyes in dismay—the Fiat had been replaced by nothing more than an oil stain.

I had two immediate courses of action from which to choose. One was to drive over to Richard Tompkins's apartment and have a look-see. The other was to scrutinize the contents of Walter's box. I decided to do both. I opened the box and rooted through it until I found a photocopy of a drivers license bearing the name of Richard Tompkins. I confirmed that the picture didn't resemble the first perp in the least, then I took note of the address, wrenched the Metro into gear, and scooted across town.

Between gear shifts, turns, stops and an occasional glance at traffic, I also managed to check out most of the contents of the box. The first item to catch my eye was his birth certificate. Richard Edward Tompkins, born at exactly 6:48 a.m. at Kingston Beach General Hospital, twenty-two years ago last October the twenty-seventh. Two tiny footprints on either side of the wording proved that he was born with two tiny feet—five tiny toes on each. I wondered if there would be any relationship between the man's adult footprints and those from when he was a newborn. I imagined myself tracking down the wooden crate, prying it open with a crow bar in my right hand while I held a gun on the perps with my left, discovering a man's body in the crate, untying a the man's shoelace, removing his shoe, peeling off his sock, and then holding a photocopy of his newborn footprints against his size twelves for a positive ID. "Aha," I'd shout, then tie the perps across the hood of my Vette and drive 'em to the authorities.

I set the birth certificate aside and fished out a senior class photograph. As I noticed how handsome Richard looked, I remembered that the photo studio that had taken all of my school's pictures had mercifully airbrushed out all of the student's many facial imperfections. It would have taken all of the Clearasil in the western world for my graduating class to have even faintly resembled the handsome kids in my class annual—smiling, row-after-row, above their lists of accomplishments both real and imagined. My list, in addition to including my genuine achievements like being on the varsity football team, listed me as being the Head Song Girl and the Senior Class Princess. Those kudos actually belonged to Stephanie Hammestein, whose picture appeared directly to the right of mine. The official explanation for the mix-up was a copy-editing error, but I always suspected that the dweeby editor had switched the accolades on purpose. I'd beat him up back in the fifth grade—my only instance of acting like a bully. Well, he'd waited until the twelfth grade to get back at me and I guess he'd taught me a lesson—that the pen is mightier than the sword! But, I—

Hooonnnnnkkkkk!!!!!

I snapped out of my reminiscing just in time to see a FedEx truck filling my entire windshield. I slammed on the brakes and swerved to the right, just in time to avert being squished like a bug. I closed the lid on the box and paid attention to my driving.

The Surfside Shadows Apartments looked as though it had been built in the fifties and then left to deteriorate in the salt air without ever receiving so much as a fresh coat of paint or even a superficial squeegeeing of the windows. A two-story, stucco-covered, flat-roofed, shoe box of a building, with twelve apartments crammed into the square footage of a typical suburban tract home. Paint flaking off the stucco, stucco flaking off the studs, studs providing a delicious meal for the termites. The apartment wasn't on the surf as its name implied, but because it was within inches of the neighboring buildings, it had to be in perpetual shadows—so at least half its name rang true. All-in-all, not a very appealing place to live. All-in-all, it reminded me of my own apartment just a few blocks away . . . except that I actually have an ocean view . . . if I stand on the toilet seat and tilt my head just right.

I tossed the keys to Richard's apartment on top of the other goodies in my gym bag. Then I walked to the rear unit on the first floor, the one that backed up to the alley, and knocked on the door. I didn't expect Richard to answer, and he didn't. I wanted to peek into the window, but a rust-stained bed sheet covered it. I looked over my shoulder to see if anyone might be watching me, saw no one, inserted the key, twisted the knob and . . . *nothing*. Instead of feeling the tumblers clicking, the knob froze in my hand. I pulled the key out, reinserted it and turned it to the left and right until I finally gave up; either I had the wrong key or the wrong apartment. I double-checked the address and confirmed that I was indeed at the right place. Next, I reached into the bag and pulled out my lock-gun. I didn't have much experience with picking locks, but the description in the catalogue had assured me that this soldering-iron shaped tool would do the trick. I'd practiced with it on my own locks at home and had actually become rather proficient with it. I held the lock-gun in my right hand, inserted the gun's needle into the keyhole, pulled the trigger, and felt the needle simultaneously striking all of the lock's bottom pins. As the force transferred to the upper pins, they rose momentarily in the chamber and created a wide gapping shear line. At that precise moment, I applied pressure on the tension wrench with my left hand and tried turning the plug. It didn't budge. I adjusted the knob on the lock-gun and tried again. Still no luck. On the third try, the plug rotated into the opening position. I turned the knob and pushed on the door—I was in.

Just enough light filtered through the bed sheet to enable me to search around without turning on the lights, but I had to do it fast because the sun was about to set. Of course, doing it fast wouldn't present much of a problem because there were only two rooms to explore; the combination living-sleeping-dining-kitchen and the bathroom. Since I'd drunk an entire Big Gulp while driving over, I figured I'd kill two birds with one stone by starting with the bathroom. While I did my impersonation of Niagara Falls, I set my gym bag on the counter, opened the medicine cabinet with one hand and rummaged through the sticky glass shelves. No prescription bottles, illicit drugs, or contraband of any sort—just the usual assortment of stuff: a couple of bottles of aspirin, a toothpaste tube squeezed from the top, a can of extra-hold hairspray, a thermometer, a throw-away razor, and a slimy can of shaving cream. Putting my keen detective mind to work, I immediately ascertained that Richard had a head, and in-and-on that head were a mouth, teeth and hair. I slammed the mirrored door closed, finished my personal business, flushed, washed my hands in the pedestal sink, dried them on the filthy towel, picked up my gym bag and stepped back into the main room. Then, with visions Hitchcock's *Psycho* playing in my head, I quickly grabbed my 120,000 volt super stunner from my bag, reentered the bathroom and whipped back the shower curtain. Fortunately, I wasn't greeted by a bloodied body, but the build-up of mildew was a pretty dreadful sight . . . even for someone with my housekeeping standards.

I walked back into the main room, still holding the super stunner. W-L's corporate policy had specifically forbidden security managers and operatives from carrying guns while on duty. They'd never mentioned anything about stun guns, so I'd bought the most powerful zapper I could carry. Most of the compact stunners packed about 50,000 volts— mine was nearly two-and-a-half times as powerful. Depress the trigger and the sparks practically flew off the contact probes and into the perp's central nervous system. Just the sight and sound of the super stunner's crackling energy intimidated the snot out of just about anybody. Actually being shot with this thing *would* actually knock the snot out of them . . . or so I imagined, I'd never actually gotten the chance to zap anyone.

I dropped the zapper back into my gym bag and surveyed the rest of Richard's apartment. It looked like a category five hurricane had hit it. Magazines on the floor, dirty dishes strewn across every horizontal surface, drawers half open, clothing hanging from hinges and doorknobs. Most people would have immediately jumped to the conclusion that the room had been the scene of a life-and-death struggle, or it had been ransacked by criminals, or a combination of both. I knew better—Richard was simply a slob. How did I come to that conclusion? Because the room looked exactly like my own, except that he preferred TV dinners and I usually dined on fast-food Mexican. I stood for a moment to appreciate Richard's collection of fine art, which consisted of a half dozen, life-sized posters of scantily clad women. The posters were duct taped to all of the walls and onto what I assumed to be the closet door. Blondes, brunettes, and redheads beckoned me with provocative poses and tempting smiles.

I finished my mini-course in art appreciation and scanned the room for a good place to begin my systematized search. A calendar he had thumbtacked to the wall next to the kitchen sink seemed like an appropriate place to start. I noted that the name Rita Sandoval was on several of the dates, including today's. As I flipped the calendar back to the previous month, I heard a rustling sound. I couldn't tell where it came from. Perhaps it had come from inside the apartment. Maybe it had come from just outside the window over the sink. Either way, it sent a wave of electricity directly up my spine and made my scalp break out in a prickly sweat. I froze in my tracks, wondering if I should dive under the kitchen table or hide beside the refrigerator. I figured that if I remained standing I'd have better leverage for pouncing on a perp, so I quickly squeezed myself between the old Kelvinator and the wall, realizing too late that I'd left my zapper in the gym bag which was now sitting on the coffee table. I held my breath and waited, hoping I wasn't about to be attacked by a group of thugs—one guy I could handle just fine, but two or more would present real difficulties. My mind shot to the preppy in old man Walter's Fiat—he, I could take care of with one arm tied behind my back. Then I pictured the wiry man with the pony tail. He'd be a different story. He'd fight dirty. He'd fight mean. He'd have a gun. I heard another rustling sound. I looked in the direction of the sound just as a rat the size of a Honda Civic scurried out from under the kitchen cabinet and across the linoleum, squeezing under a door and into the closet.

I squelched my unmanly desire to let out a blood-curdling scream. Instead, I pushed myself out of my hiding place, grabbed my stunner from the bag, and ran like a crazy man after the rodent. When I got to the closet door, I yelled out to him: "*I know you're in there you little shit*," crouched down, reached up, twisted the door knob, held the zapper forward, and wrenched the door wide open with a piercing squeak. A body fell out of the closet, its face directly in front of mine. In an instant, I gasped, caught my breath, and felt my heart pounding like a jack hammer. I shut my eyes for a moment, then opened them on the count of three. One. Two. Three. The first perp—the one with the white polo shirt and the tan khakis—stared at me with flat, cloudy, unblinking eyes. Dried blood formed a trail from a pair of bullet holes in the middle of his forehead, dripped down the side of his nose and into his gaping mouth.

I stared for what felt like hours, but was probably only seconds, as my mind reeled and my stomach churned. When my brain finally clicked into gear, I stuffed the body back into the closet and slammed the door shut. Then I ran to the kitchen sink and doused my face with cold water. I grabbed a greasy dish towel off of the counter and dried myself off, then dashed back to the closet and wiped my prints from the knob.

I ran to the bathroom and wiped down anything I'd remembered touching. Then I opened my gym bag, pulled my micro camera out and shot a couple of pictures of the closet door. I took a deep breath and creaked open the door—still using the greasy towel—and snapped a few shots of the body. I shut the door, then stood in the center of the room snapping pictures in every direction until I finished the roll.

I'm not certain exactly when I decided not to call 911. I suppose it was the moment I realized that Richard Tompkins would be the prime suspect. It wasn't that I wanted to protect the kid, it was that I'd promised his grandfather that I wouldn't get the police involved. And to be perfectly honest, it was also that I knew I'd have a hard time explaining to the police why I'd broken into the apartment in the first place. Still, it was all I could do to resist reaching over to the phone and punching 911 on the keypad. I thought more about the phone, walked over to it, picked up the receiver with the towel and punched a button with my knuckle—just one button—last number redial. I listened to the ringing on the line, wondering who would answer it—perhaps the last person the perp had talked to before he'd met his killer.

A soft, female voice answered the phone. "Walter Tompkins residence," she said. "May I help you?"

"Crystal?"

"Yes. Who is this?"

"Hank Hammond."

"Who?"

Apparently I hadn't made as strong an impression on her as she had on me when we'd met earlier today. "The man who met with Walter Tompkins this afternoon. You gave me the keys to his Fiat and to his grandson's apartment. Remember?"

"Oh yes. Have you found him? Walter is worried sick about Richard. I've told him not to worry—that Richard is probably just off on a vacation or something—but you've seen how Walter gets."

"I haven't found Richard, but I will." I heard sounds outside the apartment; a man's voice and the rattling of keys. I stared at the front door, wondering if someone was about to come bursting in with guns drawn.

"Are you still there?" Crystal asked.

"Yes," I whispered. "Just a minute." I walked to the window, pulled the dirty sheet slightly to the side, and peeked out. I saw a man enter the next-door apartment and I heard him slam the door behind him. I returned to the phone. "Crystal, are you certain that you gave me the right keys to Richard's apartment?"

"Well, yes. I think so. Why do you ask? Are you going to go to Richard's apartment?

Standing just a few feet from a dead body—even one hidden behind a door—gave me the creeps. I didn't want to take time to chat. What I wanted were answers. "Is Walter there? I need to speak with him."

"He's asleep right now and I'd rather not wake him. He's very tired. I could have him call you when he awakes."

I gave her my office number, thanked her and hung up. My mind was reeling and I couldn't wait to get out of the apartment. I grabbed my bag, sneaked out of the apartment and back to my rental car.

FIVE

Twenty minutes later I parked beneath the bold brass upper-case letters that spelled out the words *Barry Green, Attorney At Law*. For five hundred bucks a month, I probably should have insisted that my name be up there as well—preferably in neon. Actually, I probably should have insisted on a few other things too—like having a decent office. Green's office building had formerly been a fifteen hundred square foot, three bedroom, one bath house before he converted it. The living-dining room had become the reception area, complete with Lori's command center. The first bedroom was now a law library. The second bedroom had become a conference room. Barry took the largest bedroom for his own personal office. The bathroom remained as is, and the kitchen became a storage room. That's a complete accounting of all the rooms in the building. So where is my office? Between the time that I'd first spoken to Lori and the moment that I moved into the building, Lori—apparently under Green's direction—had hired a maintenance man to hammer up some two-by-fours and slap some sheet rock right down the middle of the old kitchen. My "office" was where the stove and sink had been. The only plus to the arrangement is that I have a small window that looks out onto the street . . . oh, and an exhaust fan over my desk, which actually comes in quite handy whenever I overindulge on burritos.

"You get there in time?" Lori said the moment I walked through the door—entering data into her computer without looking up.

I breathed a heavy sigh.

Lori stopped keyboarding and looked at me. "You look like hell," she said.

"I feel like hell."

"He didn't show?" she asked.

"He who?" With all that was on my mind, I didn't have the vaguest idea who she was talking about.

"Your informant—Armando." She looked at her watch. "You were gone an awfully long time if you didn't even meet with your informant. What's the matter? Did you get sidetracked at the video arcade again?"

I propped myself up against her command post. "No, no. I was thinking about something else. Armando showed up all right, and he had exactly the information I needed. After I finished with him, I met with my client for awhile. Then I drove out to where the perps had left my client's car."

Lori frowned at her monitor, made a couple of quick clicks with her mouse, then looked back up at me. "Car? What car? You told me that you were working on a murder case. Are you now telling me that somebody hired you to find his car? Hank Hammond, you are so full of it!"

"Lori, leave me alone. So far today I've witnessed a crime I can't explain; I've been shot at by a man I don't know; I've been ignored by the police; I've paid almost my last forty bucks to that Armando character; and—not more than a half hour ago—I . . ." I stopped short of telling Lori about discovering a dead body.

"And what?"

"Nothing. I just need to find Richard Tompkins." I sat Walter's leather box on Lori's command post. "I'm hoping that the contents of this thing will help me out."

Lori grabbed the box like a kid going for candy. One moment her hand was on her computer's mouse, the next moment it was holding the box under her desk lamp, scrutinizing it closely. Before I could stop her, she'd opened the lid and pulled out Walter's keys. "What're these to?

Wait, don't tell me. I'll tell you. They're automobile keys, and they're to—let me make a wild guess here—the missing car."

I grabbed for the keys. "Lori, give me those."

She yanked them away from my reach. "Hold on, Hank. Give me a chance on this. These keys belong to a Fiat. Probably an old one judging from their condition—lots of scratching and so forth. Of course they'd have to be old because Fiats haven't been imported to the states in years. I suppose someone could bring one over here himself. You know, a gray-market car. But that isn't likely. A Mercedes, Jaguar, or Ferrari, yes. A Fiat, never." She returned the key to my outstretched hand. "These keys are definitely to an old Fiat."

"I didn't know you were a car buff."

"I'm not. Quite the contrary. Cars bore the daylights out of me."

"But, how'd you know—"

"You'd be surprised by the things I know. Most of it is useless stuff, but it sure comes in handy when I'm watching *Jeopardy*. It's a good thing for Alex Trebeck that I've never actually appeared on his show, because I'd own it—*and him*—by now."

I reached over and snatched the leather box back.

"Hey, come on Hank. What else is in the box?"

I spun around and retreated into my office. "That, my dear, is exactly what I intend to find out."

I thought about closing the door behind me for privacy, but that always made me more than slightly claustrophobic. Between driving the diminutive Metro and working out of a fraction of a kitchen, I felt like I'd somehow entered a half-scale, parallel universe—like Gulliver. I sat on my squeaky, secretarial-type chair and dumped the contents of the leather box onto my Formica-topped desk.

I pushed the items I'd already examined to the side and concentrated on what was left. The first item, a photocopy of the pink slip to Richard's car—a 1968 Mustang, license number 1LJH 602—was paper-clipped to a color photo of the car. It was a gold fastback, with primer spots across the hood and front fenders. The horse emblem had been removed from the grille, a large intake scoop riveted onto the hood, and the stock wheels had been replaced with five-spoke mags. I pulled a magnifying glass out of my desk drawer to get a better look at the person sitting behind the wheel. It was hard to make out the details, but the only logical conclusion I could make was that the man waving at the photographer was Richard Tompkins. Since the pink slip was dated just about one year ago, this was the most recent picture of Richard I had to work with. I compared it to his high school picture and to the one on his driver's license. The only thing I could tell for sure that had changed since those pictures was that his hair had grown. It now cascaded over his ears and swooped across his forehead like some kind of '70's rock star's. Of course, he could have shaved it into a Mohawk the day after this picture had been taken for all I knew. I set the picture aside and picked up the three-by-five index card.

The card listed Richard's full name, address, phone number, social security number, doctor's name and phone number, bank name and checking account number, and a work phone that had been crossed out. I copied the information onto my spiral pad.

On another index card were three entries. Each stated a date, followed by a crime of some sorts. From what I could surmise, Richard had been apprehended eight years ago for shoplifting—at W-L's of course, and it was a safe bet that I'd been the one who'd busted him. Two years later he had been arrested for possessing an undisclosed amount of marijuana. The case had been thrown out for reasons that weren't noted on the card. The third arrest, about four months later, was for disturbing the peace. Walter's handwritten note said something to the effect that Richard had been caught drag racing. All-in-all, Richard's crimes didn't exactly rank up there with Al Capone's. Hell, not more than six months ago I'd been pulled over for drag racing my Vette.

The only other item that Walter had put in the box was an article clipped out of the local paper. I unfolded the newsprint and read about the armed robbery of a stereo store. Two months ago—shortly after I'd quit my job at W-L's—two men wearing matching ski masks had entered Discount Danny's Stereo's 'n' More just before closing time. The men had forced the owner at gun point into the back office and demanded that he empty the contents of the safe into a large canvas bag. Once he had finished doing as he was told, he was bound, gagged, and one of his merchandise bags pulled over his head and secured with duct tape.

The robbery was discovered an hour later by the store's security service. They had noticed that the store's alarm hadn't been set on schedule, so they phoned the store to see if everything was okay. When they didn't get an answer, they dispatched a couple of their men to the store, discovered that a robbery had taken place, untied the owner of the store, and called the police. The owner was unable to identify the perps.

Why, I wondered, was this article in the box? There was nothing that tied Richard to the robbery. And if he had been one of the two men, he certainly wouldn't have told his grandfather about it. But for some reason, Walter must have suspected that his grandson had been involved, otherwise he wouldn't have cut out the article and put it into the box. Why did Walter suspect Richard? And why didn't Walter tell me about any of this when I was at his house?

As I pondered these questions, I felt the presence of someone hovering nearby. I looked up to see Lori leaning against the door frame, her left eyebrow arched. I motioned her into my cracker box of an office. She'd surprised me with her knowledge about Fiats, so I thought I'd see what her take was on the rest of my case. She sat on the folding metal chair across from my desk and peered at the stuff I'd strewn across the desk top.

As she listened, I described in great detail about the wooden crate and the two men, boasted to her about how I'd discovered who owned the car, told her that the owner's grandson had disappeared with the car, and nearly started to tell her about the body in Richard's closet when she interrupted.

"Wait a minute." Lori set the documents neatly onto my desk and raised *that* eyebrow. "Correct me if I'm wrong, but I thought you told me this morning that you were working a *murder* case."

"Something like that," I mumbled. I could feel her smirk coming, and I could literally kick myself for what I'd said this morning.

"Well, you just got through telling me that you met your client for the first time this *afternoon*. If that's true, who were you working for this morning?" The smirk was indeed returning, just a little, and just at one corner of her mouth. "And why did you tell me it was a murder case when it's a missing person case?"

"If you'd let me continue—"

"More BS?"

"None of this is BS," I protested, and started BSing to save face. "I was doing some preliminary work this morning. I hadn't yet met with Walter Tompkins, but I had every reason to believe that he would be hiring me."

"You hadn't yet met him, but you'd talked with him?"

I hesitated while I thought up more BS. I didn't like lying, but I disliked her smirk even more. "Yes, we'd talked," I said after a moment. "There *is* such a thing as a telephone, you know. He'd told me about his missing *car*. It wasn't until this afternoon that he retained me to find his grandson."

"Let me get this straight. You'd talked to him about his missing car?"

"Right," I said so resolutely that I practically convinced myself.

"So the *murder* case you told me about this morning wasn't even a *missing person* case at that point? It was actually a *missing car* case?" Her face twisted into a half-smirk.

"Lori, do I have to spell everything out for you?" I acted as though I was annoyed with her, when actually I was annoyed with myself for concocting this whole lame-brained story. "I was watching the missing car this morning when I saw what appeared to be the transportation of a dead body. That's how it ended up being a possible murder case."

She placed her hands on my desk top and laced her fingers together, church-like, then leaned over her hands with a full-on smirk. "So the possible murder, as you're now calling it, was nothing more than two guys moving a wooden crate?"

I swallowed hard and looked down at my desk top. "Well, basically," I stammered, then looked back at Lori. "Except that one of them did

46

shoot at me. And even if he hadn't, I'm trained to spot something dirty when it's going down. I was positive those guys were up to no good, and I wouldn't be the least bit surprised to find that there was a dead body in that crate."

"Or a load of bricks, or a Grecian urn, or a load of recycled newspapers." She leaned back and spoke to the ceiling. "*But you're the detective*," she said, her voice trailing off.

"Do you want to hear the rest of it?"

"I can hardly wait," Lori said flatly, still looking up.

I was sorely tempted to tell her about discovering the Fiat driver, dead in Richard Tompkins's closet. It would probably have put a stop to her smirking attitude, but at this point I didn't want anybody to know that I'd discovered a murder and then chosen not to call the police. "Actually, there isn't any more to tell . . . yet. Right now I need to find out about those guys with the crate, especially the one who was driving the Fiat."

"Well then, let's see what we can do." Lori looked back up at the ceiling, as if the smoke stains from the room's previous life spelled something out to her. "This young man," she said quickly. "Just under six feet tall, size forty-two suit, neatly trimmed blonde hair, and a deep tan—is this correct?"

"Yes."

"Tell me about his clothing."

"White polo shirt and khakis. I told you that already."

"How many buttons were on his shirt?"

"I don't know." I looked down at my own shirt and counted three buttons down from my collar. "Three, I think. Why?"

"Was the material smooth or nubby?"

"The material of the buttons?"

"Of the shirt, Sherlock."

"Smooth, I guess."

"Banded sleeves or loose?"

"Banded, in a contrasting color." A detail I'd completely forgotten until Lori asked.

"Was there an insignia on his shirt?"

I looked up at the ceiling, right where Lori continued staring, didn't see anything of interest, then looked back down at her. "I think so. Seems to me that there was some kind of logo embroidered on the shirt, right here." I pointed to my shirt pocket.

Lori looked at my chest. "Do you remember what it looked like?"

"No, I was pretty far from him and even with the mini-telescope I couldn't make it out." As I said the words, I relived the precise moment that I opened the closet door. When it actually happened, the only information I could process was the dead body and the blood and the bullet holes. Now—in my mind—I could see the shirt more clearly and there definitely was an insignia on it. "Wait," I burst out. "It was circular and about the size of a silver dollar, with some leaves or something radiating out about an inch from either side."

"Any words on it?"

"Probably, but I don't have any idea what they were."

"Was the insignia the same color as the bands on the sleeves?"

"Yes, I'm pretty sure it would have been. At least it could have been."

"I'll bet he wasn't wearing a tacky western belt like the one you always wear."

I glanced down at my favorite belt, complete with an oversized silver and turquoise buckle I'd bought on a visit to Tombstone Arizona. "Hey, I love this belt," I protested.

"I know you do," Lori said. "That's what makes it so sad." She flashed her smirk, then continued. "The belt this man wore. Was it brown fabric with a brass buckle?"

"Uh, yes."

"And he had brown penny loafers on his feet?"

I thought for a moment. "Yes. How'd you know that?"

"How about his socks, did they match his shirt?"

"Same color as the shirt, yes. I'm pretty sure of it. What the heck are all these questions about?"

Lori reached across to my phone, spun it around to face her, and pulled the receiver to her face. "May I?" she asked me with mock politeness.

"Of course," I said, knowing that she'd damn well do as she pleased.

She turned her head away from me, punched in a number, and identified herself as Samantha Branberry. Then she spoke softly into the receiver for several minutes. I leaned forward to listen and she leaned away from me with a perfectly choreographed motion. I gave up trying to eavesdrop just as Lori wrote something down on a scrap piece of paper, turned it around and slid it across the desk to me.

I read the words on the paper—Scott Mansell—then I looked over at Lori in wonderment as she hung up the phone. "He's the guy?"

"I'd stake my formidable reputation on it." She looked at her watch, winced, and stood. "I have to get going. Good luck with your murder case." She turned and walked out my doorway. I stared out the door, then at the man's name, and then out the door again. Lori reappeared. "Oh, and by the way, his shirt was pink, not white." Then she disappeared for the night.

One of the frustrating things about Lori is that she's always right, another is that she's so damn smug about it. I didn't have the slightest idea how she'd come up with the name of Scott Mansell, but I didn't have any doubt that if Lori said it was his name, it was definitely his name. I pulled the phone book out of one of my desk drawers and thumbed through it hoping to find the dead man's address and phone number. According to US West, Scott Mansell didn't exist. I checked for the name from Richard's calendar, Rita Sandoval, with the same result.

I grabbed a burrito and a Coke at the drive-through lane of Carlita's Jr. and alternately stuffed and drenched my mouth as I headed over to Discount Danny's. I didn't know what I expected to find, but I figured that since Walter had included the article about its robbery in his leather box, it must have something to do with Richard . . . besides, even if it didn't, the merchandise I'd seen in their ads would be pretty cool to fiddle around with.

Danny's, the store with "prices so low I gotta be nuts" was on the corner of Broadway and Sixth. I weaved my way across town, and motored up Broadway. As I waited at an intersection, I looked over at a couple of what the retail people call "big boxes," stores called Toys Galore and Office Warehouse. I thought about the great little toy shops my mother used to take me to when I was a kid. All of them were "mom and pop" stores, and all of them disappeared once the "big boxes" and "category killers" came into town. The same thing happened with the stationery and office supply stores. There used to be at least a half dozen of them before Office Warehouse came in and drove them out of business.

It's hard, if not impossible, for the little guy to compete with this new breed of retailer. The category killers buy their merchandise in such monstrous quantities that they receive huge discounts from the distributors, purchasing each item for a fraction of what the mom-and-pops pay. And, whereas the mom-and-pops base their profits on gross margin percents, the big boys base theirs on gross margin dollars. What that means in lay terms is that the little stores figure their retail prices at, say, fifty percent above what they paid for it, while the big boys run at a fraction of that mark-up, concentrating instead on the total gross profit dollars they can make over the millions of units they sell. In some extreme instances, the mega stores actually sell some items for less than the mom-and-pops pay their vendors for the very same merchandise. It's no wonder that the little guys are dropping like flies. I don't know this stuff because I'm any kind of marketing genius, I just picked it up through osmosis while I worked at W-L's.

The light turned green and I drove the final block to Sixth, noticing that a new "big box" named The Electrical Outlet had come into town in the last couple of years since I'd cruised along Broadway.

As I stepped into Discount Danny's, I was assaulted with booming sounds of heavy metal, rap, oldies, classical, and—heaven help us all—disco. The effect wasn't too dissimilar from the commotion heard at a construction site with all the heavy machinery, whistle-blowing, cat-calls, crashing, cracking, and bashing. The only person in the store, a balding man with a fringe of unruly brown hair that looked like a nest under a big goose egg, came around from behind the counter the moment I walked in. I asked him to shut off the disco.

He swiveled around, waddled over to one of the receivers and flipped a switch. "Yeah, I can't stand that disco crap neither," he said to me over his shoulder. "I thought it'd died in the seventies, but the kids've discovered it again. I can't tell if they think it's camp or cool, but either way, I gotta keep up with the times."

"Even when the times take you backwards," I added, raising my voice over the remaining sounds.

"Yup, clear back to Gregorian chants if I have to. Whatever sells."

I approached him at the same speed that he approached me. We met in the center of the store, right next to about fifty cartons of VCRs stacked into a pyramid.

"Something I can show you?" he asked.

I read his badge, his name was Danny. I figured he owned the place. I can deduce these things, that's why I'm proving to be a pretty damn good private detective. The only problem was that I didn't have the slightest idea what to say to him, so I succumbed to reflex action. "No thanks, I'm just looking."

Danny had probably heard that response about a zillion times before, and obviously had learned not to pay any attention to it. "Got a great deal on CD changers. Way off list price. Nobody in town can touch my deal, I guarantee it."

I find it absolutely impossible to resist any gadget that is festooned with lots of push buttons. "Cool," I said. "How many CDs will it hold?"

"Come with me and I'll show you." He walked me over to the side wall where he had five different CD players on display. He pointed to one on the end, it had the requisite number of buttons on it to quicken my pulse. "Full function remote. One hundred CD capability. Infinitely programmable. Headphone jack with volume control. LED readout of the CD title as it plays. Manufactured by SoundScan, and it's the sweetest machine you'll find at any price."

I admired the shiny black box with all its lights and buttons and knobs the way art connoisseurs admire paintings by the masters like Renoir, van Gogh, and Norman Rockwell. Me, I'm more on Richard's level—except that I substitute Corvettes and hot rods for nearly naked women. "How much is it over at The Electrical Outlet?" I asked.

Danny's cheeks reddened, then his forehead, and then the top of his head in a perfect portrayal of a thermometer in the middle of August. "*They*," he said as if the word reeked of week-old garbage, "aren't worth your time."

"Are they cheaper?" I asked.

"*No!*" Danny slammed his hand down hard on the shelf, bouncing an entire row of expensive CD players. "You can't get this CD changer for less money anyplace in the city, county, or the whole damn state. I'm sellin' this baby for sixty percent off the manufacturer's suggested retail price. You know what that means?"

I nodded. "It means that you're either not making much money off of it, or your distributor gave you some kind of a screaming deal."

"Both," he responded quickly.

"There is a third possibility," I added. "The MSRP could be an artificially inflated one."

Danny spun around and walked quickly away from me. "You wait here," he said over his shoulder. A moment later, he returned with copies of three advertisements for the very same CD changer. He spread the ads out across the shelf, draping them over the merchandise. "Look for yourself," he said.

I read the ads. The Electrical Outlet was about thirty dollars more expensive. W-L's was another thirty above that. The third store was right about in the middle.

"How can you sell it so cheap?" I asked.

Danny pointed to the top of his ad. "Because I gotta be nuts, that's why." He rotated a finger around his ear. "Better buy it quick, before I come to my senses."

I pulled out my wallet and slapped my MasterCard on top of the ad. "I'll take it."

"Good decision, my friend. You won't regret it." Danny turned away from me and walked toward what I assumed was a door to the stock room. "I'll get you a boxed one from the back," he said without looking back.

While I waited for Danny to return with my new toy, I scanned the sales area for security devices. I spotted five video surveillance cameras, one over the cash register—or POS as the computerized ones are called—and one in each of the four corners of the store. A red white and blue decal on the counter proclaimed the premises to be protected by V.A.S.T.—Vanguard Alarm and Security Tech. Perfect! Arturo Garcia, the manager of VAST, owed me a favor for awarding him with the camera surveillance contract at the Kingston Beach branch of W-L's. I knew he'd answer any questions I asked him about Discount Danny's robbery—his confidentiality policy wouldn't apply to me.

Danny returned with my new CD changer, set it on the counter and rang up the sale. "Nice store you've got here," I said, beginning my probe for information.

"Thanks." He swiped my card through the card scanner and waited for the approval. "Been in business here for twelve years. Nobody in town knows stereos like I do."

"Isn't this the store that was robbed a couple of months ago?" I asked, trying my best to sound like I was just making idle conversation.

The approval code lit up on the credit card authorization machine and my receipt whirred out. Danny slid it over to me. "Please sign on the line down there," he said, pointing toward the red X.

I scribbled my signature. Danny compared it to the scrawl on the back of my credit card and handed the card back to me. "Yep. Two guys came in here while I was closin' for the night. Held me up at gun point. Scared the livin' hell out of me. You know how they say that your life flashes before you right before you die?"

I'd never actually faced my own death, but Scott Mansell flopping out of Richard's closet with two holes in his forehead came pretty darn close to scaring me to death. "Yes," I said.

"Well, mine flashed."

"They shoot you?"

"No, but I thought I was gonna be a goner." Danny taped my receipt to the CD changer's carton. "You want me to carry this out for you?"

"That's okay, I can handle it. Actually, I'm not in a big rush."

Danny looked around the store. "Well, I'm not in much of one either. Dinner time, nobody shops during supper. You could shoot a damn cannon off in here."

"Better a cannon than a gun," I said, smiling. "How close did those robbers come to shooting you?"

"This close," he said holding up his hand and spreading his thumb and first finger an inch apart. "I probably saved my life by doing everything they told me. I'm too old for this stuff. Somebody comes in here with a gun, I'm going to do what he says. I'm no hero. Every so often you read about some damn fool who tries to fight off a robber. You know what you call people like that?"

"No, what?"

"Dead."

My mind immediately flashed right back to the bullet holes in the dead man's forehead. "Good point. You get a look at the guys who robbed you?"

"Nope. Not at all. That's probably another reason why I'm still alive to talk about it. They wore ski masks, so I couldn't see their faces."

"But you'd have some sort of general description, wouldn't you? You'd know if they were tall or short, fat or thin, if one of them walked with a limp—"

"That doesn't do the cops any good. They need facial characteristics, hair color, stuff like that. All I could tell them was that the two guys were big, husky guys, like football players."

I pointed toward my chest with my thumb. "Like me?"

Danny appeared surprised by my reaction. "You? No, not hardly. Tall, like you, and they had wide shoulders like yours, but these were young guys with flat stomachs—pure muscle. No beer bellies or love handles on these guys, no sir."

I looked down at myself. He had a point. "Yeah, well I used to play football back in high school."

"And I used to have all my hair, but we're talkin' today, not ancient history."

I looked at the camera poised directly over out heads. "That thing do any good?"

"Nah, not with those ski masks." Danny gave me a suspicious look. "What's with all the questions? You some kind of reporter or something?"

I was used to asking the questions, not answering them. I stumbled over my words. "Independent consultant."

"What's that mean?"

I tried to think of the quickest way to end his curiosity. "Insurance. I've got some—"

"How many times to I have to tell you guys what happened?" he interrupted, his face flush again. "You better settle my claim pronto and stop harassing me or I'm going to turn you into—"

"Woah," I said, "I think you've jumped to the wrong conclusion here. I'm into life insurance sales. In fact I've got some great policies that I'd love to discuss with you."

"No, no, that's okay," Danny said quickly. He buried his face in his chest, then looked up at me with a sad looking smile. "Sorry about flyin' off the handle. But you just wouldn't believe all the red tape that I've been going through because of this damn robbery. It isn't bad enough that I nearly got myself killed, but then I had to go through all this stuff with the cops and now it's with the insurance company. It's like Chinese water torture I tell ya."

I scanned the store, his merchandise levels didn't seem to be suffering from the theft. In fact, he seemed to have plenty of stock. I would have assumed from what I saw that the insurance company had already paid the claim. "You don't look like you're going to go out of business," I said.

Danny looked me square in the eye for a moment and then he dropped his gaze just as the phone rang. I saw it as my cue to leave.

I carried my new toy out of Discount Danny's, knowing I couldn't afford it and wondering if it could be deducted as a business expense. I stared contemptuously at my baby-buggy car as I approached it and made a mental note to call about my Vette first thing in the morning.

I drove south on Pacific Coast Highway in as big a rush as the Metro could manage, which wasn't much. I'd suddenly become exhausted by everything that had happened during the day and I wanted to hurry up and get home . . . that, and I wanted to hook up the CD changer. I goosed the throttle, but the car didn't cooperate. How could it when it only about one-third as many cylinders as a real car? Just as I cursed my rental and wished it would transform into something powerful and exciting, I felt a colossal slam from the rear. The sickening sound of crushing metal filled my ears. I looked into the rear view mirror and saw the grille of a huge, dark colored Suburban doing all it could to transform the Metro from subcompact into submarine . . . ramming me toward the edge of PCH and the depths of the ocean. As I fought the wheel and screeched along the side of a fifty foot high cliff, I convinced myself that the driver of the truck was purposely running me off the road. My mind shot back to the Suburban with the suspicious cargo unloaded from Walter's Fiat. What color was the Suburban I'd seen this morning? And what color was the truck that was forcing me off the road at this very second? Were the vehicles one and the same? I wanted to look at the truck, but needed to focus all my attention on my car . . . and the cliff. I ground my foot into the brake pedal and twisted the steering wheel to the left until it couldn't turn anymore. The Metro skittered along the edge of the cliff, the right front tire dangling in midair. I leaned as hard as I could against the door, pressing my weight opposite the direction of the cliff. I reached for my seat belt, ready to unlatch the buckle, snap open the door and jump out before the tiny car hurtled into the ocean. Then, suddenly, the Geo spun completely around and skidded to a stop. All four tires had miraculously come in contact with the road once again. The engine stalled. I looked frantically around for the truck . . . it was nowhere in sight. I dried the palms of my hands on my Dockers, restarted the car and drove gingerly away. It was then that I noticed that my head lights were off and wondered if maybe I hadn't been the victim of an attempted murder after all. Perhaps the truck driver had never even seen the stupid little death trap of a car. Perhaps there really is a Santa Claus and an Easter Bunny and . . . I flipped the lights on and wondered more about the skinny man with the graying pony-tail. And about Scott Mansell. And about Richard Tompkins.

I spent the rest of the evening trying to hook up my CD changer, experimenting with different combinations of cables routing in and out of my amplifier, tuner, tape-deck, turntable, and TV monitor until finally—after over two frustrating hours—I read the instructions. They helped, but they didn't really read quite right. My guess was that they had originally been written in Japanese and then some barely literate translator had experimented from there. Nevertheless, ten minutes after referring to the directions I was listening to Mick Jagger shouting that he couldn't get no satisfaction and—soon after—my upstairs neighbor shouting that he couldn't get no sleep. I glanced at my watch—nearly midnight.

I turned off the CD player, flipped on the TV and tuned into a rerun of *The Rockford Files*. Then I cleared the stack of *Sports Illustrated* and *Hot Rod* magazines off the table in my dining alcove and sat down with a pen and my spiral pad. What, I asked myself, did I know about my case? I numbered the left side of a page with the numerals one through ten, then next to each number I wrote in a detail. *One*: Walter's grandson Richard borrowed Walter's Fiat on Friday, perhaps promising to return it on Saturday. *Two*: As of today, Monday, Richard has yet to return the car or talk to Walter. *Three*: I saw the Fiat at approximately eight this morning, driven (according to Lori) by Scott Mansell, who met with a tall, thin man driving a Suburban. *Four*: Mansell and the thin man removed a large wooden crate from Walter's Fiat, placed it into the Suburban, shot at me, and then drove away. *Five*: The Fiat was gone when I returned to the scene. *Six*: Mansell is dead in Richard's closet. *Seven*: Walter apparently suspects that Richard was involved in the hold-up of Discount Danny's. *Eight*: Richard doesn't fit the description of either of the men who robbed Discount Danny's. *Nine*: Neither Scott Mansell nor the man with the pony-tail fit the description of either of the men who robbed the store. *Ten*: Somebody driving a Suburban may have just tried to kill me.

After I finished the list, I flipped the page and started a list of questions. *One*: where is Richard? *Two*: Who killed Mansell, and why? *Three*: Is his name really Scott Mansell? *Four*: Who is the man with the pony-tail? *Five*: Where is he? *Six*: What is the connection between Richard, Mansell, and the man with the pony-tail? *Seven*: What was in the crate? *Eight*: Where did the Fiat disappear to? *Nine*: Why did Walter put the robbery article into the box? *Ten*: Who would want to kill me?

Good, I thought, I had ten answers and ten questions. Too bad the answers I had weren't the ones that addressed my questions. Tomorrow morning I'd better start getting the right answers. I fell asleep knowing that I was forgetting something.

SIX

I arrived at my office early and let myself in with my key, juggling a giant burrito filled with honey and a Coke I'd picked up at Carlita's Jr's. It was 7:45 and Lori wouldn't be in until 8:27. She had her routine down to a science. Every work day, she'd park her yellow Karmann Ghia convertible in the stall right next to our building, where it would be shaded most of the day, then she'd pick the local paper up off of the front porch with her left hand and tuck it into the strap of her attaché case. As she stood, her right hand would automatically rise to door knob level with the proper key directed at the precise angle of the key hole. Her right hand would move forward—the key sliding in effortlessly—and her left hand would perform a skilled push-pull that allowed her to walk into the reception area and close the door behind her in one seamless move. She would set her attaché on the extreme left end of her command post as she walked back to Green's office, reaching into the conference room and flipping the switch of the coffee maker on her way. She'd reach across his leather desk blotter, flip his calendar to the correct date and walk back to her command post after reaching into the conference room to pour herself a cup of coffee. She would sit down at her seat at exactly 8:30 and zero seconds—precisely three minutes after unlocking the front door—thumb through her *Things To Do Today* list, then walk into my office and begin pestering me about my case.

I decided to foul up her system by emptying the coffee from the coffee maker. I don't know why I did it, maybe I was just sick-and-tired of her perfect little routine. Or maybe I was still steamed at her for giving me Scott Mansell's name and then frustrating the hell out of me by disappearing. She knew I'd want more information and she knew I couldn't reach her since she had an unlisted phone number and I didn't have the slightest idea where she lived.

I had forty-five minutes to get some answers, and I figured Arturo Garcia would be a good place to start . . . besides, I always enjoyed getting a rise out of him. Unless he'd completely changed his routine, I knew he'd be sitting at his desk at VAST, brushing the croissant crumbs from his Caesar Romero mustache at this very moment, then sipping at his cappuccino. Some things are as predictable as the sun rising each morning and teenagers thinking that they know everything. I wolfed down my burrito, wiped the honey off my face with my hand, licked my fingers, then punched in Arturo's office number on my phone, my fingers sticking on the keys. His phone rang once with a bright, bell-like ring, then rang twice with a muffled electronic tone.

"Hank, my *amigo*," Arturo said with a deep resonance that buzzed the cheap ear piece of my garage-sale phone. "How interesting that you should call. I was just thinking of you." His voice echoed a bit and I could hear very un-office-like sounds in the background—a combination of a Laundromat, a crowd at a baseball game, and The Three Tenors trying desperately to drown it all out.

"What's going on in your office?" I asked. "It sounds like you've got a convention going on in there or something."

"I set my work phone to transfer my calls to my car. I'm actually not more than a block from your office at this very moment."

So much for predictability.

"I have a few minutes before my next appointment, Hank, why don't I just swing by and we can talk face-to-face instead of over this squawk box?"

I agreed and hung up before I remembered what an unimpressive little cracker box I worked out of. I'd made such a big deal out of my quitting W-L's and starting up my own business, and I didn't much like the thought of Arturo discovering the truth about my operation. I quickly picked up a few file folders, tucked them under my arm, grabbed my Coke and moved temporarily into Green's conference room—just seconds before Arturo walked in the front door, his double-breasted suit as refined as his silver hair. In one hand was a Styrofoam cup of cappuccino; in the other, a pink cardboard box with string tied around it. I welcomed him to my place of business and motioned him into the conference room. Arturo smiled at me as he glided through the door and toward the conference table. Then, without saying a word, he set the box on the table, untied the string, opened the box, and removed two napkins and two croissants. So, score one for predictability after all.

"I have just the one cappuccino, my *amigo*, but you are more than welcome to share in one of my pastries," Arturo said as he sat across the table from me.

I figured that a croissant would make the ideal complement to the breakfast burrito I'd just scarfed down. I thanked him and ate the whole thing before Arturo'd even finished unfolding his napkin and draping it across his lap.

"So tell me Hank," Arturo said between his first bite and his first brushing of the crumbs on his mustache, "how does the reality of running your own agency compare with a good *Simon and Simon* repeat?"

"Every bit as exciting."

Arturo's dark eyes twinkled. "Ah then, have you been involved in any car chases? And, more importantly, have you saved the lives of any beautiful women who are eternally grateful to you and are fulfilling your every desire?"

"Three car chases, seven beautiful babes, unlimited desires fulfilled . . . some I'd never even dreamed of before."

"Ah, the life of a bachelor private eye." Arturo sighed like an envious, sixty-three year old, married man. Of course, I knew that Arturo didn't envy me in the least . . . he had no reason to. Women, young and old alike, swooned whenever he entered a room—a reaction that Arturo obviously relished, but never acted on. Why should he? He'd been married for over forty years to one of the most wonderful women on the planet. The truth was that I envied him.

"Now, my *amigo*, how about the truth?" Arturo asked.

I filled him in on selected details of my case, leaving out the fact that I'd found a dead body and failed to report it. Arturo acknowledged each bit of information with an "I see," or a "hmmm," and an occasional nod of the head. Once I finished, he took a final bite of his croissant, then paused without speaking for what felt like hours, his eyes somehow becoming deeper and darker as he scanned the room.

Finally, he broke the silence. "And you think that your client's grandson, this Richard Tompkins, was involved in the robbery of Discount Danny's Stereos 'N' More."

My mouth dropped open like an empty steam shovel—I hadn't mentioned the stereo store to him. "How'd you know that?"

"Because I saw you on camera last night. And I do hope that you fully appreciate that CD player, because it is a marvelous unit. Of course, knowing you, its potential will be utterly wasted by your preference for thirty year old rock-and-roll tunes. The only way to fully exploit the nuances of your new equipment is—"

"Arturo, I wanted to talk to you for a purpose . . . and it wasn't to discuss your love of classical music."

"Maybe it was to discuss your need for a hair cut? When I saw you on the monitor last night, I hardly recognized you. Between that mop and the girth you've added during the past two months, you've certainly changed your image. Is this transformation a part of your undercover *modus operandi*?"

I glanced at my face in the reflection of the window. Arturo was right, I looked like a circa '64 version of one of the Beatles, or maybe the member of the Three Stooges who probably used a bowl as a template for chopping off his hair. I made a mental note to get a hair cut. Then I poked at my newly acquired belly—what had been trim and firm while I'd been working at W-L's had expanded rapidly in my new life. As I poked, it was all I could do to keep from letting out with a Pillsbury Dough Boy-like squeal. I made another mental note, this one to resume my old exercise program.

"If you saw me that clearly, then you must have seen the guys who robbed the place a couple of months ago. What did they look like?"

"Sorry, but I didn't see them at all. Nobody at VAST saw them because the system was down."

"Your whole system?"

"No, just over at Discount Danny's. His cameras shut off sometime in the afternoon. I immediately called over to see if everything was okay. Danny told me that the store was having some electrical problems. He said that his circuits were overloaded by having too many high powered stereos on at the same time. I offered to send a guard over to his store until his cameras were up and running again, but he declined."

"Had this ever happened before?"

Arturo folded his napkin neatly into a square. "It rarely ever happens with our other customers, but it happens fairly often at Danny's—at least three times in the past six months. He has too many things plugged in over there, and the building is very old. You know how the wiring is in those old buildings; a paper clip in a socket could blow the whole system, and he has a lot more than paper clips plugged in over there."

His comment reminded me of when I was a kid and my mom had three major fears: one was that I'd impale myself on a pair of scissors while running; the second was that I'd put somebody's eye out with a rubber band; and the third was that I'd electrocute myself by sticking a paper clip into an electrical outlet. Well, I'd done all three and I had no puncture wounds in my chest, all my friends and acquaintances still had their full complement of eyes, and I hadn't electrocuted myself . . . although I had cut the power to nearly half the house when I jammed a plastic handled letter-opener into an electrical outlet. My punishment for that escapade was something that to this day I still don't like to think about.

I asked Arturo: "You think it's more than just a coincidence that the surveillance system went out on the very night that the store was robbed?"

Arturo reopened the pink box and placed his neatly folded napkin into it. Then he reached across the table and picked up my wadded one. He put it into the box, closed the lid and retied the string. "I think I know where you're going with that question, Hank. You're wondering if someone tampered with the electrical system that feeds our cameras, so that the store could be robbed undetected."

"Precisely."

"Actually, I wondered about that as well. In fact I went over there the next morning to check it out. I looked to see if the thieves had cut the wires or otherwise specifically debilitated our system. My conclusion was that the outage was legit. The power was out to about one quarter of the store. The wiring was as fried as the Colonel's chickens. Danny Murphy is just lucky that his store didn't burn down."

I couldn't stand looking at the precisely-tied, pink box anymore. I reached over, picked it up and tossed it into the trash can . . . two points. "Why didn't Danny take you up on your offer to send a guard over while his cameras were down?"

"The almighty buck, that's why. It would have cost him about a hundred dollars."

"So it didn't surprise you when he refused your offer?"

"I knew what he'd say before he even said it; that he should have a guard for free. But he also knew what I'd say, which was 'no.'"

"You guys clairvoyant or something?"

Arturo shook his head. "Hardly. It's just that we'd had the same exact conversation every time his power went out. He knew the rules. If the cameras were down due to our error, then I'd send a guard over for free. If the cameras were down due to an error on his part, I would charge for the guard. This instance clearly wasn't our fault, and he knew it."

"Anything else you know about the robbery?"

"Only that they took him for about thirty grand in cash."

"How much in merchandise?"

"Nothing. They didn't take so much as a battery."

I found that hard to believe. If I'd robbed a store like Discount Danny's, I would've loaded up my car with all the stereo gear that would fit . . . one more reason to replace the dinky Metro.

"Do you have any idea who robbed him?" I asked.

"Only what Danny told me. He described them as young hunks— big and muscular like football players. Probably a bit like you used to be. Did I mention to you that you are looking a little soft around the edges, Hank?"

"You did, and it's not that bad."

"If you say so, my *amigo*. But, take my word for this, you need to get out and either start chasing criminals or chasing women, because if you don't, pretty soon you'll be looking just like that fat detective on the reruns. What's his name?"

I knew who he meant—Cannon. "Barnaby Jones," I said innocently.

"No, he's the older gentleman . . . and quite thin. I'm talking about the one who looks like Broderick Crawford and every time he gets into his Lincoln, the car practically bottoms out."

"Mannix."

"No," Arturo said with disgust. "Joe Mannix was played by Mike Connors, a former basketball champ who could hardly be described as obese."

"I thought Mike Connors starred in *The Rifleman*."

"*No*, that was *Chuck* Connors, who was also a former basketball player. I'm talking about that big, round detective."

"Columbo?"

"Screw you, my *amigo*."

"I didn't think I was your type, especially now that I'm fat like Jim Rockford."

Arturo's eyes locked on me and turned hard. "Don't you make fun of Rockford, he's my favorite."

"He's not real," I said. "He's just a character on TV played by a guy named James Gardner."

"Garner!" Arturo's voice practically reached across the table, grabbed me by the throat and strangled me. For such a normally genteel sort, Arturo was certainly easy to get a rise out of. No wonder he'd nearly cracked under pressure when he'd been a cop.

"Calm down, Arturo. You're talking about Cannon. You know how I remembered?"

"How?"

"'Cause you're acting like a loose one right now." I looked at Arturo and waited for him to laugh. I had a long wait. I finally gave up and asked him some more questions. "Is there anything else you could tell me about the robbery?"

"I've told you all that I know." His voice was distant and his eyes searched the ceiling.

"What about the store itself?"

Arturo didn't respond. I thought that he was, at the very least, ignoring my question—at the most, that he'd taken a mental trip into outer space.

"Arturo?" I waved my hand in front of his face. His body snapped abruptly and his eyes refocused. "Did you notice anything unusual about the store itself?"

"It's probably nothing," Arturo answered, his demeanor returning to normal, "but Danny didn't have nearly as much merchandise as usual. Some of the shelves were practically empty and he had bare flooring where he normally had cartons of equipment stacked up on display."

"You can't sell from an empty cart," I muttered.

"What?" Arturo cocked his head.

"Oh, I was just remembering what Mr. Eaton, the store manager over at the Kingston Beach W-L's used to say whenever our stock got low. He'd call the corporate buying office and scream at them about how he couldn't sell from an empty cart. The corporate inventory system was so screwed up that they never had any idea when we needed more merchandise."

"Well, Danny's cart was very close to being empty two months ago. I thought that he might be having troubles with his suppliers and that

66

perhaps they weren't shipping any product to him. I was concerned that he might not be paying his bills on time. In fact, as soon as I returned to my office, I asked my bookkeeper to see if Danny was up-to-date in paying us."

"And?"

"Like clockwork. Absolutely no problems. And the next time I visited his store the shelves were full, so I assume that he must have just had a momentary glitch in receiving merchandise."

While Arturo talked, I looked down at my spiral pad and the questions and answers I'd written the night before. My eyes fixed on the name that Lori had given me. "Arturo, have you ever heard of a man named Scott Mansell? Young guy, kind of preppy looking."

"No, I can't say that I have. Who is he?"

I debated whether to tell Arturo about the dead man I'd discovered at Richard's. I decided to pass. No sense telling too much, too soon. "He may be the man I saw driving my client's station wagon yesterday morning."

"Sorry, but I never heard of him. Do you think that there is any connection between this Mansell fellow and the robbery at Discount Danny's?"

I shook my head. "I don't see how. He doesn't fit the description that Danny gave to me or to you."

"How about your client's grandson? Does he fit the description?"

"Not at all."

"Then why does your client think that his grandson was involved in the hold-up?

I shrugged my shoulders. "I'm not really sure at this point. I think my client suspects his grandson might have been involved somehow."

"You're *not sure*? You *think*?" Arturo looked at his watch and stood. "What kind of a PI are you, Hank?"

I realized that my statement had sounded more than just a little stupid. After all, I should know what my client thinks about the relationship of his grandson to the holdup. I also—at this very moment—remembered that I hadn't heard back from Walter after I'd left a message with Crystal. "It's a long story," I said, hoping my response would keep me from appearing completely inept.

"Aren't they all? Well, you're just going to have to spare me the details because I have to leave to meet with the man who took your place over at W-L's. What do you know about Treet?"

I couldn't help myself from making a face like I'd just smelled rotting garbage. I didn't know much about Greg Treet, but what I knew I didn't like. Why the brass couldn't see through that brown-noser was beyond me. "A little," I said as I stood. "For the past few years he ran security at the W-L's store in La Jolla. When I quit, W-L's moved him—against his strenuous objections—into my spot at the Kingston Beach store. Since Kingston Beach does about double the volume of La Jolla, he ended up with a pretty good promotion."

"That's not how Treet sees it."

"He doesn't think it's a promotion?" I tried not to sound wounded, but the fact was that I was still pretty proud of the fact that I'd been the security manager of what corporate called an "A" store. La Jolla was a "C" store, at best.

"He's telling everyone that he was brought in to clean house. He says that you left the place in a mess."

I pushed my chair hard against the wall. "That's a bunch of bull."

"Hey, don't yell at me. I'm just telling you what he said."

"If I did such a terrible job, then explain how I brought down the biggest drug ring in the history of Kingston Beach? Huh? And tell me why the Chief of Police awarded me that check for ten thousand grand."

Arturo paused, then finally said in a sing-song voice: "You're not going to like this."

I leaned over and rested my hands on the table. "Try me."

"Treet says that if he'd been the security manager at Kingston Beach, the drug ring never would have even gotten its foot in the door. To hear him say it, you deserved to get the ax instead of a reward. He's—"

"He couldn't have done half the job I did," I interrupted, my blood pressure pushing up against my scalp and my fists slamming the table.

"He's saying he could've. And he's implementing a whole variety of new procedures over there as we speak. Apparently they worked quite well for him over in La Jolla."

"Like what, for instance?"

"I don't know all the details. Maybe he'll tell me when I meet with him."

"Fine. You give him a message for me when you see him. Tell him he's a sniveling little liar."

"No can do, my *amigo*. I'm going to be very, very nice to Mr. Treet. There is simply no way that I'm going to jeopardize my company's chance of regaining the contract at the Kingston Beach store. I—"

"Wait! You said regaining. What do you—"

"We lost the contract as soon as Treet took over your old position. It's handled internally now. He and his staff monitor the security cameras instead of having VAST do it. And they respond to the alarms if they go off after the store has closed. That's the way he did it in La Jolla, and he claims that he saved thousands of dollars by doing the work in-house instead of using a service like mine. I'm going to meet with him and try to sweet talk him into using VAST again . . . at a discounted rate."

"For less than you charged me?"

Arturo looked down at the table and answered me quietly. "I'll do whatever I can to stay alive in this business my *amigo*. If I don't, I'm toast. So Hank, I'm going to be sweet as pie to your Mr. Treet."

"Toast. Pie. Treet. I can't believe that you'd sell me out like that and kiss his butt."

"Temper, temper. I didn't say that I'm actually going to like the man, I'm just going to do my best to charm him into liking me while I present him with a discount that he hopefully won't be able to refuse." Arturo looked up at me. "Hank, as far as I'm concerned, anyone who defames you is lower than a snake's belly. Still, I have to make a living."

"You owe me Arturo."

Arturo said nothing.

"Arturo," I said.

"What?"

"I said that you owe me."

"What do you want from me? I can't refuse to work with Treet just because he says that you did a crappy job."

"I'm not asking you to do that."

"What then?"

"I want you to ask your guys at VAST if they've ever heard of Richard Tompkins or Scott Mansell. If they have, you give me a buzz and fill me in. If they haven't, you tell them to ask around. Okay?"

"Certainly." Arturo glanced at his watch and winced.

"And find out what you can about a skinny guy with a graying pony tale who may hang around with them."

Arturo pulled a digital organizer out of his breast pocket and began keying in some words. "What's his name?"

"I don't know. You tell me after you and your boys have snooped around a little. Okay?"

"I suppose."

"And one more thing—"

Arturo looked up at me. "You just don't stop do you?"

"I need to know who'll develop a roll of film for me without asking me any questions and without giving any answers to anybody else. Can you do that for me?"

Arturo snapped his electronic organizer shut, returned it to his pocket and reached out his hand. "Give the film to me. I'll get it done for you at our lab. We use a system that's so secure that even the person operating the equipment won't see the results. It's similar to the equipment used at the one-hour film processing services, except that the finished photos and negatives go straight into an envelope that is automatically sealed with pressure sensitive adhesive. The system cost us a lot of money, but we think it's worth it for maintaining total confidentiality. I'll call you as soon as your pictures are ready."

I remembered that I'd unloaded the camera in my apartment and left the film on my coffee table. "I'll have to drop the roll past your office."

Arturo shrugged. "Whatever works for you."

"Thanks, I owe you."

"That's right, my *amigo*. One hundred dollars per roll of confidential processing." Arturo flashed me a gigantic smile, turned and walked out of the office.

I picked up my files and returned to my cubby-hole, just as Lori stepped into my doorway and my phone rang. I motioned Lori away and answered my phone.

"Hello my good man." Walter sounded bright and full of energy. "I'm sorry I didn't call you last night, but I slept completely through the evening. I just awakened and Crystal told me of your call. Have you any news about my grandson's whereabouts?"

I decided not to alarm the old man with news about the dead body in his grandson's closet. "I'm working on it at this very moment and I've come across a name that may be of help. Did Richard ever mention a man named Scott Mansell?"

"No, can't say that I've ever heard that name before. Why? Has this Mansell fellow disappeared too?"

Disappeared from the land of the living, I thought. "I think he may have been the last person driving your Fiat and I thought maybe you'd know who he is and where he lives."

"Sorry, but I never heard of the boy. Did you find my car?"

"I'm working on that Mr. Tompkins—"

"*Walter!*"

"Walter."

"How many times do I have to tell you not to call me Mr. Tompkins. I'm beginning to wonder if you remember anything I say to you. Now tell me everything you've accomplished since you began my case."

"I know the name of the man who was driving your car," I said defensively.

"What about my grandson?" Walter shouted.

"I told you, I'm working on that."

"And my car?"

"I'm working on that too, Mr. Tompkins."

Walter exploded into the receiver. "You know, I'm the one who's supposed to be hard of hearing, but you're the one who keeps repeating himself over-and-over again and telling me absolutely nothing. I'm beginning to wonder about you, young man. I'm paying you to get results, so you better not be wasting my money."

"I'm not," I protested.

"Not getting results?"

"Not wasting your money."

"Well you just keep it that way, because I am not your ordinary, run-of-the-mill old fool, thank you very much." Walter hung up.

I slammed my phone down and looked up to see Lori standing in my doorway, coffee mug in hand, its aroma filling the room.

"Trouble?" she asked.

I nodded. "Impatient client."

"Would some information about Scott Mansell be of any help?"

I leaned across my desk. "What do you have?"

Lori smiled and cocked her head. "As soon as I finish my coffee, I'll put you in touch with him."

"And just how do you propose to do that, are you going to conduct a seance?"

She looked at me with a puzzled expression. "No, it's much more mundane than that." She glimpsed at her watch, then back at me. "I don't suppose you have a pair of shorts, a T-shirt and some tennis shoes with you."

"No, why?"

"Do you have any appointments in the next couple of hours?"

"No, why?" I was getting pretty good with this response.

"Because you're going to need to drive over to your apartment, pick up a change of clothes, and then wait for me to drive past and pick you up. Then we'll be off on an adventure."

I slumped in my chair, doubtful that her so-called adventure could measure up to anything that had happened to me yesterday. My mind replayed the moment when Scott Mansell's body fell out of Richard's closet and practically into my face, then it flashed to the gunshots at the

Dumpster and then to the Suburban nearly running me off into the Pacific Ocean.

Lori drummed her perfectly manicured fingernails on the side of her mug. "Well, are you going to go with me or are you going to continue to sit there in a trance like some kind of zombie?"

"Why do we have to go together? Can't you just tell me where to go?"

"Oh, believe me, there are *many* times that I'd love to tell you *exactly* where to go . . . including this very moment." Lori gave me the famous smirk. "I'll meet you at your place in twenty minutes." She took a sip from her coffee mug, the steam rising past her mischievous eyes.

SEVEN

Exactly twenty minutes and zero seconds after I'd pulled out of the office parking lot, Lori stood on my porch ringing the doorbell. I'd barely had time to stuff my shorts and shirt into my gym bag, on top of my collection of spy toys. When I heard the bell, I picked my bag up off the dinette table and threaded my way to the front door. I say "threaded" because I'd created an obstacle course between the table and the door consisting of the CD player box; its corrugated cardboard and molded Styrofoam packing materials; a couple dozen car magazines that somehow had never made it back onto the closet shelves; a pair of pillows I'd used to prop my neck against while watching *Magnum* three nights ago; a large bowl holding about fifteen or twenty unpopped popcorn kernels; three empty Coke bottles; and a football.

"Nice place you have here," Lori said as she scanned my combination living-dining-anything room. "I simply must have your housekeeper's name."

"Actually, she didn't show this week," I said with feigned distress. "Good help is so difficult to find these days." I locked the door behind me as Lori and I walked out to her Ghia. She opened the car door for me, a courtesy that I wasn't so sure I felt comfortable with. Next thing I knew, women would begin opening up doors for men at stores and restaurants. Of course, there wasn't any question in my mind about who'd still be expected to pick up the check after a meal.

The drive to the Coastal Country Club took about a half hour. The Ghia's top was down, the sky was blue, the sun was warm, and the ocean sparkled—all the ingredients for a wonderful ride, except that during the entire trip I kept glancing back over my shoulder, looking to see if the Suburban was following us. There was another problem too—Lori drove, well, like a girl; lugging the engine, upshifting too soon, downshifting too late, obeying the speed limits, and braking unnecessarily through the winding portions of the road as we rose higher up the cliffs above the Pacific Ocean. It drove me absolutely nuts and made me wish I were blasting along in my Vette.

Tall trees—don't ask me what kind they were, I only recognize palm and Christmas—lined the approach to the gated entrance of the country club. When we approached the gate, a man in a polo shirt and khakis that I recognized as matching the ones Scott Mansell had been wearing, stepped out of the booth for us—finally, I knew how Lori had figured out Mansell's name and where he had worked. Lori handed the man what appeared to be a credit card. The man looked at it and returned it to her.

"Please enjoy yourself Mrs. Green," he said as the gate raised and we motored forward.

I raised an eyebrow. "Mrs. Green?"

"Barry is a member and he lets me use the facilities. The only catch is that I have to pretend that I'm his wife."

"Oh, I thought for a moment that the two of you were actually married and that you'd been keeping it a secret from me. That would explain your unlisted number."

Lori drove the Ghia up a narrow, flower-lined road toward a parking lot. "Not hardly. He's not my type."

Actually I'd been wondering what type Green was. After eight weeks of leasing office space from him, I still hadn't met the man. But then, I didn't know too much about Lori either. I decided it was time to find out about her.

"Yesterday, on the phone, you identified yourself as Samantha Branberry. Today you're Mrs. Barry Green. Is there actually a person named Lori Reed, or is she just a figment of my imagination?"

Lori smiled as she coasted the Ghia into an end parking place. "Samantha Branberry was actually a girl I knew back in grade school. Whenever we had a substitute teacher, I'd sit in her seat and she'd sit in mine. Then we'd both see how much trouble we could get ourselves— and each other—into. I've been using her name ever since, whenever I'm doing something that isn't quite kosher. It's much more fun that way."

We climbed out of her car and walked up the marble steps to a huge, four story building. The brass sign at the entrance read "Fitness Building," but it looked more like the White House to me. I noticed that all the employees were dressed like Scott Mansell.

"What department does Mansell work in?" I asked Lori as we stepped into the building.

She didn't answer, instead she gave me some instructions: "You go change into your shorts and meet me over there." Lori pointed across the large, glass-walled room we'd entered, toward a double door. The panoramic view of the Pacific ocean distracted me for a moment—the blue sky, the puffy white clouds, the sparkling blue water punctuated by the sails of wealthy people's boats. I imagined myself on a sailboat with a half-dozen bikini-clad beauties as my crew.

"Hank." Lori interrupted my reverie. "The men's locker room is over there. You'd better get going. Class starts in less than five minutes."

"Class?" I said as I looked toward the locker room door. When I turned back to face Lori, she'd disappeared.

I found an empty locker and changed into my basketball shorts and a loose-fitting T-shirt designed to resemble the top half of an Indy 500 driving suit. I'd already been wearing a pair of Reebok running shoes, just in case I had to chase after a perp. Moments later I was next to Lori in a formation of about two dozen grunting women of a vast variety of shapes and sizes, bouncing and thrusting and arching and kicking and swinging to the sound of disco music from the seventies—there was no doubt about it, I had just entered hell.

A boxy brunette with calves more solid than granite, led the exercises. If ever there were a masochistic killer, she was it. I squatted and jumped; reached and stretched; and twisted and pulled until I thought my legs would fly off and my torso would burrow itself into the polished wood floor like a bit in a Makita drill. I huffed and puffed and sweated and strained, always at least three moves behind the instructor. Then I looked over at Lori. She looked just as calm and serene as if she were resting on a chaise lounge, sipping a margarita—not so much as one bead of sweat appearing on her forehead. Lori must have sensed that I was staring at her, she looked over at me and gave me her famous smirk.

"You're breathing heavily," she noted with amusement.

I nodded, sweat flipping off my nose with each nod.

"Maybe this will teach you not to mess with my coffee, Mr. Hammond." More of her famous smirk.

"What are you . . . talking . . . about?" I panted between deep knee bends.

"I know I put coffee in the machine before I left work yesterday."

Lori began running in place. I looked around . . . everyone else was running in place too. I followed suit, pumping my legs up-and-down and swinging my arms back-and-forth in an exaggerated characterization of a marathon runner.

"You," Lori continued, "for some unfathomable reason, emptied it out before I arrived at the office this morning."

I gave Lori my best attempt at a look of innocence.

"Don't give me that look, Hank Hammond. I'm wise to you."

Busted, I thought, pledging to myself that I'd never again do something stupid like messing with her coffee. "So that's . . . what this . . . is about . . . Coffee? . . . Not Mansell?"

"Oh, I'm quite sure the information you need about Scott Mansell is here. I did my part. I found out that he works here, and I got you into the country club. Now it's time for you to do your part and start acting like a detective."

"Right," I said as I turned and ran to the locker room, my arms and legs finally in synch with the in-place running of the exercisers.

"I'll meet you in an hour, Hank," Lori called out to me. "I'll be relaxing up at the juice bar, overlooking the ocean." I waved my arm to her and nodded, just before slamming myself through the locker room door and into a private world where I could collapse onto a towel-covered bench. I couldn't believe how beat I was. It had only been a couple of months since I'd left W-L's and in that time I'd packed on this lousy gut and reduced my stamina to the point that I had trouble keeping up with a bunch of middle-aged socialites. I tried to convince myself that it had been the choreography and the disco music that had zapped me of my strength, but I knew better. When I'd worked at W-L's, I used to show up an hour earlier than anyone else so I could work out on the exercise machines in the sporting goods department. I'd considered it my own free health club membership. Since I'd left, I'd been too cheap to join a real one and the nearly immediate results were depressing.

I felt more human after showering and changing back into my Dockers, western belt and sport shirt. I suppose that my attire didn't really fit into the country club culture too well, but then I've never really fancied myself as much of a navy blue blazer and ascot kind of guy anyway. I decided that I'd talk to a few of the employees, do my best to convince them that Scott Mansell was an old friend of mine who I hadn't seen in a few years, and find out as much as I could about him. The first four people I spoke with didn't have any idea who I was talking about, but then I met a young woman named Terri. She was so tan, blonde and pretty that she struck me as being the perfect female counterpart to Mansell. Too bad she smelled like a flower shop and chewed gum like a cow chews its cud.

She told me that Scott Mansell hadn't showed up for work either yesterday or today. Poor attendance doesn't necessarily mean that someone is dead, but when Terri told me that she'd met Richard Tompkins, I knew Lori had identified the right man.

"I'll never forget Richard," she said, rolling her eyes. "He made a pass at me within the first ten minutes we met. He was kind of cute, so I went along with it. The very next day, his wife called me up at work and told me that she'd kill me if I ever so much as looked at him again. The jerk had never even told me he was married."

Walter had never told me that Richard was married, a rather important detail for him to have omitted. "You ever see him again?" I asked.

Terri snapped her gum a couple of times. "No way! I don't need any trouble like that. Besides, there are plenty of other guys out there to chose from."

When I asked her about the man with the gray ponytail, she made a face like she'd just swallowed a spoonful of Kaopectate.

"I've seen him with Scott," she said, "but I don't know anything about him except that he looks like a creep." Then she looked me directly in the eye. "Don't I know you from someplace? You look kind of familiar."

"I don't see how. Maybe I just have one of those faces."

Terri cocked her head. "Are you a member here?"

"No, I'm just visiting."

"Has your picture ever been in the newspaper or something? I could swear that I've seen you before."

Sweat started beading up on my forehead. The publicity I'd been so proud of could be about to backfire. "Me? No way," I said.

Terri continued looking at my face. "You didn't used to work at W-L's did you?"

My heart stopped. "No," I lied, "why?"

"Because that's where I used to work, at the La Jolla store."

I breathed a sigh of relief . . . I'd never even been in Treet's old store.

"In fact, that's where I first met Scott," she continued. "Then we both came here. He couldn't wait to quit his job as a stocker and start working in the tennis shop."

"So, you're his girl friend?"

Terri held up the ring finger of her left hand. In the place where a ring had been was the only un-tanned part of her hand. "Not after he took off without calling me."

79

"Yesterday?" I asked.

"You got it. We were supposed to go out last night and he didn't even give me a call. Can you imagine someone actually standing me up?"

I looked her up and down. "No," I said.

"Me either."

"Have you called him to find out if he's okay?"

"There's no phone on his boat."

"He lives on a boat?"

"Yeah, the *Flying Fish*. It's tied up at the Captains' Coast Marina."

"Well, did you go past his boat to see how he was doing?"

Terri rolled her eyes up and rocked her head from side-to-side. "Of course not. I don't want him to think that I'm desperate for a boy friend or that I'm actually all that interested in him. There are plenty of other guys around. You know, what's that saying?" She closed her eyes, then opened them big as saucers and looked straight at me. "So many men, so little time. That's it." She clasped her hands behind her back, thrust out her chest so far that it strained her polo shirt, and giggled as my eyes practically popped out of my head. "I don't have to chase after men. They chase me."

"I'm sure they do." I smiled. Terri didn't smile back. I decided I'd better get as much info as I could and move along. "Were you wearing Scott's ring when you had your little fling with Richard?"

"Of course I was wearing it, he was my boy friend. Only it wasn't a fling! I only just went out with Richard once. It wasn't really any big deal. Why, what's it to you?"

I faked a response: "I just remember that Scott used to be pretty jealous and I wondered if he and Richard might have had a fight over you."

"I wish!" Terri popped her gum, blew a small bubble, then sucked it back into her mouth. "That would've been kind of fun."

"What about Richard? Do you think he was jealous of Scott being your boy friend?"

"You're really starting to bore me, mister."

"Sorry, it's just that I haven't seen Scott in awhile and I was curious." I debated whether to ask more questions, then decided to just plunge right in until she stopped me. "Is Scott still driving a Suburban?"

Terri wrinkled her brow. "What's that?"

"A big four-wheel-drive truck. His was black."

"No way. He's not into that whole sport-utility thing."

"How about an old Fiat station wagon. Have you seen Scott driving one of those lately?"

As soon as I saw the reaction on Terri's face, I knew I'd gone too far with my questioning.

"What did you say your name is?" she asked.

"I didn't."

"Well, what's your name? In case I see Scott and I decide to tell him about some guy who's been bothering me."

"Branberry," I said. "Sam Branberry." I offered my right hand to Terri. She responded by putting both of her hands on her hips and frowning.

"Well, Mr. Branberry, I'm sick of all your questions. So, if you don't mind, I'd like to get back to work and I'd appreciate it if you didn't bother me again. Because if you do, I'm going to tell my manager that you've been harassing me. Do you understand?"

I nodded and Terri turned on her heels and walked away as quickly as her size fives could carry her.

Lori and I slithered down the hill in her Ghia. I found myself clinging to the dashboard's grab handle and tugging on my seat belt to make certain it was properly latched. A taste of my own medicine perhaps? How many passengers had I frightened out of their wits with my impersonation of an IndyCar racer? None lately, at least not since I'd been driving the itty-bitty rental car. But the fear that grabbed my body and soul while riding with Lori didn't come from the speeds we were traveling, it came from her awkward and utterly inappropriate negotiating of the turns. The woman may be smart, but that didn't make her a driving whiz. I almost commented about it, then I remembered how swiftly and effectively she'd punished me for my coffee prank. I decided it was best to keep my big mouth shut.

As we dropped down to the flatlands, my blood pressure dropped commensurably and my mind snapped back to Richard's disappearance and Scott Mansell's murder.

"Lori," I said as she stopped at a red light. "Would you mind driving past Mansell's boat slip on the way back to the office?"

She looked at her watch. "I can drive past, but that's all I can do. Barry allows me an extended break for my exercise class, but I can't be gone too long."

"He won't know how long you're gone," I said. "He's not even in town. Fact is, I'm beginning to wonder if this Green person even exists. The guy is never in the office."

Lori looked over at me and winked. "That's exactly why I have to get back to the office. Who do you think runs that place? Without me, it would absolutely fall apart."

After working with her for the past two months, I knew that she was right. "Just a few minutes," I said. "I promise. It's only a couple of blocks out of our way."

A car behind us honked. Our light had been green for at least fifteen seconds, but there was no way in hell that I was going to tell her. After the second honk, we chugged off in second gear. "Okay," she said.

I glanced at my gym bag and remembered the film I'd picked up in my apartment. "Oh, and just one more thing. Could we make one other stop along the way?"

"No. I told you I have to get back to the office."

"It won't take long."

She sighed. "Where is it?"

I gave her the address to VAST and she gave me an icy stare. "That isn't even close to being 'on the way.'"

"But I have to get my film there as soon as possible. It has to be developed right away."

"Why don't you just take it to the drug store next door to our office? They offer one hour service."

I didn't want to argue, but didn't have any choice. "Because the film can't go to just any processor."

Lori looked at me instead of the road. "Why not?"

"Because it's evidence and it has to be handled very confidentially."

Lori grabbed the film from me. "Evidence? How exciting. Here, you give it to me. I can drop it off after I've dropped you off."

"What do you mean, dropped me off? Aren't you going to wait for me? I'll only be a minute."

"What if Scott Mansell is on his boat? Won't you want to talk to him? Won't you want to ask him questions, interrogate him, apprehend him, or whatever it is that PIs do when they've tracked down a perk?"

"Perp," I corrected.

"Whatever." Lori pulled up to the entrance of the Captains' Coast Marina, then made a quick U-turn when she spotted the locked gate. "I guess you're just going to have to forget it. You can't get past that gate, let alone near his boat."

"Oh, I can get in all right," I boasted.

Lori pulled to the side of the road and parked with her engine running. "You're going to break-and-enter aren't you?"

"I wouldn't exactly describe it as breaking and entering."

"What would you call it then?"

"Entering. I don't intend to break anything."

Lori revved up the VW's engine. "That does it for me. I'm out of here."

"So you're not going to wait for me?"

"Not on your life. I'm not going to be an accessory to burglary."

"I'm not going to steal anything."

"Whatever. Now, please extricate yourself from my car so that I can go back to performing my chosen profession. I have a law office to run. And it's probably a pretty damn good thing that I do, because I have this sinking feeling that you're going to need a lawyer real soon."

"Do me a favor Lori. Don't use the word sinking when I'm about to board a boat. Okay?"

Lori smirked.

I unbuckled my seat belt. "About the film——"

"What?" Lori snapped.

"Ask for Arturo Garcia. Tell him that this is from Hank Hammond. Then give him the cassette and this." I pulled off one of my Reeboks and removed a tightly folded bill from the insole. "Tell him to keep the change."

"What in the Sam Hill is this?" Lori exclaimed, staring at the money.

"It's a hundred dollars," I said.

"I know that. But since when does it cost a hundred dollars to develop a roll of film?"

"I told you it was evidence. Confidential evidence."

Lori arched an eyebrow and took the money. "Hank, am I going to be in any danger?"

"From Arturo?"

"No, not from Arturo. From this stink-soaked hundred dollar bill that you've been saving in your shoe." She held it up gingerly between her thumb and first finger. "How long have you been saving this, since the Johnson administration?"

"Close. My mother always said to wear clean underwear and to carry emergency money, just in case."

"In case what?"

"She never told me that, but I'm pretty sure that this qualifies. You tell Arturo that I'll go past his office and pick the prints up later today."

Lori shook her head. "Okay, but this is most definitely against my better judgment." She revved up her engine and stuck the shift lever into fourth gear. "Now, get going before I come to my senses and turn you into the police."

I grabbed my gym bag, opened the door and began stepping onto the sidewalk. "You wouldn't."

"I might. I'm still pretty steamed about my coffee this morning." Lori popped the clutch and the Karmann-Ghia jerked and stalled. "Don't you say a word," she said. Then she restarted the car, jammed it into first, and took off just as I'd managed to get both my feet on the pavement.

I walked back toward the entrance to Captains' Coast Marina, trying my best to look as though I belonged in an area where I was utterly, hopelessly unfamiliar. I'd only been on a boat once before, and it hadn't been a pleasant experience. About fifteen years ago, midway between Newport Beach and Catalina Island—on a tiny eighteen foot sailboat with a young woman to die for, I nearly did. Or, at least I felt like I'd died. Caught in mildly choppy seas, I lost all of my lunch—along with most of my pride. Since that day, I've steadfastly avoided anything to do with boats. The mere thought of setting foot on one practically turned me green. Today I had no choice . . . I had to get inside Scott Mansell's boat.

I sat on a concrete bench that faced the marina, breathing the salt air and trying to figure out how to get inside. Wrought iron fencing, easily fifteen feet tall, ran the entire length of the marina. I knew that I couldn't jump high enough to grab the top of the iron bars, and I certainly couldn't squeeze between them. There were only three ways I could think of to accomplish my mission. The first was to steal a boat from a less secure marina and sail it into Captains' Coast from the ocean-side. The second was to carjack the driver of one of the Cadillacs or Jaguars as they entered the marina through the gate. The third plan—and the only one I considered for more than a nanosecond—was to somehow bypass the gate's security system.

I waited until there was a break in traffic and walked, as quickly and nonchalantly as I could, to the gate. I looked both ways to make certain that nobody was watching, then grabbed the iron bars with both hands and struggled in vain to slide the gate to the side. I'd been pretty sure that it wouldn't work, but it never hurts to give things like this a try. I didn't think that my next idea would work either, but I had to at least make an attempt. I walked back to the brick monument that stood on the driver's side of the entrance and poked a few buttons at random into the key pad, hoping to somehow guess some boat owner's secret access code that would make the gate slide open. I knew that I had just about as much chance of accomplishing that feat as I did in determining the winning lottery numbers, something that I'd failed at for over one hundred consecutive weeks. After inputting several combinations of numbers, I gave up. At this point I knew that I had no choice but to hide someplace close to the gate, wait until a boat owner drove up and input the proper code, and then sneak in during the short time that the gate remained open. I scanned the immediate vicinity for a place to conceal myself, and decided that my best choice—actually my only choice—was to curl up into a ball behind a shrub barely larger than a portable television.

I crouched for so long that I lost the circulation to both my legs. They felt like someone had opened them up and poured 7-Up into them. Just when I didn't think that I could take it any longer, a woman in a silver Mercedes approached the marina. I watched as she pulled up into the entryway, powered her window down, punched in her secret number, waited until the iron gate slid to the right, pulled slowly past the gate, and waited with the trunk of her car nearly flush to the gate as it slid closed. A very careful woman, one who didn't allow any opportunity for someone to sneak in during the fifteen seconds that the gate was open. I hoped that the next person wouldn't be so careful.

A gray Lexus coupe with a really cool set of custom wheels whipped into the entry and stopped. Perfect, I thought, this driver wouldn't waste any time pulling through the gate. Just as I'd predicted, he did his open sesame routine, chirped his tires and sped into the marina. I grabbed my gym bag and started toward the gate, stumbling momentarily as my legs recovered from their cramps. The gate reversed direction and began sliding closed. I sprinted the last few yards and slipped in just before the gate shut, nearly dropping my bag on the wrong side of the gate. I darted toward a parked maintenance truck and hid behind it while I caught my breath, then I took a quick look in every direction until I was sure that no one had spotted me. The coast was clear and I walked away from the truck just like I belonged in the marina and knew what the heck I was doing.

I didn't have any idea where to find the *Flying Fish*. After all, there were probably a thousand or so boats tied up in the marina, each one more impressive than the last. How could a young kid like Scott Mansell afford a boat, I wondered as I reflected on my nearly empty checking account. I gazed at the parking lot with all the luxury cars parked side-by-side. That's when I saw it. Sticking out like the proverbial sore thumb, right between a pair of Mercedes Benzes, was Walter's old station wagon.

I repressed my instinct to run to the Fiat, realizing that to do so could attract attention. Instead, I slowly sauntered to the car and peered obliquely into the windows. The wooden crate I'd seen yesterday morning was in the back, or at least it appeared to be the same crate. But I distinctly remembered that the crate had been lifted out of the Fiat and into the Suburban. What was it doing back in the station wagon. I looked more closely at the crate to see if there were any identifying labels on it. No labels, but there was a design that I couldn't quite make out stenciled in black across one end of the crate. And there was something else I noticed—something that appeared suspiciously like dried blood along the edge of the lid. My heart began pounding wildly. There had been a dead body in the crate, I thought. I'd been right all along. I looked around to see if anyone was watching, then moved to the driver's door and tugged on the handle. It was locked. I tried each of the other doors and the tailgate without luck. I reached into my pocket for the Fiat keys that I'd removed from Walter's leather box, but just as I did so a grizzly man wearing a watch cap and pulling a red wagon filled with boating paraphernalia, walked up to one of the Mercedes Benzes parked next to me.

"Beautiful day for sailing," he said to me as he unlocked his trunk. "Gentle breeze, probably only eight or nine knots. Much better'n yesterday." The man tossed his gear into the trunk and slammed it shut, then he looked over at me. "I don't recognize you. Are you new to Captains' Coast?"

Since I didn't know the difference between port and starboard without supreme concentration, I knew better than to try to pretend that I actually owned a boat. "Oh, I'm just visiting from out of town."

The man eyed me from head to toe. "How did you get past the gate?"

"My cousin has a boat here and I'm supposed to meet him. He gave me his access code."

"He's not supposed to do that," the man snapped. "It violates our security rules. What's your cousin's name?"

"Scott Mansell."

The man made a clucking noise with his tongue. "That young man has been warned about this before."

"I'm sorry. I didn't know it was against the rules."

He smiled slightly. "Now don't get me wrong. I'm not mad at you, but I sure as blazes am mad at him."

"I'll tell him when I see him. Actually, I could use your help. I forgot which slip is his. You don't happen to know where he parks his boat do you?"

The man's eyes moved from my hairline down to my toes, over to the Fiat, then firmly locked on my face. "He *parks* at slip seventy-nine. His is the Nicholson 58, the red and green one over there." He pointed across several boats toward a beautiful yacht with twin masts, then reached forward to shake my hand. "I'm sorry, I didn't catch your name."

"Sam," I said. "Sam Branberry."

"Robert Wilson. Pleased to meet you." He pointed in the opposite direction of Mansell's boat at a smaller one with blue and white sails. "That's my Cal 25 over there. She may not be a raving beauty like your cousin's, but I love her just the same. I'm going to be making a few trips back-and-forth from her to my car with this little red wagon. You wouldn't be interested in giving me a hand would you?"

I begged off, telling him that I needed to get over to Scotty's boat. I had no idea if anybody ever called Scott Mansell "Scotty," but I thought it somehow lent some authenticity to my charade.

I practically ran to the boat, then hopped over the cables and onto the back of it. There was an odd shaped door that led into the cabin; part of it was horizontal and part of it was vertical—all of it was locked. I reached into my gym bag and pulled out the lock-gun. My fingers and palms were slippery with sweat. At any moment, Robert Wilson or any other boater could pop along and confront me. What would I say? What would I do? There was simply no good way to explain what I was doing breaking into a dead man's boat. I fumbled through at least a dozen attempts to pick the lock until it finally gave way. I tossed the lock-gun into my bag and then tossed the bag into the cabin as I climbed down into what looked to me like a miniature, teak-lined living room. To the left of the living room was a kitchen and to the right was a navigation area filled with an impressive assortment of switches, lights, gauges, radios, and digital panels. Ahead of these was a narrow hallway with two doors on the left side, one on the right, and a larger one at the end. I picked up my bag and grabbed the zapper from inside, then I walked into the hallway and opened each door in sequence.

The first door opened into a head—the only nautical term I was intimately familiar with. It took me less than fifteen seconds to thoroughly peruse it. The second door opened into a bedroom with a pair of small beds. It didn't look like Scott Mansell, or anybody else, had ever spent much time in it. I closed the door and went to the next one. The third door opened into another bedroom, this one with bunk beds. I took a quick look around and then walked the final steps to the door at the end of the hall. Something made me nervous. I don't know what it was, maybe it was the way the boat creaked as it rocked gently back-and-forth. Maybe it was the narrowness of the hallway or the ceiling that brushed against my hair every time I stood up straight. Whatever it was, it made my heart race and my forehead trickle with sweat. I reached for the door, turned the knob and pushed it open with the nose of my zapper. The room was completely black. I stumbled through the room, groping for a cord to open the shades and let sunlight in through the portholes. I found the cord and yanked on it, the room turned bright. On the bed, staring at me with unblinking eyes, was Scott Mansell . . . still very dead.

I gasped . . . just as the room went dark again and I slumped to the floor.

I awoke with a mouthful of carpet fibers and a headache worse than any hangover I'd yet experienced. I ran my fingers over the throbbing knot on the back of my head . . . it felt about the size of a baseball—the knot, not my head. Once I realized who and where I was, I scanned the floor for my zapper. Of course, the perp had taken it . . . another two hundred bucks down the drain. Luckily, I'd fallen on top of my gym bag. Otherwise, whoever had conked me over the head probably would've taken all my PI gear. I slowly raised myself into an ape-like stance, my head spinning like a top. After several unsteady moments I evolved to an erect stance and stared across the room at Scott Mansell. His skin was a color I'd never seen before on a human. I couldn't tell exactly what the color was, but it made my epidermis itch and my stomach turn somersaults. I walked forward very slowly and touched his face—it was cold and clammy. I pulled my hand back and rubbed it furiously on my Dockers to generate some warmth. Then, as the gears finally began meshing in my brain, I realized that Scott Mansell might not be the only other person on board.

I reached down and picked up the chromed winch handle that had obviously been used to smash my cranium. I held it like a Louisville Slugger as I walked to what I assumed to be a closet, stood to the side of the door and threw it open. No one lunged out at me . . . no one shot at me . . . no one zapped me. I peeked in and was greeted with a view of clothes and miscellaneous stuff. I closed the door and walked warily to an open door on the opposite side of the room. I stepped into the private head, slid the frosted shower door to the side and peered into the empty stall. Then I walked back through the bedroom and into the hallway. I opened each of the doors—looking into the rooms for any sign of the person who'd knocked me out—as I made my way back into the living room.

I stepped into the kitchen, traded the winch handle for a towel, and retraced my steps, wiping off every knob, every door, every surface that I'd touched. I even wiped off the spot I'd touched on Mansell's forehead, just to be on the safe side—for all I knew, forensics could take a fingerprint off of dead flesh. Then I made a beeline to the nearest head, stooped over the toilet, and lost my breakfast burrito and croissant. I swore that this would be my absolute last time aboard a boat.

I climbed out of the *Flying Fish*, and onto the dock as I scanned the marina; gym bag in one hand and winch handle in the other. There didn't seem to be any people in sight. I dashed along the dock to get another look at Walter's car. As I approached the parking lot, I could see it disappearing in the distance.

EIGHT

The cab dropped me off four blocks from my office. I didn't want to leave a trail from Scott Mansell's dead body that led directly to me or to my business, so I'd walked a few blocks from the marina and hailed a cab from a motel. I told the cabby to drop me off at Totally Tofu, a too-trendy place that I wouldn't normally visit in a thousand years. It wasn't that I was suddenly getting hip, I just wanted to go where nobody could possibly recognize me. I jumped out in front of the restaurant, went in, washed my hands until my skin practically came off, then walked out and back to my office. I'd given the cabby a phony name during the ride, and I'd made up a story about being a visitor from out of town named Sam Branberry. I probably should've just sat in the back seat with my mouth shut, but I had so much nervous energy that I'd nearly exploded.

When I walked into the office, Lori immediately stood and whisked me into my cubby-hole, sat me down and closed the door behind us. Her movements were quick and fidgety, unlike anything I'd ever seen with her before.

"Scott Mansell is *dead*," she whispered as she hovered over my desk.

I simply stared up at her for several seconds. "How do you know that?" I finally asked, hoping she hadn't heard it on the radio. The last thing I wanted to learn was that Scott Mansell's body had been discovered and that somebody fitting my description had been seen hanging around his boat.

"Because of these." She reached into her handbag and pulled out an envelope filled with my pictures from Richard's apartment.

I was relieved that Lori hadn't learned about Mansell's murder from a news report, but I was more than just a little upset that she hadn't followed my instructions. "I told you that I would pick these up," I said testily.

"I thought I was doing you a favor. Arturo said it would only take his lab a few minutes to develop the film, so I waited. When I returned to the office, I just couldn't resist looking at them."

She took each of the pictures out of the envelope, one-at-a-time, and laid them across the surface of my desk. Just what I needed, another viewing of the dead body—over-and-over-again—in living Kodachrome.

"I told you I was working on a murder case," I said lamely.

"You said *possible* murder case."

"Well, now it's more than just possible."

Lori shook her head. "*Impossible.*"

"The case?" I asked.

"No. Y*ou!*"

My phone rang. I stared at it and then at Lori.

She stared at me. "Well, aren't you going to answer it?"

"You're the secretary. You answer it."

Lori reached across the pictures and picked up the receiver. "*Rank* Hammond Investigations," she said. "Yes, he's here. Sure thing." Then she hung up and glared at me.

"Well?"

"Well what?"

"Who was it?"

Lori hesitated, then blurted out: "The police. You're wanted for the murder of Scott Mansell."

My blood instantly drained from my face and settled someplace around my ankles. I tried to ask Lori a question, but my tongue had suddenly assumed the consistency of a dead fish.

Lori looked down at me with her famous smirk. "*Gotcha*. It was Arturo Garcia on his car phone. He's a couple of blocks away and he wanted to know if you were in. He should be here in a few minutes."

I gathered up the pictures, stuffed them into their envelope and tossed them into my top desk drawer just as Arturo's voice filled the outer office.

"Hank, my *amigo*. Are you here?"

Lori opened my door and motioned Arturo to enter. Arturo stepped through the doorway, scanned my tiny room and shook his silver-haired head. "No wonder you chose to meet me in your conference room this morning."

"His conference room?" Lori smirked in her patented way.

Arturo smiled and winked at her. "Let him pretend, Lori my dear."

Lori's smirk enlarged to ever greater proportions, happy to have found a co-conspirator.

I couldn't take much more of the abuse. "I hope you're both through making fun of me, because I'd like to get going on my case."

"Sorry my *amigo*. It's just that I have closets at my office that are bigger than this. In fact, I have drawers that are bigger than this." He looked over at Lori and smiled again. If I didn't know better, I'd swear that he was flirting with her . . . and that she was lapping it up. I don't know which bothered me more, the ridiculing or the flirting.

"Lori was just leaving," I said.

"I'm sorry to hear that," Arturo said in his most charming manner.

Lori flashed her perfectly straight teeth toward Arturo. "My pleasure to see you again Arturo," she said. Then she gave me a dirty look and walked out to her command post.

After she'd left, Arturo wiggled his eyebrows up-and-down like Groucho Marx. "Very nice indeed," he said.

"Watch your mouth," I said protectively.

Arturo approached my guest chair—actually a folding metal chair—and dropped onto the hard seat. "A little touchy aren't you? I must have struck a nerve."

Before I could respond, Arturo started in on topic of much more interest to me—Greg Treet.

"The man who replaced you at the Kingston Beach store is a first class ass, my *amigo*."

I leaned forward on my elbows, eager to hear any dirt about my successor.

"First of all," Arturo continued. "He arrived forty-five minutes late for our meeting. I showed up precisely on time and told the woman in the office who I was. She asked me to wait for him over in the HR lobby. I didn't know what she was talking about, and my face must have shown it because she quickly clarified it to mean *human resources*. Whatever happened to good old terms like personnel?"

"It started with those propeller heads in data processing," I said. "They decided that they wanted to be called MIS, for *management information systems*. Then personnel decided they wanted their own initials too, but didn't want to be called the P department so they came up with *human resources*. It even happened in my area. They're not security anymore, they're LP—"

"Which would be *el pee* in my first language," Arturo said with a chuckle.

"*Sí*, Mr. Garcia," I said. "But here it means *loss prevention*."

Arturo shook his head in disgust. "No wonder no work gets done in corporations, everyone is spending time making up new names for departments. Now, where was I? Ah, yes. So I walk over to *HR*, sit down with several other people, who are all nervous because they're about to either be hired or fired. After twenty minutes I'm so sick-and-tired of waiting that I went back to the woman at the office and she tells me that Mr. Treet is out with Mr. Eaton and she isn't sure when they'll be back. At this point, I am absolutely furious, but I can't very well walk out because I really would like to have Treet's business. So I walked back to human resources and sat for another half hour. I keep looking at my watch, but . . ."

I glanced at my watch. As much as I liked hearing gossip about what a jerk my replacement was, I had a murder case to solve. "Arturo," I interrupted. "Can you do me a favor?"

"You don't want to hear about what's going on at your old store?" Arturo said, sounding a little hurt.

"Sure I do. But my wheels are over at my apartment, and I thought you could continue with your story while you drive me over there. I'd really appreciate it."

Arturo stood. "Let's go."

As we left the office, Lori smiled at Arturo and batted her eyes like a school girl. I demonstrated my authority by telling her to answer my phone and take messages. She responded by telling me that she'd solve the murder case before I returned. Arturo smiled back at Lori and raised an eyebrow at me.

"So it is a murder case you're working on," he said as we climbed into his cop-like Chevrolet Caprice.

I faced the windshield. "I can't talk about it."

Arturo gave me a dirty look, slid the Chevy's shift lever into drive and we slunk out onto the street.

"So what did Treet do to tick you off so much," I asked. "Besides making you wait for him?"

"He never had any intention of resuming a business relationship with VAST. He told me his store needed a complete break with the past. In fact, he said that the only reason he wanted to meet me was to see what kind of person would be friends with a loser like Hank Hammond."

I let out a yell. Arturo slammed on the brakes. My face lunged for the windshield. Just before certain contact, the shoulder belt grabbed me and threw me back against the seat. The Caprice skewed sideways before coming to a full stop half-way into an intersection.

"What the hell was that about?" Arturo exclaimed as he turned the ignition key to restart the car.

"The guy called me a loser!"

The engine kicked in and Arturo threw the car into gear and drove off, leaving a trail of honking drivers in his wake. "Don't ever do that when I'm driving. I thought you were warning me that a car was about to run into us."

"Sorry."

Arturo opened a tin of Altoids, removed one of the mints and placed it into his mouth. He didn't offer one to me. "Now, do you want to hear the rest of what I have to say or are you going to continue to distract me?"

"I already apologized, Arturo."

"Apology accepted." Arturo passed the tin to me. "Have one, they're curiously strong."

I popped a half dozen into my mouth and bit into them—my mouth nearly exploded. I stifled the temptation to let out another yell and instead thanked Arturo in a voice that sounded like I'd just inhaled a balloon full of helium.

"Mr. Treet," Arturo continued, "told me that using VAST had been a gigantic waste of money and that by doing his surveillance in-house he would be able to reduce his budget by something like twenty percent. When I challenged his figure, he just told me that he didn't want to hear what an old, has-been cop had to say."

"Ouch, that hurts."

"You're damn right, it hurts. But you know what else he's done? He fired one of the men who used to work for you—Lou Gaston. As it turns out, he was one of the nervous people waiting over in human resources. He probably knew that he was about to lose his job.

"Lou? Lou Gaston? I don't believe it. He was the best. He was my right hand!"

"Well, as of now he's unemployed."

"Treet can't do that. Human resources can't do that. They've got rules, policies, and procedures up the ying-yang. They can't just fire somebody without notice, especially somebody like Lou who has an unblemished record."

"Treet told me he can do whatever he wants because he has Eaton's full support. In fact, Treet has already replaced your friend Lou with a creature named Al Metzger. Have you ever heard of him?"

"Nope. Should I?"

"I don't know."

"What's he look like?"

"Tall, about six-three, and very skinny. He reminds me a bit of a hungry coyote. And he is very strong and mean looking . . . exactly like a hungry coyote. He has gray-streaked hair—"

"In a ponytail? I asked quickly.

"No, but I could spot that he had recently received a haircut."

I broke out in a sweat. This could be the break I needed, although it was certainly coming from an unexpected place. "What did Treet tell you about Metzger?"

"Nothing."

My heart sank.

"But I do have some information which I think will be of interest to you." Arturo pulled into my apartment's parking lot and up to my assigned stall. When he saw my rental car, his train of thought went completely out the window. "What's that little pink car doing in your parking place? Don't tell me you have a lady friend waiting for you in your apartment."

"No such luck. My Vette's in the shop, and that's my rental."

Arturo laughed out loud. "And what happened to the body? Did someone think it was a can of sardines and attack it with a can opener?"

I told Arturo about last night's encounter with the Suburban.

"That, on top of being shot at yesterday morning? Plus, Lori mentioned something about you working on a murder case. You wouldn't care to give an old, has-been cop any details about that would you?"

I wanted to, but there was already one person too many who knew about the murder—Lori. "Can't," I said.

"Don't you mean won't, my *amigo*?"

I kept my mouth shut and Arturo knew better than to press. "Tell me about Lori, is she married?"

"I think she's single."

"You think? You don't know? What's the matter with you. You're working with this wonderful woman, who is obviously quite crazy about you, and you don't know anything about her?"

"I never thought about her that way, and I doubt very much that she thinks of me that way either."

"Oh right. The way the two of you were looking at each other and the way you both talked, it was as if you were already married to one other."

"That would be the day. We're like water and oil."

"Does she like your Corvette?"

"I'm not sure. The only thing she ever said to me about it was that she'd never known a guy with a Vette who didn't need one."

"What do you suppose she meant by that?"

"Beats me, but she smirked while she said it."

Arturo looked at the Metro again, staring at the rumpled rear and scraped side. "Did you call the police about that?"

"No, the police were the last people I wanted to see . . . then or now."

Arturo shook his head and made a *tut-tut* sound with his tongue. "Hank, my *amigo*, I hope you that aren't getting in over your head with this private detective business."

Me too, I said silently to myself. "Not to worry," I said aloud. I started to get out of Arturo's Chevrolet when I remembered that he hadn't yet told me about the information he thought would be of interest to me. "Was there something else you were going to tell me?" I asked.

"Yes," Arturo said, "and I think you are going to like it. It's about Scott Mansell." He reached into the back seat and retrieved a notebook computer with a small printer attached to it. He fired it up and read from the monitor as several printed sheets started spitting out. "Born twenty-four years ago in Long Beach, California on October the twenty-seventh. Attended Robert A. Millikan High School where he graduated at age eighteen. No record of him attending college. Some very serious credit problems a few years ago, but it appears that they have been resolved within the last two—"

"How much do you figure a yacht is worth?" I blurted out.

Arturo looked at me like an uninvited guest. "I thought that you would be interested in this information."

"I am. In fact it's what triggered my question. I don't know much about boats, but the one that Scott Mansell lives on must be worth at least a few hundred grand. If he had such a problem with debt, how could he buy such a big yacht?"

"He couldn't, not with credit. Must have paid for it with cash . . . or, perhaps it isn't even his boat. He could just be staying on it, maybe in exchange for keeping it ship shape. Maybe he pays rent. Maybe it belongs to his father. There could be several answers."

I tried to remember the details of my conversation with Terri. I was pretty sure that she'd said the boat belonged to Mansell, but pretty sure isn't good enough. Besides, who knows what a guy like Mansell would tell a girl like Terri, just to impress her. Men were always misrepresenting themselves to women, and women to men—I had the proof of that . . . two failed marriages.

"What else is on that computer?" I asked.

"As I was saying, Mansell started clearing up his debts two years ago. Beyond that, there are no felony or misdemeanor convictions in our county. But, there are two convictions in Orange County, both approximately three years ago. The first one was for discharging a firearm. He was found guilty and received a fine, plus court costs. The second conviction was for theft. Once again, he was found guilty. That time he paid restitution and was given twelve months probation. I don't know about any other counties because I can't run a state-wide search in California, I have to do it county-by-county. That hurdle is courtesy of the fine folks up in Sacramento who care more about protecting the privacy of criminals than protecting the lives of good, decent, law-abiding citizens."

"Do you know what he shot at or what he stole?"

"No, and I don't have his driving history or earnings history yet. It takes at least a week to get salary information from the Social Security Administration, and about two days for a driving history. But what I can tell you is that he doesn't hold any professional licenses, like you need to be a pharmacist, nurse, insurance agent, teacher, et cetera."

"The guy works in a tennis shop," I interrupted. "You don't need a license to sell balls and rackets. Before that, he worked at W-L's—in the same store where Treet used to manage security—excuse me, *loss prevention*—before he transferred to mine. Did you pick that up on your computer?"

"Sorry, I can't get any information on places of employment, only on earned income. But I do have more on him." Arturo looked over the newly printed pages and handed them to me. "Here. His home address is on the cover sheet. Apparently he lives on a boat."

"I already know where he lived."

"Oh, right." Arturo appeared sheepish, then looked at me quizzically. "*Lived?*"

"*Lives*," I corrected, then changed the subject. "You were able to get all this information from your computer?"

"I used VAST's Research Information Inquiry System. We have on-line access to TRW, Equifax and Trans Union for credit data. For criminal information we go through the National Crime Information Center's computer. I can get this information even when I'm out in the field. Pretty good for an old has-been cop, isn't it?"

"Very. Did your guys come up with anything else on Mansell? Anything that they'd heard on the street?"

"No. None of them know anything about him."

"And Al Metzger? Do they know anything about him?"

"I only just learned his name about an hour ago and I haven't checked with my men yet. I haven't even had a chance to run him through the system." Arturo tapped the computer. "Would you like me to do it?"

"It wouldn't hurt."

"It might." Arturo held out his hand. "These searches cost. You owe me $150 for Mansell. Metzger'll cost you another one-fifty."

I winced. "You're charging me? I thought we were buddies."

"I have to charge you. I do run a business, you know. And you claim to be running one too, although by the looks of your office, I—"

"Can't you do a 'two-fer?'"

"I need every cent I can get, especially now that I've lost the W-L's account in the Kingston Beach store. . . thanks to you and your grandiose idea about becoming the next Paul Drake."

I wrote out a check for three hundred dollars and handed it to Arturo. He held it up to the light and squinted at it.

"Maybe I should run a credit check on you before I accept this," Arturo chided. "I've seen that miniature office of yours," he looked out the windshield at my smashed up Metro, "and your itty-bitty widdle car. I'm not so sure that you've got three hundred dollars to your name, my *amigo*."

I thanked Arturo for his vote of confidence, stuffed the report on Mansell into my gym bag, hopped out of the Chevy and walked over to the crunched up Geo. Just as I unlocked the door and began crouching down to squeeze myself in, Arturo yelled out his window at me.

"Hey. The engine in Treet's Corvette is bigger than yours."

The words *maybe he needs it* popped into my mind, but I found my mouth asking how much horsepower he had.

"I'm just kidding, my *amigo*. I just wanted to give you a little rise, I don't have any idea what he drives." Arturo grinned like an adolescent.

I sunk into the smashed up, pink Metro and started the three-cylinder engine, wondering how many horses were under *its* hood . . . probably one old gray mare . . . that ain't what she used to be. As if reading my mind, the Metro coughed and stalled. Arturo waved good-bye to me and motored smoothly away. I restarted the rental in a cloud of blue smoke, floored it and drove away in the opposite direction.

I careened onto Ocean Boulevard and immediately found myself face-to-face—or rather, bumper-to-bumper—with Walter's station wagon. I could hardly believe my eyes; the continuously disappearing Fiat was so close that I could almost reach out and touch it. I cinched up my seat belt, patted the little Metro's dashboard, and told it in the most soothing of tones that I'd never bad-mouth it again if it didn't allow the Fiat to escape. At that very moment, the engine went dead and the Fiat disappeared, swallowed up in a sea of moving traffic.

I restarted the car, called it every filthy name in the book, and took off in hot pursuit of the Fiat . . . wherever it may be. I thought I caught a glimpse of it—or maybe it was another station wagon—turning right onto Camino del Oro, so I cut into the right lane and did likewise. The wheezing engine had so little torque that I had to down-shift just to get out of my own way. I speed-shifted back up to third with so much force that the shift lever nearly broke off in my hand. Then, to gain enough oomph to pass an elderly man in a Town Car, I down-shifted again. Then back up to third and almost immediately into fourth. Then down to third again, up to fourth, and finally into fifth. I threw the shift lever back and forth so much that I might as well have been rowing the car toward the Fiat. But, the important thing was that I was making progress . . . Walter's wagon was only three car lengths ahead.

The light ahead turned red and the Fiat came to a stop in the curb side lane. I locked my brakes and slid to a halt directly behind the Fiat, pushed the emergency flasher button, yanked up on the parking brake while flinging open the door, and jumped out. Or almost jumped out . . . I'd forgotten to unfasten the seat belt. I broke free of the belt and rushed forward to the Fiat. The light was still red, but I didn't know for how long. I grabbed the Fiat's door handle and wrenched open the door. The driver turned toward me with the very same panicked look that my movie date Thelma Hooper had given me years ago when the shark had jumped out of the water in "Jaws."

I grabbed for the driver's arm, just as he threw a tight fist directly into my jaw. My mouth clacked shut and suddenly my world spun like carousel. I shut my eyes and immediately heard trumpets . . . and wondered if I'd just entered heaven. The trumpets blared louder. I opened my eyes, shook my head, and realized that drivers were honking at me and that the driver of the Fiat was clambering out the passenger's door. I reached across the seat and grabbed his shirt. The sleeve ripped off at the seam. I scrambled across the center console, being particularly cautious as the car's stick shift came precariously close to my own similarly shaped accessory. The driver ran down the sidewalk and I followed . . . my adrenaline surge propelling me forward.

When my escapee looked back over his shoulder at me, I knew for the first time who I was chasing.

"Richard," I yelled between great gulps of air.

He whipped his head around to look at me again while he continued running.

"Richard Tompkins, stop." I yelled.

He shot off to the right between two buildings.

NINE

I detoured off the sidewalk and raced across yellowed Bermuda grass toward the open space between the buildings. I stumbled momentarily as I stepped onto the cracked concrete that filled the gap between the backs of two matching apartment houses. I scanned the area. Four doors on the left. Four doors on the right. The same number of windows. The same number of ripe garbage cans. An eight-foot fence blocking any exit at the rear. No Richard.

I stopped . . . listened . . . heard nothing. Could he have entered an apartment through its back door? What were the chances of one of the doors being unlocked? Zero, I thought. What were the chances that he'd have climbed into one of the garbage cans? An impossibility, I figured. I quit wasting time thinking and ran for the fence. I wrapped my hands over the two-by-four stringer on top and performed a chin-up so I could look up and beyond.

Whap! A large piece of something slammed across my face. I let go of the fence and dropped to the ground. I tasted blood dripping into my mouth and my nose felt strangely numb. I heard the sound of footsteps running away. I inhaled deeply through my mouth, reached up onto the fence again and pulled myself up-and-over . . . just in time to see Richard dashing into an alley.

I ran, wanting more than ever to get my hands on that boy. At first, all I'd wanted to do was find him for Walter. Now I wanted to beat the crap out of the little squirt. Where was my gym bag, filled with my goodies now that I really needed it? I wanted to reach into the bag, grab the stun-gun and administer a shock to Richard that would set his hair on fire. Then I remembered that I'd left my bag back in the Metro, and that my zapper had disappeared when I'd been conked over the head on Mansell's boat. But that was okay, right now I knew that I was gaining on the little twerp and that my hands would be all the ammunition I would need.

Richard rounded a corner only a few strides ahead of me. We'd run in a giant circle and the Fiat and the Metro were now only half a block ahead, still blocking the intersection. I ran like I was going for the gold, my heart pumping furiously and my temples pounding. I sprinted up behind Richard and lunged forward with my hands reaching for his shoulders. *Contact!* I pulled him down onto the sidewalk, pinning him beneath me.

"Don't kill me!" he shrieked in terror, closing his eyes and wincing like a frightened baby.

My hand had instinctively formed a fist, but I couldn't bring myself to hit such a pathetic looking creature, even after he'd just smashed my face with a board. "I'm not going to kill you," I said.

Richard opened his eyes, then grabbed toward his pants pocket and pulled something out of it. I instinctively grabbed for the object, realizing too late that it was my missing zapper. 150,000 volts ripped through my body. I could've sworn that my skeleton had caught fire and that my skin had been beamed all the way to Jupiter. I felt Richard wriggling underneath me in an unsuccessful attempt to free himself . . . finally something positive about my recently added girth. Thirty seconds later, the zapper's effect had worn off and I did what I should have done the minute I'd brought Walter's grandson down to the cement . . . I punched him in the nose as hard as I could. Then I grabbed the zapper from him and shoved it into my Dockers.

Richard's head flipped sideways and a combination of blood and tears streaked his face. "I give up," he sputtered. "Just don't kill me."

I repeated what I'd already told him: "I'm not going to kill you."

He opened his eyes, batting his eyelids as if they could somehow protect him. "Then, like what are you chasing me for?"

I reached for my pocket. Richard immediately cringed. "Don't shoot me!" he screamed.

I felt like slapping him. I pulled my wallet out of my pocket and extracted one of my business cards. I held it up for him to read. "Open your eyes!"

"No way!"

"I have something to show you."

"Whatever it is, I don't want to see it."

I shook my head in disgust, or pity, or wonderment. "My name's Hank Hammond. I'm a PI. Your grandfather hired me to find you, and his Fiat. Though I'm not so certain at this point that either you or the car are worth the effort."

Richard opened his eyes and read my card. "Wow! You're a PI. Cool! Just like that Paul Drake guy."

Finally somebody had gotten it right. I immediately started to like Richard . . . just a little. "You're in a lot of trouble and we need to talk." I let go of his arms, but continued to sit on his body.

"So, like, you're on my side?"

"I am, but I'm thinking about asking your grandfather for combat pay."

"Sorry about hitting you with the board."

I glared at him. "And?"

He brushed his hair out of his eyes and wrinkled his forehead. "And what?"

"Aren't you going to apologize for turning my body into a lightning rod?"

He grimaced. "Oh yeah. Sorry about that too."

"And?" I paused until I was sick of waiting. "How about an apology for hitting me across the back of the head with that winch handle over on Scott Mansell's boat?"

"I'm sorry man, but I thought you were the guy who killed Scott."

"You didn't do it?" I asked.

"Of course not. I wouldn't hurt a flea."

I glanced down at my bloodied shirt, then felt my nose, then moved my hand to the back of my head. "I guess you didn't mistake me for a flea then."

"I'm really, really sorry about all that, man."

"Don't worry about it, just make sure you don't ever do it again."

"Promise."

"Now let's go someplace where we can talk." I stood up and Richard did the same. I wasn't concerned that he'd try to run away from me again; I had eight inches of height and about seventy pounds on him . . . and at least half of those pounds were muscle.

While we walked to the cars, Richard told me how much his grandfather means to him. He spoke about Walter as though he were talking about his own father. I could tell that Richard loved the old man with all his heart—it was actually rather sweet.

The emergency lights were still flashing on my Metro. My Metro? I didn't much like the sound of that. Drivers were maneuvering past our cars as though they didn't exist . . . people are just too damn busy—or scared—these days to stop and help when a car appears to be disabled.

"Hand me the keys to the Fiat," I said to Richard. He obeyed me instantly. I instructed him to sit in the passenger's seat and not to move until I returned. Then I walked quickly back to the little Geo, started it up and parked it against the curb. I grabbed my gym bag and as I walked back to the Fiat, I reached into the bag and palmed a pair of stainless steel handcuffs. Once I'd squatted into the driver's seat, I reached over and cuffed Richard to the dashboard. It was probably overkill, but I didn't want to lose this kid . . . besides I'd spent sixty bucks on those cuffs and I wanted to give them a try.

"Hey, what're these for?" Richard protested.

I drove off in a cloud of blue smoke. "I've had a dead body disappear on me, I'm sure as hell not going to take any chances on a live one."

"You're talking about Scott, huh?"

I nodded while I negotiated through traffic. "I found him in your closet. Then I found him in his bed. What do you know about that?"

Richard practically hyperventilated his response. "I found him in my closet too. I'd just gotten back from Mexico with this girl I've been seeing, and I was really beat."

I remembered the name noted on Richard's calendar. "Rita?" I asked.

"Right. How'd you know that?"

"I'm a detective, remember?"

Richard made a stupid face and I wondered if it was permanent or temporary. "Oh yeah," he said.

"Was Rita with you in your apartment?"

"No, I was alone. I'd dropped her off at her place over in La Camino." Richard stopped talking and stared blankly at me.

"Continue," I said as I shifted up a gear.

"Well, as soon as I got home, I went straight to the bathroom and washed up. Then I threw my clothes on top of the hamper and walked over to my closet to grab a pair of boxers. That's what I wear when I sleep—"

"Thanks for sharing."

"When I opened the closet door, this dead body came tumbling out. Scared the crap out of me."

"What'd you do then?"

"I put on my shorts."

I made a face. "And?"

"Then a pair of sweat pants and a shirt. There was, like, no way I was going to be able to get any sleep with a dead body in my apartment."

"Did you know who it was?"

"Sure, I knew it was Scott the minute I saw it . . . him . . . whatever."

I listened to Richard while I tried to figure out where we could go that would be private . . . and safe.

"I didn't know what to do, but one thing I did know was that I couldn't have him around my place. The first thing I did was to get my thirty-eight from my night stand, only it wasn't there."

"Probably the murder weapon."

"Yeah, that's what I thought too."

"What next?"

"Then I ran down to my garage—"

"You have a garage?"

"I rent one about a half block from my apartment. It's owned by this little old lady who doesn't have a car. I pay her fifty bucks a month. It's a screamin' deal, man." Richard looked down at the handcuffs. "You sure I need these things?"

"Let me think about it. Keep on with your story."

"It isn't a story, man. It's the truth."

"Why did you run to the garage?"

"To get my car. I've got this really cool '68 Mustang. Crager mags, bored out 302 with—"

"Richard. Any other time and I'd love to talk cars with you."

"You like cars? I never would've guessed, not with that thing that you drive."

"Richard!"

"Yeah, right. Well, I opened the garage door and there was my grandfather's station wagon parked right next to my Mustang. Scott must've returned it and parked it right where I'd asked him to. So, like, it was perfect for hauling him away, especially since it already had this empty wooden crate in the back. I drove the wagon up close to my apartment, then I carried the crate inside and stuffed him into it. I put the crate on top of my skateboard and pushed it out to my grandfather's car and loaded it in. Then I drove over to the marina, put the crate on one of those little kid's wagons that they have sitting around, and wheeled him over to his boat. Then I put him into his own bed."

I looked over my shoulder at the back of the station wagon. The crate was missing. "Where's the crate now?"

"I broke it into pieces and tossed them into a Dumpster behind my apartment."

I shook my head.

"Bad move, huh?"

"Very bad," I said. "There's a good chance that the cops'll find the scraps and they'll have Mansell's blood and your prints all over them."

Richard shrugged his shoulders. "Oh well."

I shook my head. The boy was dumber than a rock. "How'd you get into the marina?" I asked.

"Scott had told me his access number. It was a real easy one to remember."

"It would have to have been," I said almost to myself.

"What?"

"Nothing. How'd you get into his boat?"

"With his key. He had his keys in his pocket."

I turned right into the parking lot of the Humpty Dumpty Motel, a cheap flea-bag that I thought I could afford. I parked at the far end of the lot and shut off the engine. "I need you to listen to me Richard. You are in a huge amount of trouble. It's only a matter of time before the police start looking for you."

"Why me?"

"Didn't you park your grandfather's Fiat near Scott's boat, right where somebody would have seen it?"

"Yeah."

"And are you absolutely certain that nobody saw you wheeling his body over to his boat?"

"Well, he was in the crate. I don't see how somebody—"

"Did anybody see you?"

"I don't know."

"Did you wear gloves when you transported the body?"

"Nope."

"Did you wear any when you were in his boat?"

"Nope."

"I rest my case."

Richard stared out the window and wagged his head from side-to-side. "Man! I can't believe this is happening to me. I didn't do anything wrong. All I did was get Scott the heck out of my place and put him where he'd be comfortable. It's not like I killed him or anything." He turned to look at me. "You think the cops are waiting at my apartment?"

"If they aren't now, they will be soon."

"And at my job?"

"You can bet on it."

"Damn! This is really the pits, man. That's the best job I've had in years and now you're telling me that I can't go to work. My boss was nice enough to give me a few days off. He's going to be really ticked off if I don't come back. I've got to call him and let him know."

"You're going to stay put and you're not going to talk to anybody but me until I can straighten this whole thing out."

"Straighten it out?"

"Your grandfather hired me to find you and also to help keep you out of trouble. Well, I've done the first part. Now it's time for me to do the second."

"So are you going to uncuff me or what?"

"First, I'm going to check you into a room using a bogus name. Then, depending on how I feel about you, I'll decide whether to uncuff you or not."

"Well, you're going to have to uncuff me to get me out of this car and into the motel. Right?"

I ignored his comment, reached into the glove compartment and pulled out a rag. Then I pressed a button on the dashboard and watched as streams of wiper fluid covered the windshield. I hopped out of the Fiat, dabbed the rag in the fluid and wiped the blood off of my face while inspecting my ugly mug in the car's side-view mirror. No doubt about it; I looked like hell, but at least now my face was clean. I left Richard cuffed in the car while I paid cash for a room using the name of Sam Branberry. I requested, and received, the room underneath the far end of the motel's sign. It sported the caricature of a dizzy-looking egg with a crack in his forehead. With my own head aching from two unnecessary wallops, I felt a certain affinity for the egg. But that wasn't the reason I'd selected the room . . . it was just that for security reasons, I wanted Richard at the very end of the building. I inspected the room before returning to the car. Just a simple room without any frills—no telephone, no chocolate mints on the pillow, no fancy shampoos or shower caps; just a lumpy bed and a television that required quarters before you could turn it on.

Richard didn't like the room very much, but he liked not wearing the cuffs. He told me that he'd met Scott about a couple of months before he'd been laid off at a car wash. Scott was a regular customer and a big tipper, so Richard had always made a point of doing an extra special job when he detailed his van. When Scott learned that Richard had lost his job, he set up an interview for Richard at a print shop that his cousin owned. The cousin had just fired a man for stealing, and his name was Al Metzger. Richard replaced Metzger and started his new career, just over two months ago.

Scott would stop by the shop every once-in-a-while, sometimes to order some printing and sometimes just to shoot the breeze. Last week, he'd complained about how his van had broken down and how he didn't have time to get it fixed before he needed to deliver something. He said that he hated to waste money renting a van. Richard had been trying to figure out a way to repay Scott for getting him the job, so he offered to loan his grandfather's station wagon for a few days. Richard borrowed the Fiat from Walter, and then gave it to Scott. Richard never thought to ask Scott what he would be delivering . . . in fact, Richard didn't even have any idea what Scott did for a living.

All Richard knew about Scott was that he would sometimes come to the shop on his cousin's day off and place an order for some bar-coded labels. He was always in a rush for the labels and he needed them to be printed immediately. He told Richard that if his cousin ever asked what he'd printed for Scott, to just say that it was business stationery and not to elaborate on it. Scott also ordered some other printing that Richard was supposed to keep secret from his employer. Richard wasn't sure, but he thought that they were envelopes.

Other than that, Richard didn't seem to know much about anything. He claimed to know nothing about the robbery of Discount Danny's, and he claimed that he had no idea why his grandfather had clipped out the article. When I asked him about his criminal record, he readily admitted that he'd swiped some cassette tapes at W-L's, back when he was in high school. He couldn't remember who had apprehended him, but he described the man as being a big, football player type, tall like me, but a lot more fit—I knew exactly who he meant. Richard also said that he'd been caught with a couple of joints back before he'd quit using pot; and that he and some of his friends had gotten drunk once and removed the mufflers on their cars, revved up their engines at two in the morning, and promptly been arrested for disturbing the peace. Stupid things, all of them—consistent with the stupid act of moving Mansell's body—but hardly the acts of a killer. But then, what do I know about killers except that I've never met one?

"Tell me about your wife," I said.

Richard looked at me like I was from Mars. "I'm not married."

"Divorced?"

"I've never been married in my life. Why do you ask?"

"Terri, over at the Coastal Country Club, told me that you and she'd gone out once."

"So?" Richard grinned. "Just because she and I climbed into the sack once, that doesn't mean that we were getting married."

"She'd slept at your apartment?"

"I didn't say anything about sleeping, did I? But, yeah, she'd been to my place. Why?"

"She said that she received a threatening phone call from your wife, right after you and she'd—"

"Screwed our brains out?" Richard bragged.

"Gone out on a date," I corrected. "But you're telling me that you weren't married to anyone at the time."

"Not then, not now, never. That's really weird. Maybe she just made it up."

I remembered the tan line on Terri's finger. It had been obvious to me that she'd been wearing Scott's ring for a fairly long time. "Wasn't she Scott's girlfriend when you—"

"Screwed her brains out?"

"Richard, this isn't funny," I snapped. "I'm trying to keep you from the gas chamber."

Richard looked sheepishly at me. "Sorry, man. Yeah, Terri and Scott were going together, but that didn't mean that he owned her or anything."

"Did he know that you'd gone out with her?"

"Not as far as I know. I sure as hell wasn't going to tell him, and I'd be pretty surprised if Terri had told him that we'd screwed our—" Richard put his hand up to his mouth, then dropped it. "That we'd gone out on a date."

I left Richard in the room, along with a couple of candy bars I'd bought for him from the motel's vending machine, a pocket-full of quarters for the TV, and instructions not to even think about setting foot outside the door.

"Sure thing, man," he said as he flopped back onto the king-sized bed. "Hey, I could really use a pizza when you come back here. I'll buy."

"With what? Do you have any money with you?"

"I got a Master Card in my wallet."

I shook my head. "That would be just great. Then I could be arrested for killing Mansell because the cops would think that I'm you."

"Works for me," Richard said.

I shut the door behind me, climbed into the Fiat and drove off to where I could hide it until I unraveled the murder and could finally contact the police. I decided to call Lori and ask if I could borrow her garage, but I knew that I should call Walter first and let him know that his grandson was safe. I pulled my cell phone out of my bag and punched the buttons. When the phone didn't respond, I remembered what I'd forgotten—to pay the phone bill. Oh well, a personal visit would probably impress the old man more than a phone call anyway.

As I drove to Walter's, I drove through the neighborhood where I'd left the Metro and decided that I ought to check on it. Not that I really cared about the little piece of junk, it's just that I couldn't remember if I'd locked the doors or not and the neighborhood wasn't exactly what I'd describe as upscale. All I needed was for my rental to be stolen. I was relieved when I turned onto the block and saw the car parked in the distance. Then, as I got closer, I discovered that the car was sitting up on concrete blocks and all four wheels and tires were missing. The good news was that in the Metro's present condition, no one could steal it. The bad news was that I now had to buy tires and wheels in addition to getting the car's body repaired and painted . . . either that, or face certain cancellation of my insurance. This case was costing me too much—I figured that with the car repair, I was at least a couple of grand in the hole.

I peeled out from the curb and drove to Walter's. Crystal must have been looking out the window, because she came running out onto the porch. For a moment I thought that she was glad to see me, then I realized that she was far more interested in the car.

"You found it!" she said, slightly out of breath. "Where was it? Is Richard okay? Walter is going to be so pleased. He's been very upset, you know. Upset because Richard disappeared and upset because he hasn't heard enough from you." She looked at the blood on my shirt. "What happened?"

"Cut myself shaving," I said unconvincingly. "Where is Walter?"

"In his room. Come on, let's go into the library and I'll bring Walter in to see you."

I followed Crystal's swaying hips into the mansion. Just as we entered the foyer, she turned and whispered to me. "It's not just the car is it? I mean, you have found Richard, haven't you?"

"Yes."

"Is there anything that you should tell me before I get Walter?"

"Like what?"

"Oh, I don't know. Is Richard okay? Because if he isn't, I don't want Walter to hear it the wrong way. He's very fond of that boy you know."

"Richard is fine," I said.

"*He is?*"

"Does that surprise you?"

Crystal shook her head. "No, no, no. I'm glad he's fine. It's just that I'd imagined the worst. I'm, I'm *so* relieved."

"I'll just wait in the library," I said. "Please tell Walter that Richard is fine and that I'd like to speak about the situation with him."

Crystal disappeared down the hallway. I sat in the same wing-back chair I'd used during my first visit with Walter. Several minutes later, Walter entered the room. He appeared to be wearing only a wool robe and a pair of leather slippers. He sat on the sofa, lowering his head then taking a deep breath.

"So you found him," he said, at last.

"Yes sir, I did."

"Then where is he?"

"He's in trouble Mr. Tompkins—"

"*Walter!*" He slammed a clenched fist down on the coffee table. "How many times do I have to tell you? My name is *Walter*, it isn't *Mister.* Good land, my boy. Do you have nothing between those ears of yours? I am so sick-and-tired of feigned respect and," he suddenly looked very pale, "ah, I think I just figured it out. You're here and Richard isn't. You're going to try to hold me up for more money. Is that it? You won't let me see my grandson until I pay you thousands of dollars. You're no good! You're holding him for ransom. I never should have hired you without checking you out first. Well, you're not going to get away with this. No siree, you're not. No money. No money. No money. No money." He slammed his fist down on the table with each "no."

I waited for Walter to finish his tirade. When he finally stopped, he shut his eyes and slumped back into the sofa. Worried, I rushed over and called his name. He opened his eyes. "What the hell are you doing?" he asked.

"Checking to see if you're all right."

"I'm perfectly fine. Just because I'm diabetic, everyone thinks that I'm going to black out without any notice. It just doesn't work that way."

I backed away from him. "I didn't know you were diabetic. You just scared me when you slumped back and closed your eyes. Now, are you ready to listen to what I have to say about your grandson?"

He nodded.

I told Walter about the murder, the transportation of the body, and that I had hidden Richard until I could either find the real killer or figure out a way to prove that Richard hadn't done it. The old man took the news terribly, weeping like a baby.

"My grandson did not kill anyone," Walter said emphatically, "he couldn't."

"I know that."

"It looks bad for him doesn't it?"

"Very bad."

"Then you must find whomever is responsible for this." He pulled ten, one-hundred dollar bills out of a pocket in his robe and pushed them across the coffee table toward me. "Here. Whatever it takes, you have my support."

I pocketed the cash. "Thank you."

"Thank you. Now, where is Richard? I need to see him. I need to talk with him."

"I can't give you that information. Once the police discover the body and examine the evidence, they'll be looking for Richard. One of the first things they'll do is to watch you. If you go to visit Richard, you'll lead them right to him."

"Then don't tell me where he is. Just give me his phone number and I'll call him instead."

I shook my head. "That could end up being the same as telling you where he is. Besides, there's no phone where he's staying."

"Then have him get to a phone and call me."

"Sorry, the cops'll have a tap on your phone in no time. You're just going to have to take my word for the fact that Richard is fine . . . for now."

"Then you're just going to have to get a move-on and find the killer. The sooner you accomplish that, the sooner I can see my grandson."

I knew a cue when I heard one. I promptly stood. "You're right. I'm on my way."

Walter stood, slowly and deliberately, wobbled for a moment, then looked past me through the leaded window. "That's my station wagon," he wheezed as he tottered past me to get a better look. "You didn't tell me you'd found it." He turned to face me. "I'll take those keys back now."

"I'd rather not give them to you just now. I think it would be much better if I hid the car, just like I've hidden Richard."

Walter held out his hand, palm up. It shook like a leaf in the breeze. "Nonsense. That's my car and I demand to have it returned to me."

"I don't think—"

"Well *I* think. And you know what I think? I think that you're a charlatan. Now, you give me my keys this instant. Give them to me before I call the police."

"You wouldn't do that."

"Like Hades I wouldn't." He hobbled over to the phone, picked up the receiver and punched 911.

"*Don't do that.*"

Walter scowled at me then spoke into the receiver. "I want to report a theft in progress."

I tossed his set of keys on the coffee table . . . and kept Richard's set in my pocket.

"Never mind," he said to the phone. "I was mistaken. So sorry to bother you." He hung up the phone, snatched the keys, dropped them into the pocket of his robe, then looked over at me. "I'm glad you came to your senses, young man."

I wished that he would come to his senses. I decided to try reasoning with him. I figured that if I failed, I could still drive the Fiat away using Richard's keys. I looked Walter straight in the eyes and spoke in the most sincere and convincing voice that I could muster. "Walter, that car needs to be hidden away. The police will be looking for it, and this would be a logical place to start. I guarantee you that once the police find it, they will discover evidence that will incriminate your grandson. Is that what you want?"

Walter wagged his finger slowly at my face. "What I want is for you to leave and to not come back until you have some good news to tell me." He pulled his little black remote out of his pocket and pressed the button. Moments later, Crystal entered the room.

"Yes?" she said, smiling at Walter and ignoring me.

"You call a cab for Mr. Hammond. He's about to leave."

Crystal pirouetted out of the living room. I watched with interest as she sashayed into the foyer and then out of my sight. Once she'd disappeared, I turned to face Walter. He put his hand on my arm, smiled and began speaking.

"I'm sorry to have to pull rank on you son, but I'm the employer and you're the employee. If I say that I get the keys to my car, well then, that's the way it has to be. Do you understand?"

I nodded, guilty in the knowledge that I would soon be using the other set of keys to drive off in his car.

"Good. Then we understand each other clearly. So, it shouldn't come as any surprise to you when I ask you for my grandson's set of keys."

"Your grandson's keys? I don't—"

The telephone rang. Walter answered it. "Yes," he said into the receiver. "Certainly. Yes, I am the party who just called. Am I safe? Why, yes I do believe that I am. It is very considerate of you to follow up so efficiently. Does me proud to see my tax dollars going to work. What was that? You want to know if the theft is still in progress?"

Walter looked at me, then pointed into his robe pocket. I pulled Richard's keys out of my Dockers and reluctantly dropped them into Walter's pocket before he had a chance to say something stupid to the police.

"No, no. There is nothing to be concerned with. It was all a mistake on my part. I do apologize. Thank you for your concern." Walter hung up the phone just as Crystal entered the room.

"Your cab has arrived," she said to me. "I can walk you out if you like."

I didn't like the part about leaving the Fiat at Walter's, or the part about my leaving in a cab. I did like the part about walking with Crystal.

I turned to say good-bye to Walter, but he'd already sat down on the sofa and appeared to be asleep.

As Crystal and I walked through the foyer and out onto the porch, she asked me if what she'd overheard was true.

"How much did you hear?" I asked.

"Only a little bit. It sounded like you said that Richard is wanted for murder."

"If he isn't yet, he will be soon."

"Who did he kill?"

"Nobody. He didn't kill anybody."

"But who's dead?"

"I think the less I say, the better."

Crystal reached out and rested her hand on my forearm. "Are you sure that you can't tell me, Hank?" Her eyes drew me in.

TEN

The cabby must've taken me for a tourist, because he started driving a purposely circuitous route to my destination. Once I'd set him straight, he drove me straight to Totally Tofu. Just as I'd done after my earlier cab ride—it seemed so long ago, but had actually only been a few hours—I exited the cab, walked into the restaurant, used the rest room, then walked four blocks to my office. Lori was stationed at her command post, keyboarding fast and furiously. The door slammed behind me. Lori raised her right hand to the same height as her head, waved it mechanically, and returned it to the keyboard without missing a vowel or a consonant. I walked into my cubby-hole, grabbing my phone as I rounded my desk.

My first call was to the shop where they were supposedly fixing my Vette. The jerk told me to be patient. Well, that's not actually what he said. He told me to keep my pants on and to quit bugging them. Against my better judgment, I then asked if he had any wheels or tires that would fit a Geo Metro. He told me he didn't, but that he knew who would—Toys 'R' Us. Very funny. I slammed the phone down, then punched in the number for a tire shop up the street. Their price was way out of line, so I slammed the phone down again. Then I remembered Armando at Tony's Imported Car Service. I punched in the number and, after several rings, he answered.

"This is Hank Hammond," I said, waiting for a sign of recognition. When none came, I tried again. "The PI. You know."

"I know, man. What do you want? I can't talk to you on this phone unless it has to do with repairing a car."

I told him about my wheels and tires. He said that he had some that would fit, but weren't exactly original equipment. I told him that I didn't care, as long as the wheels were round and the tires held air. We haggled over the price and finally agreed that he'd drive over to the Metro and install them as soon as he got off work . . . which was in about fifteen minutes. Perfect! I gave him my MasterCard number and slammed the phone down again out of habit.

Lori appeared at me doorway. "What's all that slamming about?"

"Just wrapping up a few details on the case."

"Is that blood all over your shirt?"

"No, it's red dye number two. Better steer clear, it's poisonous."

Lori ignored my comment. "So, have you figured out who killed Scott Mansell?"

"No, but I'm getting close."

Lori gave me a puzzled look. I agreed to fill her in on the details if she agreed to drive me to where I'd parked the Metro. She marched right out to her command post, shut down all of her office equipment, set up the coffee for tomorrow morning, and returned to my door way—all within less than two minutes.

"Well, what are you waiting for?" she asked.

As she drove me to my rental, I told her about finding Mansell's body in Richard's closet and then finding it again in Mansell's boat. I told her about chasing Richard in his grandfather's car and the ensuing scuffle. I told her that I believed Richard was innocent and that I'd hidden him away so that the police couldn't find him. I told her about reluctantly returning the Fiat to Walter.

"So who killed Scott Mansell?" she asked when I finished telling my day's events.

"I wish I knew," I said.

Lori turned the corner and began laughing hysterically. I looked over at her. What on earth was so funny? She stared directly ahead, through the windshield. I followed her gaze. Immediately ahead, parked on the side of the road, was the pink Metro . . . complete with a set of four deep-dished, gold-toned mini wheels and ultra-low-profile cruising tires that protruded at least a foot from the wheel wells. All that was needed to complete the picture were neon lights under the chassis and a bass speaker booming obnoxiously from beneath the back window. That's when I noticed that there was no back window, it had been shattered by vandals.

"I really like what you've done to your car," Lori said with a smirk as she parked.

I hopped out of her Ghia with my gym bag in hand and slammed her door. "See you in the morning," was all I could manage to say. Maybe Lori had been right; now—more than ever—I needed my Vette.

I picked up a frozen pizza at a 7-11, then drove to the Humpty Dumpty Motel to check on Richard. The sun had set and the neon sign was flashing . . . or at least the first third of it was—*HUMP . . . HUMP . . . HUMP.* I don't know if the message was subliminal or obvious, an accident or intentional, but it had attracted a half dozen women in hot pants, tube tops and big trashy hair. They all waved and smiled at me as I pulled into the parking lot.

Aside from the fact that Richard was out of quarters for the TV, he seemed fine. I handed him the pizza and he not-so-tactfully pointed out that he had neither an oven nor a micro-wave. I told him to unwrap the pizza and place it on top of the TV. He did as he was told and I pulled out my 150,000 volt zapper, placed it against the pizza and squeezed the trigger over-and-over again until the cheese bubbled and the pepperonis sizzled.

"Righteous, man," Richard said has he blew on the pizza to cool it off. "You find out who killed Scott?"

"I'm working on it. You come up with any ideas?"

"I've been thinking about it ever since I ran out of quarters. The only names I ever heard Scott mention were Terri and that Metzger guy."

"The one whose job you took? Scott knew him?"

"Yeah, I guess so."

"And Scott talked to Metzger after he'd been fired?"

"Yeah. I heard him on the phone with him a couple of times when he was at the print shop. He'd talk real quiet like he didn't want me to hear what he was sayin'."

"Did you?"

"Didn't hear nothin' except the guy's name. Scott would dial the number, then I'd hear him say 'Metzger,' then he'd talk real quiet."

"Why didn't you tell me this earlier."

Richard shrugged his shoulders. "I don't know."

"What else do you know about Metzger?"

"That's it, man."

"You know what he looks like?"

"Nope."

"What else did you think of?"

"Well, you asked me about that robbery at Discount Danny's and I told you that I didn't know anything about it. Maybe this isn't anything, but I remember seeing some stuff from the store when I cleaned out Scott's van. You know, back when I worked at the car wash."

I looked longingly at the pizza. "Tear me off a piece of that. It's got to be cool enough to eat by now."

Richard grunted and walked into the bathroom. A moment later he came back with a couple of wash cloths. He tore off two pieces of pizza and handed one to me as he stuffed the other one into his face. Then he wiped tomato sauce off his face with one of the wash cloths and tossed the other one to me. "Pretty good stuff," he said.

"The pizza or the stuff in Scott's van?" I asked.

"The pizza. The stuff in the van wasn't nothin' but cardboard. You know, like packing cartons. Except these were flattened out. I remember that they were from Discount Danny's 'cause he uses this really cool lookin' logo, a couple of big D's. It's one of those designs where you can't tell what it is at first and then it hits you, like, *bam*." Richard struck his palm against his forehead. "Well, there were a bunch of cartons in Scott's van with that design on it."

My mind flashed back to the marina and to the design I'd seen on the crate inside Walter's Fiat. "Like the design stenciled on the end of the wooden crate you stuffed Mansell's body into?"

"Hey, well yeah. I guess so. Sure."

"What did you do with the cartons?"

"I threw them away. I mean, that's what I was paid to do . . . that, along with vacuuming, washing and drying."

"Did Mansell ever mention Danny to you?"

"He never mentioned anybody to me, 'cept Terri."

"And he never mentioned what he planned to do with those bar-coded labels?"

"Nope. He just acted real paranoid like he didn't want his cousin to find out about them."

"Didn't you ask him any questions about them? Weren't you the slightest bit curious?"

"I got this feeling that I shouldn't be askin' him. You know what I mean?"

I didn't answer Richard, my mind was already thinking about what the bar-codes could have been used for. It seems like every business is using bar-codes these days—FedEx uses them to direct packages to the proper geographical areas, retailers use them for inventory control and pricing information, cars have them inside their door jambs, et cetera, et cetera. There must be at least a thousand uses for them, and one of the uses —*Scott Mansell's*—wasn't legit.

"You got any more quarters?" Richard asked. "For the TV."

I fished around in my pocket, found a dollar's worth and tossed them onto the bed. They bounced on the mattress like kids on a trampoline. "Anything else you can think of that could help me figure out who killed Mansell and why?"

Richard popped one of the quarters into the TV, tuned it to MTV and started bobbing and swaying to the sounds of a group that should have been called Snotty and the Nose Rings. "Nope. Sorry man."

I left, not certain if it was because I was through interviewing Richard or because I couldn't stand what passes for music these days.

Whatever happened to the good old days of Jimi Hendrix, The Doors, Led Zeppelin and the other groups played real music?

The drive to my apartment was excruciating. The tires rubbed the fenders every time I hit a dip, and I felt as though everybody was staring at me thinking that *I* was a dip. I did a double-take when I spotted a red Vette in my assigned parking spot. It looked like mine. Could it be? I parked in the visitor's lot and practically ran away from the Metro lest anyone actually see me near it, and examined the Vette. *Damn*. Same year. Same color. Different car. I walked away dejectedly toward my apartment. As I neared my porch, I heard footsteps behind me . . . gaining. I speeded up—they speeded up. I slowed—they continued running . . . closer. I listened carefully as I moved forward. Then I stopped, turned, and threw a punch at the precise moment that I knew my pursuer would be within a foot of me. My fist connected to his face with a loud crack. He dropped to the ground. I pounced on the man and pulled his head back by his hair.

"Hank, what in the hell are you doing?" the man said through his already swelling lips.

"Lou?" I said, suddenly recognizing Lou Gaston, my former operative at W-L's. I stood up and offered him my hand.

Lou looked me up-and-down, then grabbed my hand reluctantly and pulled himself up off the ground. "My new boss fires me and my old boss punches me out. This just ain't my day." He looked at my bloody shirt. "From the looks of you, it ain't yours either."

I was tempted to tell him what my day had really been like, but realized it would be about the stupidest thing I could do. Loose lips sink ships, and my lips had already gotten too loose around Lori—in the figurative sense at least. I thought about the irony of keeping my case secret from the man who had been my most trusted operative, yet divulging almost every detail to a secretary.

"No, it's not my day either," I responded. "What're you doing here? And why did you sneak up on me like that?"

"I've never been fired before and I needed to talk to someone. You're the first person I thought of. And I wasn't sneaking. If I had been, you wouldn't have heard me."

I mulled his comment over. I hoped he wasn't right about my inability to sense when someone was sneaking up on me, but considering that I had a huge bump on the back of my head, I suspected that he might be right. "You want a beer?" I asked.

"Is the Pope Catholic?"

I invited Lou into my apartment. After I changed into a clean shirt, I popped open a couple of Buds and listened as he griped about how W-L's had gone to hell in a hand basket since I'd left. Hearing Lou tell me how great a boss I'd been made me feel pretty good about myself, but hearing that Treet was going around trashing me to everyone who would listen was about the last thing I wanted to hear. Still, the more Lou told me about Treet and the changes he'd begun implementing at my old store, the more I thought that something very screwy was going on.

I commiserated with Lou over his job loss and assured him that, no, he wasn't a loser, he'd just been screwed by Treet. After finishing two six-packs—he had eleven beers and I had one—I drove Lou to his house and to his wife, explaining to her that I hadn't thought that he was in any condition to drive. She thanked me, put her arms around Lou and gave him such a big kiss that—for just a moment—I thought that being married again might not be such a bad proposition.

She asked me how I liked Lou's Corvette. "He always wanted one like yours," she said. "Then, the very day he bought one, he got fired."

I couldn't believe that Lou and I hadn't talked about his Vette. He must've really been upset, and I must be slipping. I love talking about cars . . . especially Vettes. *Damn*, I really wanted my car back.

I pulled out of Lou's driveway in the bashed-up, pink cruiser cupcake and drove straight to my old store—time to give Treet a piece of my mind for firing Lou and for trashing me, and to see if I could figure out what he was up to.

Lorraine Reynard, the lead clerk in the general office, greeted me like a long lost friend, which was entirely appropriate since we'd worked in the same store for fifteen years. I'd always considered her to be a sort of a mother figure, although I suspected that she wouldn't be too flattered with that since she was only about ten years older than I. She told me that Treet was off for the evening, along with Eaton and every other remaining member of management. When I asked her who was in charge of the store, she shook her head, raised her eyebrows and explained that she was.

"These budget cuts just don't quit," she said. "I can hardly get my work done. Instead of doing what I'm supposed to be doing, I keep getting 'bonged.'" She pointed toward the ceiling. "My bell starts ringing and I have to run off to shoes or linens or designer dresses or wherever there's a complaining customer or a lackadaisical employee or a malfunctioning register or any one of about a million other things going wrong. That's what we used to have managers for, but Eaton wants more money for his bonus at the end of the year so he's cut the staff to shreds. We hardly even have any sales people anymore. The store's going down the dumper, Hank. Eaton couldn't care less about his employees . . . what's left of them."

"I heard that Treet fired Lou Gaston and then he hired some new guy named Al Metzger. What's that all about?"

Lorraine wrinkled her brow. "Took me completely by surprise. One minute Lou was here, doing a great job as always. The next minute, he was gone. I figured he was laid off like so many of our other employees. You know, Eaton doesn't even have the guts to call it what it is. He never uses words like 'laid off' or 'terminated' or 'fired' or 'canned.' He uses 'down-sized,' 'right-sized,' 'position reviewed,' 'transitioned,' and 'deployed.' Well, I figured that Lou had been canned and wouldn't be replaced. But I was wrong. The next thing I knew, Treet had hired this germ Metzger."

"What do you know about Metzger?"

Lorraine tapped her pencil on the counter top and glanced from side-to-side. "He gives me the willies. Always looking at me, you know? I've heard the other women talking about it too. He leers at all of us. Gives us the creeps."

"Is he working tonight?"

"Nobody from loss prevention is on tonight."

"No one?" I couldn't believe what I'd just heard. "What if there's a shoplifter? What if some creep is hassling one of the girls in the junior's department?"

"If something like that happens, I get 'bonged.' It's already happened twice tonight. First there was a middle-aged woman down in accessories getting ready to take a handbag—"

"Let me guess. She's five foot four; a hundred and thirty pounds; black hair, obviously a dye-job; expensive clothes and jewelry; and about fifty-five years old?"

Lorraine's mouth dropped open. "You really are good, Hank. That's her. How'd you know?"

"Her name's Harriet Kuebler and her husband is the president of Bayside Bank. She used to come in here at least once a week and steal something. Classic klepto. I thought she ought to be locked up, but Eaton let her husband pay for her thefts in advance in exchange for us not apprehending her."

"You've got to be kidding. How much did he pay Eaton?"

"He wouldn't tell me."

"Did he ever tell you what account he put the money in?"

"He said something about it going into a reserve account. It didn't sound kosher to me, but what do I know?"

Lorraine arched her eyebrow. "You know a lot, Hank."

I accepted her compliment, then moved the conversation back on track. "You didn't apprehend Mrs. Kuebler tonight did you?"

"Heavens no. My instructions are to just burn the shoplifters. Go over near them and stare until they get spooked. This woman did what all of them do when they see me, she dropped the bag and left the store. We didn't catch her, but we didn't lose any merchandise, so I guess we come out even."

"You've been 'bonged' for two shoplifters so far tonight?"

"Not a shoplifter per se; a tag switcher. A teen-aged kid took the price tag off a box of sale Nikes and put it on a box of regular stock. A customer saw him do it and she told an employee who called the operator who 'bonged' me. I got down to the department just as he was about to hand the merchandise over to the salesperson. He almost got away with it. Once the salesperson had scanned the price tag it would have been all over—the kid would've had a hundred dollar pair of shoes for twenty-eight bucks."

I knew the practice well. In the 'good ol' days' back when sales people knew their merchandise and before computers had replaced common sense, we would enter every sale by hand. The sales person would look at the merchandise, then look at the price tag to confirm the information before ringing it up. Later that night, the entire transaction—along with every other transaction from the day's business—would be audited for accuracy. Today all that the sales people do is swipe a scanner over a bar-coded tag and then utter something unintelligible like '*cashorcharge*' and stare blankly at the customer . . . usually never even bothering to stop chewing their gum. Once the transaction is completed, the sales and inventory information is beamed via satellite to the corporate mainframe in Los Angeles, compiled, and then laser-printed onto fan-folded sheets of paper that nobody even reviews and in a month probably could reach from earth to Jupiter and back again.

"I wish I had a dollar for every time someone switched a tag," I said.

"You and me both. Then I could retire from this place."

I switched the subject. "Do you know anything about Metzger's background? Where he lives? Where he used to work?"

"Nothing, except I can tell that he's friends with Treet."

I heard the familiar '*bongs*' over the Muzak. When I'd worked at W-L's, three 'bongs' meant that an employee had spotted a shoplifter and I was to call into the store operator to learn which department to go to. Now I heard two bongs, followed by one more.

They're playing my song," Lorraine said. "Two bongs, space, one bong. Time for me to salivate like Pavlov's dog." She picked up a phone, punched zero, identified herself, and listened for instructions. "I'm on my way," she said into the receiver.

"Where to?" I asked.

"Infants department. A toddler just went *number two* on the linoleum and I've got to clean it up."

"Why you?"

"Eaton laid off the janitors at the same time he laid off most of management. Come to think of it, I miss the janitors a lot more than most of those prima donnas." Lorraine disappeared to the back, then reappeared with a bucket and a mop. "I don't know how I'll ever get my work done tonight with this kind of *crap* going on . . . literally." She pointed to the papers on her desk. "I've got to have that production report on Eaton's desk by 8:00 a.m. I miss the deadline and I'll be canned—excuse me, I mean *deployed*—by 8:01."

"How close are you to finishing it?"

"If I didn't have to provide janitorial services, I'd have a fighting chance."

I reached out for the mop handle. "I'll clean it up. You continue with your real work."

"I can't let—"

"Yes you can. Just do me one favor."

"Anything."

"Let me spend a little time in the store tonight."

Lorraine gave me a funny look. "We're open until ten. You've still got an hour until closing."

"I want to be able to go into the back areas . . . unsupervised."

"Why would you want to go back there?"

"Let's just say that I'm conducting an investigation."

Lorraine looked at the mop in my hand and the bucket in hers. "But Treet will have me fired—"

"He won't know if you don't tell him."

"Are you working on a case . . . as part of your detective business?"

"Yes."

"And it has something to do with Treet?"

I winked. "I can't say anything. It's confidential."

Lorraine smiled. "And this Metzger character—he's involved too?"

"A logical assumption," I said obliquely.

"And you could get them into trouble?"

I smiled and said nothing, although I nodded ever so slightly.

Lorraine handed me the bucket. "Deal."

"I'll need the master keys."

She fished a gigantic ring of keys out of her handbag and slipped them around my finger. I picked up a W-L's employee badge from the counter, pinned it onto my shirt and headed off to the infants department. Duty—or was it *doody*?—had called.

I seemed to have inadvertently discovered the ideal stealth cloaking for snooping. Nobody, it seems, pays any attention to a janitor. Employees—what few there were—didn't acknowledge me and customers looked right through me. When I finished cleaning up the mess, I pushed through the double-doors that led into the back corridor and began my investigation.

Both Arturo and Lou had told me that Treet had changed a number of loss prevention procedures and practices. Between the new ones that he'd implemented and the short-sighted operational "efficiencies" that corporate—and Eaton—had mandated over the past couple of years, the systems had deteriorated to zip. Arturo was particularly incensed that Treet had replaced VAST's camera surveillance system with his own; Lou's biggest gripe—other than being fired—was that Treet had forbidden him to enter the security holding room. Therefore, that was precisely the first place I went.

I walked through the corridor to the freight elevator, thumbed the down button and waited. The elevator arrived with a buzz and the cage-like doors opened like a whale's mouth. I climbed in, held the 'close' button while pushing the button marked 'dock.' A hundred whirring moments later, the doors spread open and I walked out onto the receiving dock.

The security holding room was located just inside the transfer dock doors that opened to the parking lot behind the store. The procedure mandated from corporate was that whenever "high risk" merchandise was unloaded from the company's transfer trailers, it would immediately be delivered to the security holding room and secured until it could be delivered to the selling department. "High risk" merchandise was defined as anything of exceptionally high value that was easy—and tempting—to steal.

When I'd first started at W-L's, we would physically check in all the merchandise as it was unloaded from the trailer and carefully compare what we had received to what was on the manifest. That way, we knew if we had received the correct quantities. The merchandise was then double-checked once it arrived in its selling department. Corporate, in its never-ending quest to increase efficiency and reduce payroll, had eliminated these steps a little more than two years ago. Starting then, we simply unloaded the trailer and assumed that what was in the trailer was what we were supposed to have. It seemed like a pretty sloppy business practice to me, but when I questioned it I was told that with the new computerized systems at our central distribution center, it simply wasn't possible for a mis-shipment to occur.

I couldn't argue with the fact that the new procedure saved a great deal of time at our store, and there seemed to be enough security precautions to ensure that the merchandise couldn't be stolen out of the trailers between the distribution center and the store. The doors of the trailers were locked and a laminated paper seal with a coded number printed on it was attached through the lock and the trailers' doors. The number of the seal on the trailer sent to my store would be phoned to me—the store's security manager—and I would be present at the dock to verify the seal's number before it was broken, the doors were unlocked, and the merchandise was unloaded. As a further precaution, the distribution center secured all "high risk" merchandise onto pallets with special security bands to prevent the removal of any items without it being obvious that the banding had been tampered with. Additionally, either I—or in my absence—Lou, was required to physically lock the palleted merchandise into the holding room, unlock it when the selling department was ready to receive it, and then remove the banding.

As I walked onto the dock, I looked up at the surveillance cameras and wondered who was monitoring them. Arturo had told me that the

TV screens were all lined up in Treet's office, but who could possibly be watching them now if Treet and Metzger were both off for the night? Probably just videotaping, I thought, for future review in fast motion.

I eased along a wall, away from the view of the cameras, and pulled a blonde wig off of one of the mannequins that stood like silent witnesses to my actions. I squeezed the wig onto my head, figuring it would work fine as a temporary disguise.

I resisted the temptation to look at my reflection in a Mylar display as I walked over to where I could see the holding room. It was immediately obvious that Treet had made a major change to the room; a change I didn't approve of. When I'd been security manager, the room's walls had been constructed from heavy-duty, chain-link fencing. I liked the idea of having the room open to view, making it easier to monitor and more difficult to steal from without being detected. I also liked knowing that the video cameras, located strategically throughout the dock, could look right through the fencing and into the room at all times.

Now the fencing had been covered by plywood—nobody could possibly see into the room. I remembered Lou's complaint about not being allowed into the room. *What had Treet been doing in there that he'd been keeping from Lou?* I pulled out Lorraine's master ring as I marched straight to the holding room's door. Just as I reached forward to try the first key, I heard a rustling from inside the room.

ELEVEN

I darted back, looking for a place to hide. I wanted a vantage point that would not only give me a clear view of the holding room's door, but would also provide me with cover. I knew that the recycling area would have plenty of extra-large corrugated cartons like the one that I'd hidden in during the drug-ring investigation. I ran over to the recycling bin, grabbed the biggest flat-folded carton I could find, and quickly formed it into a cube. I cut an inconspicuous hole in the side with a box-cutter, returned the cutter to the work station, then I carried the box out onto the dock and placed it where I didn't think it would be noticed. I climbed in and folded the top over my head.

Ten minutes went by with nothing happening except that the one beer I'd had with Lou had worked its way through my system and wanted out. Then the door to the holding room opened and I watched as Treet walked out pulling a flat-truck—a large flat cart that resembled a quadruple-sized child's wagon. On the flat-truck were several cartons of merchandise. Treet checked his watch as he wheeled the cartons to the roll-up dock door. I could hear the door creaking as it raised to the ceiling. I couldn't see what was happening, so I jumped up and shifted the box to the left while my body was momentarily suspended in mid air. Treet must've heard my movement, because he turned, pulled a gun out from under his shirt tail, and looked in my general direction. Then he walked closer but not directly toward me; I prayed that he hadn't spotted my hiding place. I waited perfectly still, stifling a sneeze and crossing my legs tightly. Then I heard the sound of a car or a truck engine, and Treet turned away from me. I reached into my pocket and grabbed a key. It didn't feel familiar. I looked down and recognized Lou's infra-red key fob that activated his doors and ignition. I used the key to cut a ragged hole in the cardboard carton while I mentally cursed myself for not remembering to give the key to Lou's wife. I peered out the hole and had a perfect view of the cartons, the open dock door, and Metzger standing next to the open tailgate of a black Suburban. I peeked through the first hole and watched Treet as he walked toward Metzger, returning his gun to his holster.

The two men quickly unpacked the cartons and loaded dozens of smaller boxes into wooden crates that were in the back of the Suburban. Crates exactly like the ones I'd seen Mansell and Metzger transfer from the Fiat to the Suburban yesterday morning—exactly like the crate that Richard had used to transport Mansell's dead body. After they packed all the boxes into the crates, Metzger tossed the large cartons into the trash compactor and Treet rolled out another similarly loaded flat-truck from the holding room. The two of them quickly packed the last of the boxes into the wooden crates in the back of the Suburban. When they finished, Metzger swung the tail gate shut and drove away as Treet rolled the dock door back down. Treet then wheeled the flat-trucks off to the side of the dock, tossed the last of the large cartons into the compactor, brushed off his hands, then walked over to the holding room, slammed the door shut and secured the padlock.

I took a deep breath as Treet turned and looked directly at my carton. Did he notice that it was out of place? After all, there was no logical reason for a big carton to be in this part of the dock. He stared at the carton as I stared through the hole at him. Would he notice the hole? Could he see my eye examining his every move? I wished I had my gym bag with me. I wanted my zapper, my handcuffs, anything to use against this man.

He walked toward me. My right leg jittered nervously and my hands instinctively transformed themselves into fists. There were perhaps seventy feet between Treet and me . . . then fifty . . . then twenty. He seemed to have spotted the hole in the carton . . . or had he? When he stepped to within ten feet of my hiding place, the freight elevator banged to the floor and the caged doors opened. Treet turned toward the elevator. Then he walked out of my view. I waited, hoping I could hear who had entered the dock . . . praying it wasn't Metzger.

"Just checking things out before I leave," Treet said to the new arrival.

"I didn't expect to see you down here. I thought you'd gone home hours ago."

I immediately recognized the second voice as belonging to Lorraine Reynard. I exhaled, realizing at that moment that I'd been holding my breath for minutes.

"Monitoring security in a store like this is a twenty-four proposition," Treet answered. "I like to show up when people don't expect me."

Lorraine walked to within my view, then turned her back to me and waved me a subtle warning . . . she must have recognized my old hiding method from my famous drug bust.

"I'm glad I found you here Mr. Treet," she said. "I think I'm going to need you." She walked across the dock to the wall phone, picked up the receiver and punched a number.

Treet followed her to the phone. "What is it?"

"Trouble on the third floor. We need to get there fast."

Lorraine walked quickly to the freight elevator. Treet stared at my carton.

"Come on!" she said, her voice rising anxiously. Treet turned from me and ran to join Lorraine.

Once the elevator doors slammed shut, I crawled out of my hiding place, folded it flat and returned it to the recycling bin. Then I ran to the holding room. I pulled the ring of master keys out of my pocket and tried every one of them on the padlock . . . none of them fit. I thought about my lock-gun in the Metro, turned around and sprinted toward the stairs that led to the selling floors. Half way to the stairs, a thought hit me. Why had Treet and Metzger tossed the cartons into the trash compactor instead of putting them into the recycling bin?

I doubled back to the compactor, opened the steel door and pulled out one of the cartons. It looked like every other carton I'd ever seen that'd been unloaded from a W-L's trailer—same material, same corrugation, same manufacturer, same label indicating the store number, same bar-coding on the label.

Then I noticed something strange. The store number wasn't right, it was the store number for the Newport Beach store. I pulled another carton out of the compactor. Its label had the store number for the Cerritos store. It didn't make any sense. It should be impossible for the Kingston Beach store to have received merchandise that had been intended for other stores; the distribution center's system simply wasn't capable of making that type of mistake.

I looked at the labels again. Something else was wrong, but I couldn't figure out what it was. I cut the label off of the two cartons with Lou's Corvette key, then retrieved a carton from the recycling bin that had the proper Kingston Beach store's number on the label. I cut it out and stuffed all three into the pocket of my Dockers. Then I sprinted for the stairs and clambered up, three steps at a time.

Once on the main floor, I detoured over to the general office and placed Lorraine's master keys in her desk drawer. Nobody saw me do it because with Eaton's new staffing, nobody else was even scheduled in the general office. Instead, there was just a phone so customers could speak with some disembodied voice in the corporate office—so much for personalized service. I walked out of the office area and onto the selling floor, pausing for just a moment to catch a glimpse of myself in a full-length mirror. Much to my dismay I saw the mannequin's blonde curls cascading across my forehead. I looked around to see if anybody was watching me. When I was convinced that they weren't, I wrenched off the wig and tossed it into the nearest wastebasket. Then I walked quickly to the closest exit and ran across the parking lot to my dainty little car. I unlocked the door and reached for my bag, debating whether I really needed to go back into the dock and break into the holding room.

My indecision was handled for me . . . the gym bag was missing. Not only that, but the radio had been ripped out of the Metro's dashboard and the shift knob had been removed. Somebody had climbed in through the broken back window and ransacked the car. I looked on the bright side . . . at least I still had wheels and tires.

I was bone tired when I arrived at my apartment complex. During the course of the day, I'd been knocked unconscious; had a two-by-four slammed across my face; nearly been electrocuted by my own zapper; and discovered Scott Mansell dead. . . for the second time in as many days. All of this on top of chasing Richard down and tackling him; punching out my friend Lou Gaston; nearly being caught spying on Treet and Metzger; and having my rental car broken into . . . twice. Things were getting to be a bit much.

I auto-piloted the Metro home in a trance-like stupor, nearly ramming the back of Lou's Corvette as I pulled into my parking spot. Luckily, I saw the back of his car before I actually made contact. I jammed the Metro into reverse—slicing my palm on the bare shift lever—and parked it in the visitors' lot. After I tended to my wound, I returned to the car and did my best to secure it from future thefts by duct-taping Saran Wrap over the gaping back window area. As an afterthought, I wrapped enough duct tape around the end of the shift lever to give it a little padding. Then I returned to my apartment, and prepared to collapse the moment I slammed the door behind me.

The phone rang the instant I staggered into my living room. I reached for my cordless with my good hand, said "hello" and walked to the bathroom to finally relieve myself of the beer.

"Hank, my *amigo*. I'm glad I reached you. I have something that will be of interest to you."

I recognized the voice as Arturo's. "Shoot," I said.

"What's that sound?" he asked. "It sounds like Niagara Falls over there."

I zipped up, held the receiver up to my head with my shoulder and washed my hands. "I don't hear anything. What's so important that you had to call me up at eleven at night?"

"I thought that you might want to know that someone over at the Captains' Coast Marina reported to the police that there were two suspicious men on Scott Mansell's boat. The caller said that one of the men hauled a large wooden crate to the boat and unloaded something from it onto the deck. He said that the second man came about a half hour later, boarded Mansell's boat and then fussed around with the lock for about ten or fifteen minutes until he finally unlocked it. He also said that when the two men left—separately—they each ran like scared rabbits. Rather vivid descriptions of both the men—one of them fit you to a tee, although you wouldn't be very flattered."

I dried my hands by waving them in the air. "What have the cops done about the report?"

"They're at Mansell's boat right now. Discovered Mansell's body in the cabin. They've dusted the scene for prints and already identified one of the suspicious men as Richard Tompkins. There's an APB out on him. They haven't ID'd you yet, so you'll probably be safe for awhile. But your friend Tompkins is going to be toast real soon unless he stays out of sight."

"Thanks for the info, Arturo. Anything else?"

"Only that Tompkins was seen driving away in an old Fiat station wagon. They don't have the license number, but it won't take long for the cops to figure out who it belongs to."

"Terrific," I said flatly. I made a mental note to call Walter's house to make certain that the car was well hidden. I told Arturo about meeting with Lou and what I'd subsequently discovered over at W-L's.

"Doesn't surprise me in the least. I knew Treet was dirty the moment I met him. He and Metzger have probably already unloaded the hot merch by now."

"That'd be my guess."

"What do you suppose it was?"

Just as Arturo asked me the question, my eyes locked onto the box that the CD changer I'd bought at Discount Danny's had come in. It was still where I'd left it . . . right on the floor in the middle of the living room. "Stereo stuff," I said to Arturo. "That's my guess. The boxes were the right size and it's exactly the type of merch that fits W-L's 'high risk' definition."

"But wouldn't W-L's miss it?"

"Not if Treet has figured out a way to adjust the distribution of merchandise from the corporate distribution center out to the stores."

"You mean funnel more merch to his store than it's supposed to receive?"

"Bingo."

Arturo chuckled. "Impossible! VAST has surveillance cameras all over the distribution center. At least I didn't lose that contract. I don't see how anybody could reroute the merchandise. It takes humans to do that, and there just aren't very many people working in that building now that it's computerized. Besides, the allocation of merchandise is all set up on spreadsheets. If somebody altered the spreadsheets, it would show up."

"I didn't say that I knew how Treet is doing it. I only said that I think he's figured out a way to get more merchandise sent to his store than it's supposed to receive."

"Well, I'm telling you that it can't be done."

"Because of the computers?"

"Precisely."

"And I say that's all the more reason that it *can* be done, and I'm living proof of it. I'm the only PI in existence who can't get a gun. Why not? Because of a glitch in Uncle Sam's computer. Those machines only do what they're told." I pulled the bar-coded labels out of my pocket, set them side-by-side on the floor next to the CD changer's box, and examined them. "And I think Treet has figured out a way to give those computers exactly the information that he wants them to have."

Arturo sighed. "I think you give him too much credit. I think he lucked into a misdirect and decided to take advantage of it."

"You think what I saw tonight is just a one-shot deal?"

"That's my guess."

"Well I disagree—and I think that if I dig into it I'll find that Treet was doing the same thing over at the La Jolla store before he moved over to take my place at Kingston Beach."

"You think too much."

"One of us has to—and you know what else I think?"

"You're going to tell me whether I want to hear it or not, so let's hear it."

"I think all of this links up with Discount Danny's. I'm betting that the merchandise I saw going out of W-L's tonight ends up at Danny's. And I'm also betting that somehow this whole thing relates to that robbery at Discount Danny's two months ago, but—for the life of me—I can't figure out how."

"You know what I think? I think you've been watching too many reruns of *Simon and Simon*."

"Maybe you're right, Arturo. But, talking about reruns, there's one that I'd like to have a tape of . . . and it's a show that only you would have. How about letting me view some tapes taken by the surveillance cameras at W-L's distribution center?"

"I could do that, but you're wasting your time. If anybody at the DC has been doing anything suspicious, one of my men would have seen it while he was viewing the tape 'live.'"

"Humor me."

"I always do. You can pick them up on your way to work tomorrow morning."

"Thanks Arturo."

"You're welcome Sherlock."

Before getting ready for bed, I mentally kicked myself for not checking Richard into a room that had a telephone. I considered driving out to the Humpty Dumpty, just to make sure that he was all right, but I was just too bone-tired to drive clear across town. Instead of calling Richard, I called Walter's house to make sure that the station wagon was where the police couldn't find it. Walter was asleep, but Crystal assured me that everything had been taken care of. She told me that Walter was furious with me for refusing to tell him where I'd hidden Richard, and had

143

instructed her that if she spoke with me, she should demand that I reveal his exact location or I'd be fired. I politely refused. She pressed again and when she finally realized that I wasn't going to tell her she said that she understood, asked if Richard was still okay and told me to give him her regards. Ten seconds after the phone call, I fell sound asleep on the living room floor . . . still in my clothes.

TWELVE

It took all my willpower to walk past Lou's Corvette and climb into my rented joke. I must admit that I did waver for more than just a moment. In one hand I literally held the keys to a car that looked so much like mine that I could almost cry; with a high performance V8 putting out a zillion horsepower, and probably capable of blasting from zero to sixty miles-per-hour in under four seconds. In my other hand I held the keys to a seventy horsepower, three cylinder buzz-box that probably took ten times as long to reach the same speed. One car was sleek, shiny, and red; wore a set of BFGoodrich Z-rated tires; and sported a five speed transmission so robust that King Kong could speed shift without breaking it. The other car was cartoonish, smashed-up, and baby girl pink; rolled on ludicrous, skateboard-like wheels with rubber bands for tires; and sported a glob of duct tape on top of a shift lever so spindly that one good shift could snap it in half like a dried twig. One car was *me*, the other was PeeWee Herman. The more I looked at the Metro, the more I hated it . . . and the more I realized that I needed my Vette. Yes, *needed* it.

I drove the Geo past Arturo's office to pick up the tapes. He wasn't in, but a baby faced kid who practically 'yes sired' me to death, seemed to be expecting me and handed me six tapes . . . but only after I provided him with suitable identification and signed his log book.

I drove to the office, parked the Metro next to Lori's Ghia, walked through the front door and was immediately engulfed in the smell of

145

freshly brewed coffee. Lori looked up at me and smiled, walked over to her computer, pressed a couple of keys, then reached out to her laser printer at the precise moment that a sheet of paper appeared in the output tray.

"I have something that I think will be of interest to you," she said with almost a melodic quality to her voice. She handed the newly printed page to me. On it, were the following words:

"Scott Mansell was killed at approximately 11:00 a.m. on Sunday of this week. He was standing in Richard Tompkins's closet, with the door closed, at the time he was shot. The cause of death was two thirty-eight caliber bullets, most likely fully jacketed by brass or copper, which were fired through the door and into his forehead. Death was instantaneous."

"Where did you get this?" I asked.

"I wrote it."

"I figured that. What I want to know is where you learned this information."

Lori pointed to her head. "As Hercule Poirot would say, I used my little gray cells."

I wrinkled my brow. "Hair Cool who?"

Lori gave me her patented smirk, this time with a bit of a twinkle in her eye. "Poirot," she said.

"Like Ross Perot?"

"*Hank!*"

I recognized that tone of voice—my mother and father had both used it whenever they'd become completely exasperated with me. I knew it was time for me to shut up and listen. "I'm sorry. Go on."

"Hercule Poirot was Agatha Christie's grandest sleuth. You do know who Agatha Christie is, don't you?"

I nodded as though I knew, but I wasn't really certain if she was a writer of mysteries or of cook books. One thing that I did know was that I was tired of Lori's word games and patronizing.

"Now that I've been coached for *Final Jeopardy*," I said disdainfully, "how about filling me in on the pertinent information."

"Just the facts ma'am, nothin' but the facts. Is that it?"

"*Joe Friday*," I exclaimed. "Finally somebody I can relate to." I smiled. Lori laughed out loud. "Yes, I would very much like the facts . . . ma'am," I said.

Lori moved around from the back of her command-post to join me. "It's really quite simple. I looked at the pictures you took of Scott Mansell in Richard Tompkins's closet. Then I started writing down all of my observations. What caught my eye first was the color of his body. It was greenish-red—quite unlike anything I'd ever seen before. The second thing I noticed was that his jaw looked slack, but the rest of his body looked stiff. The third thing I noticed was that the bullet holes were perfectly round and that there was no other damage to his forehead.

"After I noticed those things, I logged onto the Internet and within just a matter of minutes I knew approximately when he'd been killed and what kind of bullet he'd been shot with."

I stood there shaking my head.

"You don't believe me?" she asked with a hurt voice.

"Oh, I believe you all right," I said. "It's just that I can't believe that you did all this. I didn't know you were such a propeller head. Tell me more."

"Well, I remembered you saying that his body was cold and clammy. That, plus the resolving rigor mortis and the skin coloration, means that he was killed approximately eighteen hours before you discovered him. Give-or-take."

"You learned all that from your computer?"

Lori nodded.

"And the type of bullets?"

"I learned all about bullets from the Internet too, then I simply used the process of elimination to figure out what type the murderer used. Couldn't have been solid lead because lead would have flattened out as soon as they hit the closet door. Couldn't have been 'dumdums' because they would have expanded on contact and created greater damage than what I saw in the photographs. Same thing with soft, split-nose, hollow-point or jacketed bullets with exposed cores. So that means that Scott

Mansell was shot with either full metal jacketed bullets or with Teflon-coated 'cop-killer' bullets. Actually, it could be either type. I'm just guessing that they're jacketed because they're more common."

"But what makes you so sure that Mansell was inside the closet with the door closed when he was shot? Isn't it more likely that he was shot in the living room or bedroom and then stuffed into the closet?"

Lori returned to her command-post, reached into a drawer and extracted an envelope. "Because of this," she said as she pulled out a picture I had taken of the closet door.

"Hey," I objected. "Those pictures were in my desk."

"So what's your point?"

"I don't like people going through my things, that's my point. And what would happen if I needed to look at those pictures and I couldn't find them because you'd put them in your desk?"

Lori's smirk spread across her face. "I take it that you don't want to know what I figured out, and how?"

She had a point. "Get on with it," I said. "But I want my pictures back."

"Here." Lori gave me envelope that contained all the pictures except the one I'd taken of the closet door, which she set in front of me. "See those black dots on the door? Don't you think that they could be bullet holes?"

I couldn't see what she was talking about. "What dots? What bullet holes?" "These." She pointed to some black dots that were partly camouflaged by the coloration of the poster that was duct taped to the door. "Knowing you, you probably focused all your attention on the bikini-clad model and never even noticed these marks."

I cleared my throat. "That's a definite possibility."

"So? What do you think?"

"I think she's absolutely gorgeous!"

"Hank! About the bullet holes."

I looked closer at the picture. I hadn't noticed any bullet holes in the door when I'd been in Richard's apartment, but since I'd arrived right at sunset, the apartment had been fairly dark. The camera's flash had illuminated the room nicely for the photographs, and I could now clearly make out the black dots on the closet door. They looked like bullet holes to me, but I was still skeptical.

"Well," she prompted. "What do you think?"

"What I think is that there are some black dots on the door. Actually, it would be more accurate to say that they're on the poster that's on the door. I suppose that they could be bullet holes, but they could also be thumb tacks or felt pen marks or defects on the negative for that matter."

"So you still think that Scott Mansell was killed and then dragged into the closet?"

"Well, it does make more sense. Why would someone shoot a man who is inside a closet?"

"I don't know the answer to that. But then, I'm not the detective . . . *you* are. But answer me this: If Scott Mansell was dragged into the closet *after* he'd been killed, where are the heel marks?"

"What do you mean, heel marks?"

"Look at the carpet in the picture. That carpet is the same kind that I used to have at my place and I swore that I'd never have it again. Do you know why?"

"It clashed with your furniture?" I answered lamely.

"No, it looked perfect with my furniture. The reason I hated that carpet was because every time someone so much as scuffed a foot across it, it left a mark . . . an indentation." Lori pointed a perfectly manicured finger at the carpeting just in front of the closet door. "Now, if someone had dragged Scott Mansell's body across that carpet and stuffed him into the closet, where are the marks leading up to the closet?"

I held the picture up closer to the light and closer to my eyes. There weren't any marks in the carpet. And the black dots did look much more like bullet holes than thumb tacks or pen marks or anything else for that matter. Lori was definitely onto something.

"You, my lady, are brilliant," I said.

Lori curtseyed and perhaps even blushed. I'm not certain because that's one of the things I miss by being somewhat color-blind.

"Will this information help you to figure out who killed Scott Mansell?" Lori asked excitedly.

"I'm not certain just yet, but it could. It very definitely could." I motioned toward the stack of video tapes. "You want to watch some movies with me?"

"What kind of movies?" she asked suspiciously. "They don't star that girl on the poster do they?"

I wiggled my eyebrows up-and-down. Lori gave me a very offended look. I finally told her that the tapes might explain how hundreds of thousands of dollars worth of merchandise was probably marching right out of Weisbach-Lander's distribution center and into the waiting arms of Greg Treet. I also told her that since she'd done such a great job with her deductions from the snapshots of Mansell and the closet, that I'd be a fool not to use her skills with the tapes as well. We walked back to the conference room and I popped the first cassette into the VCR. Soon, Lori and I were watching a grainy, black-and-white tape showing the distribution center's parking lot.

"This isn't going to win any Academy Awards," Lori said. I agreed, ejected the tape and inserted another one.

"At least there are some people in this one," I said as we watched a few smock-attired employees punching a time clock and disappearing down a hallway.

"Is that Sean Connery?" Lori asked as she pretended to swoon. I replaced the tape with the third one.

"Well, this is real interesting. Wake me when it's over," Lori said.

I, on the other hand, could barely contain my excitement. "Actually, this is exactly what I'm looking for."

"All I see is a conveyor line with cartons rolling along on it."

"Look closely," I said. "What else do you see?"

"Well, the cartons are traveling along the conveyor line, and the conveyor line is fairly high. Maybe twenty feet above the floor."

"Right."

"And every so often a big paddle-like thing gently swats one of the cartons , diverting it onto a sloping conveyor that runs perpendicular to the main conveyor. It looks to me like there must be at least fifty of these sloping conveyors, and fifty paddles—"

"Actually, there are forty-four of them. One for each Weisbach-Lander's store. The Kingston Beach store is store number twenty-eight, so my guess would be that the twenty-eighth sloping conveyor would be the one that directs merchandise down from the main conveyor to the specific transfer dock that's devoted to my old store."

"And somehow the twenty-eighth paddle knows when to swat the cartons that should be going to your store?"

"Well, Treet's store actually."

"Right." Lori looked away from the TV screen and into my eyes. "But how does the paddle know which cartons to swat?"

I pointed to the screen at a large metal box suspended above the beginning of the main conveyor. "See that? It's a scanner. Just like the ones that the sales clerks use at the store, except more powerful. It reads the bar-codes that are on the cartons as they pass beneath it."

Lori squinted at the screen and pointed. "On those labels?"

"Exactly. Those labels still have the store's number printed on them so that humans can tell which store the merchandise should be delivered to. But, that's really just an hold-over from the old days when people did the sorting instead of the scanner, computer, and conveyor. Now, as you can see, the distribution center is practically human-free."

Lori nodded. "It's actually kind of creepy. Watching this tape is like looking at a ride at Disneyland with no people on it."

"Printed on the label, underneath the number," I continued, "is the store's bar-coded information. The bar-code is much more important than the number because it tells the *computer* which store the carton should be transferred to. It works like this: The carton rides along the conveyor. The scanner reads the bar-code on the label and sends the information to the computer. The computer tells the system which paddle should swat the carton. The designated paddle swats the carton and sends it down the dedicated conveyor for the store that is indicated on the bar-code. The carton rolls down the store's conveyor and directly into the trailer that is sent to the store at the end of the schedule."

Lori frowned. "I don't see how this has anything to do with stealing merchandise *out* of the Kingston Beach store."

I pulled out the three bar-coded labels I'd cut off of the cartons. "Take a look at these. Do you see anything different between them?"

"That's easy. The first one has 011 printed on it. The second one says 013. The third one has 028."

"Very good. Eleven is the store number for the Cerritos store. Thirteen is for Newport Beach. Twenty-eight is for Kingston Beach. Now, look at the labels again and see if there is anything the same about them."

Lori took a little longer to respond, shook her head, and then answered me. "Well, they're all white with black printing. They're the same size and shape. They all use the same font."

"Look closer at the bar-codes. I didn't even notice it myself until about a minute ago."

Lori focused on each of them—one at a time—then looked up at me. "The bar-codes all look the same."

"Exactly! Somebody printed up labels that trick the computer into distributing too much merchandise to the Kingston Beach store. The numbers on the first two labels may be for Newport Beach and Cerritos, but the bar-codes on them are for Kingston Beach. Somebody printed these labels to trick the distribution system. My guess is that there are phony labels interspersed with legitimate ones in the security staging area where cartons containing 'high risk' merchandise are held prior to being placed on the main conveyor and distributed to the stores. Once the buying office's computer determines how many cartons should go to each of the stores, an employee in the security staging area slaps the appropriate labels on the cartons."

Lori interrupted me. "So there are still some employees left at the DC."

"Just in a few areas."

"So you think that one of the employees in the staging area is deliberately misrouting merchandise to the Kingston Beach store by using these misprinted labels?"

I picked up the three labels and stacked them on top of one another on the counter. "It's likely that those employees don't even know that the labels have been tampered with. They have forty-four stacks of labels, one stack for each W-L's store." I slid the stack of three labels in front of Lori and looked at her. "What store number is on that top label?"

"Eleven."

"All right. Now assume for a minute that each of the labels in this stack have the number eleven printed on them."

Lori neatened up the stack. "Okay. That would mean that all these labels are for cartons that are to be delivered to the Cerritos store."

"Cartons of high risk merchandise," I corrected. "Like TVs, VCRs, and stereos. Now imagine that instead of three labels, you actually have a hundred, or . . . better still . . . a thousand of them, each one with the number eleven on it."

"Okay."

"And let's assume that you are now working in the security staging area at W-L's distribution center and you receive a print-out that tells you to send thirty of a certain type of stereo to the Cerritos store. What would you do?"

Lori put her hand on the stack of labels. "I'd take thirty labels from this stack and stick them onto thirty cartons of stereos. And then what? I'd push the cartons onto the large conveyor?"

"Exactly! And the cartons would travel up the conveyor to where the scanner would read the bar-codes on the labels and distribute the cartons. And we both know that the top label—the one you're touching right now— would direct a carton, not to Cerritos, but to Kingston Beach because of the bar-code. Now, what if one out of every third 'Cerritos' labels is actually a 'Kingston Beach' label, or maybe it's one out of ten, or one out of twenty? Whatever the ratio, it's going to send vastly more merchandise out to the Kingston Beach store."

Lori unstacked the three labels and picked up the one with the number thirteen on it. "And the same thing would happen when I placed labels on cartons destined to go to Newport Beach—"

"And probably Glendale, and Westminster, and Puente Hills, and on and on. By printing up these labels, someone is redirecting who-know-how-much 'high risk' merchandise to the Kingston Beach store."

Lori nodded her head, slowly at first, then faster. "But who would have printed them?" she asked after a moment of silence.

"Richard Tompkins—"

"So your client's grandson is in even more trouble than we thought. Not only is he wanted for murdering Scott Mansell, but he masterminded a scheme to divert merchandise into your old store so it could be stolen."

"Richard couldn't mastermind an effective tic-tac-toe strategy. He only printed the labels; he didn't have any idea what they would be used for."

"Well then, who did he print the labels for?"

"Mansell."

"*Terrific*," Lori said, her entire body sagging. "That ties the murder victim right back to Richard again. It might even provide the police with a motive."

I shrugged. "I know. *Damn!* Here I am, the only witness to Treet and Metzger stealing gobs of merchandise right out the back of my old store, and I can't do anything about it because it implicates Richard in the theft and the murder." I ejected the tape and shut off the VCR.

Lori cocked her head the moment I mentioned Treet and Metzger taking the merchandise. "Hank, there's something that doesn't make sense. If all that merchandise gets diverted to the Kingston Beach store, wouldn't somebody there notice that they were getting too much? And wouldn't somebody at the Cerritos store, and the Newport Beach store, and all the others notice that they didn't get enough?"

"You're right," I responded. "It doesn't make sense. In a company as large as W-L's you'd expect that there would be so many checks-and-balances that this sort of thing couldn't happen . . . and it wouldn't have happened prior to W-L's automation, computerization, and expense reductions. Up until a little more than two years ago, each store was on its own individual inventory. Back then, we in the stores knew exactly how much inventory we were supposed to receive, and we'd check the merchandise off on a manifest whenever we unloaded a trailer. But then the company went to a corporate-wide inventory and each store just accepted whatever was delivered without counting it. We wouldn't know how much we were supposed to receive, and we wouldn't know how much we actually did receive. I questioned it at the time, but a lot of people with titles that were much more impressive than mine told me that the new way would be just as precise and far more cost effective."

"Sounds pretty stupid to me."

"Well I certainly saw the flaw in it at the time, and so did somebody else."

Lori smirked and I didn't mind it in the least—this time, her smirk wasn't directed at me. "Treet!" she said.

"Bingo! He, Metzger and Mansell were all in on this. They probably have been for quite a while. In fact, I'll bet that they were doing the same thing over at the La Jolla store before Treet transferred to Kingston Beach. Come to think of it, that would explain why Treet tried to turn down his transfer. I couldn't think of a good reason for him to not want to go to a big volume store that was literally only a twenty minute drive from his small one. He probably already had enough bogus labels in place at the distribution center to redirect merchandise to the La Jolla store for years—"

"And he had to set it up all over again when he transferred to your store." Lori completed my thought. She and I were definitely getting onto the same wavelength.

I continued: "Treet needed to put new labels into the DC's security staging area, and he needed to revise the security procedures at my old store. Well, I know about what he's done to my store. And I know that Mansell arranged for Richard Tompkins to get that printing job . . . replacing Metzger who'd been fired well after he probably printed the La Jolla labels. Mansell knew that Richard wasn't the swiftest guy around, and he knew that he could get him to print him anything he wanted."

Lori shook her head. "I see another problem. How could they get into the DC to replace the labels?"

"Easy as pie. Store security managers rotate through the DC, ostensibly as part of their on-going training, but I always assumed it was just another way for W-L's to save money by reducing the security staff at the DC down to the bare minimum."

Lori handed the labels and the photo of the closet door back to me. "But none of this helps Richard. In fact it just further implicates him."

I nodded.

"So what are you going to do?"

"I'm going to drive out and talk to Richard. Maybe now that I know what the bar-codes are being used for, it may trigger something in his empty little mind."

"Is there anything else you want me to do for you?"

I shook my head. "Hey, you seem to have done quite well without any instructions from me. You just put your little gray cells to work."

The Metro started with a gasp; the three cylinders suddenly reduced to two operable ones. I chugged and bucked and wheezed for several blocks until the temptation became too great for me. I did, after all, have the keys to a perfectly good Corvette in my pocket. I detoured past my apartment and pulled the Metro up next to Lou's car. As I unlocked the door to the Geo, I aimed Lou's key fob at his car and squeezed the remote to unlock it. At that very instant the Corvette exploded into a thousand pieces of flying shrapnel, a yellow fireball reaching high into the sky. The Metro rocked on its suspension and the passenger's window exploded into the interior, throwing bits of jagged glass against my face. Smoke filled the air and sparks glittered like a magician's finale. Scorching heat singed my face. I threw the pink hatchback into reverse and backed as fast and as far away as I could. Then I stared out the windshield at what had once been my friend's prized Corvette . . . for all of two days.

Neighbors poured out into the parking area. I heard sirens. I knew that I couldn't wait for the cops—they'd have too many questions and I only had the wrong answers.

I jammed the little Geo into gear and wobbled out the back of the lot, at the precise moment that a black-and-white entered through the front.

Just as I thought that my day couldn't get any worse, I unlocked Richard's door at the Humpty Dumpty and discovered that the room was empty. I washed the blood and shattered glass off my face, sat on the foot of the bed and rested my head in my hands.

THIRTEEN

My hope was that Richard had simply grown tired of sitting in the motel room, had gone out for a quick walk, and would be back in a couple of minutes. My fear was that whoever had tried to kill me by bombing the Corvette had gotten his hands on Richard. Somewhere in between these thoughts, was the concern that the police had apprehended Richard. I waited in his room, killing time by snooping through the drawers for who-knows-what. After about five minutes, I figured it was time for me to get out of there.

I started to climb into the Metro to drive off, but made a quick detour to the motel's office instead. The man who had checked me in the day before sat on a torn vinyl chair, watching *Geraldo* on a ten inch black-and-white.

"Hi," I said, trying to compete with a screenful of women-who'd-slept-with-their-sister's-husbands-while-their-dogs-watched. "I checked into room eighteen yesterday."

The man looked blankly at me for a moment, then returned his attention to the screen. When *Geraldo* was replaced by an ad for a psychic hot-line, the man swiveled around, picked up a clipboard and ran his finger down the dog-eared chart under the spring.

"Branberry," he said, looking up at me with absolutely no interest.

"That's me."

The man nodded. "I know that. What I don't know is who that other fella is in your room. Now, I'm not sayin' that I care what you and your friend do in your room . . . consentin' adults and all that. I'm just sayin' that I need to know when there's two people usin' a room 'cause I gotta charge you extra."

My face flushed for no good reason. "I didn't actually stay here last night," I explained. "My friend did. I just paid for the room."

The man looked back at the chart. "One day's worth. You takin' another day? 'Cause if you ain't, you're bumpin' up against check-out time and you'll have to get your stuff outta there . . . and you gotta give me back my keys."

I handed him three twenties. "I'll take another day."

"For you and your friend?"

"I told you, it's just for him."

He put my twenties into a drawer and pulled out a rumpled ten. "You sure 'bout that?"

"Positive."

He tossed the ten onto the counter. "There's your change."

Like the professional investigator that I am, I moved skillfully into my info gathering phase. "My friend isn't in the room. You didn't happen to see where he went did you?"

The commercial had finished and Geraldo was back with his two-timing sisters. The man swiveled away from me and toward the TV, giving me a front row view of the lice dancing in his greasy brown hair.

I leaned over the counter and raised my voice. "I asked you a question."

He looked over his shoulder at me. "I don't answer questions 'bout what the Hump's clientele do. Keeps things simpler . . . for me and for everybody." He turned back to the TV.

I'd heard somewhere that PIs and hoods used to refer to their guns as their "persuaders." Thanks to Uncle Sam's wonderful computer system I didn't have a gun, but I did have a ten dollar bill sitting on the counter. Judging from the looks of this guy, I was pretty sure that it'd persuade him to give me the desired results. "There's ten bucks in it for you if you remember anything about my friend leaving the motel."

He swiveled around quickly, reached his hand across the countertop, and snatched the bill like a lizard. "He left at around midnight."

"Did you see where he went? Was he with anyone?"

His hand returned to the counter, palm up. "My memory's fadin'." He smiled for the first time, exposing a row of teeth as imperfect as a picked-over sale shelf at W-L's.

I only had a five and a twenty left. I pulled out the five.

He shook his head back-and-forth. "That old memory of mine just ain't what it used to be. Needs some bigger joggin' to clear out the cob webs. Know what I mean?"

I slapped the twenty into his hand. It snapped shut like a Venus fly trap.

"He left alone. On foot. Didn't come back neither. Least I didn't see any lights come on in the room later that night."

"You would've noticed?" I asked.

"Yeah, I would have. Now, if you don't mind, I'd like to return to my program." He swiveled around to face the TV and I walked out with five bucks in my wallet and the feeling that I'd just been had.

I couldn't help but notice the woman as I walked toward my rental car. She was lounging on a chaise next to the pool, wearing a tiny bathing suit and big hair. I recognized her as one of the mini-skirted, crop-topped purveyors of extra-curricular activity that I'd noticed on the corner the night before.

"Excuse me miss," I said as I walked toward her.

She slid her sunglasses down her nose and looked over the top of them at me. "Sorry honey, business hours are from six p.m. to two a.m. Check back with me then."

"That's not what I had in mind. Actually, I'm looking for a man—"

"Whatever floats your boat, honey. There's Raul, he's stays over in room twelve and—"

"No, that's not what I meant. I'm looking for a friend of mine. I was supposed to meet him here. I was thinking that maybe you might have seen him."

"You got a name?"

"Branberry, Sam Branberry." Funny how that name has become so natural to me.

"That's not your name," she said authoritatively.

"What makes you say that?"

"I meet a lot of guys in my line of work and most of them give me phony names. I can always tell when they're doin' it. They don't look me in the eye. They may try to, but the gaze is always off by just a bit . . . just like yours was." She looked me straight on. "So what's your name, honey."

I hesitated.

"I ain't gonna burn you. Anybody asks me about your name, I'll just say that it's John Doe."

I figured that I didn't have anything to lose. "Hammond. Hank Hammond."

She reached her hand up regally for me. "Well Hank, pleased to make your acquaintance. My name's Goldie. Name matches my hair. Made it up myself."

I wondered if she meant that she'd made up her name or her hair, and figured she probably meant both. I shook her hand. "Nice to meet you Goldie. Now, about my friend."

"Well, what's he look like?"

I described Richard.

"When was I supposed to maybe have seen him?"

"Maybe around midnight. Probably would have been on foot, walking away from the Humpty Dumpty."

Goldie closed her eyes and leaned her head back as the sun beat down on her face. "I saw him." Her eyes opened. "It'll cost you."

Somehow, I knew that was coming. "I only have five bucks on me."

Goldie laughed. "That ain't gonna do it, Hanky. I need fifty. I never do nothin' for less than fifty." She appraised me from head-to-toe. "I'll take your watch though. It looks like it's worth at least a hundred."

"I need the watch."

"Then I guess you ain't going to get the information." Goldie shoved her sunglasses up to cover her eyes and leaned back on the chaise.

I leaned over her. "Goldie, I really need to know what happened to my friend. It could be a matter of life-or-death."

She slid her shades back down her nose and stared directly at my waistline. I automatically sucked in my gut.

"That belt buckle, what'd it cost you?"

I leaned over and looked at my favorite silver and turquoise buckle. I'd bought it in Tombstone Arizona and thought that it gave me a certain desperado look. "A hundred and seventy-five."

"You got screwed."

You're the expert, I thought.

"It's not worth more than fifty. You give it to me and I'll tell you about your friend.

I didn't have time to argue. I unbuckled the belt, whipped it out of my Dockers loops and handed it to her. I figured that if anybody happened to be watching, they'd probably expect that my next move would be to drop trou and go at it with Goldie right on the chaise.

Goldie examined the belt and buckle for a few moments, then set it down next to her. "I was standin' over there." She gestured toward the intersection with her chin. "He left that room over there." She pointed with her thumb to room eighteen, right underneath the large, cracked egg. "Then he walked along that sidewalk and right past me. *Right past me!* Can you believe it? The guy wasn't interested in me in the least. Actually, it kind of hurt my feelings. Anyway, he went over to a phone booth and made a call. Then he walked away real fast and I never saw him again."

"Which way did he go?"

"East." She shook her head. "Maybe it's west. Actually, I don't know which direction it is. All I know is that he walked toward Bissell Street and that's the last I ever saw of him."

I drove along Bissell Street, trying to figure out who Richard might have called and where he might have gone . . . and why. Nothing unusual or enticing stood out from the sea of chain restaurants, mom-and-pop stores, and other typical slices of Americana on Bissell or any of the other nearby streets. I wheeled back past the Humpty Dumpty, then stopped at the pay phone that Goldie said she'd seen Richard using.

I'd hoped to find a message etched into the phone's paint—something like "Hank, everything is fine. I just decided to check into the Hilton so I could watch TV without using any more of your quarters. Come on over." Unfortunately, the only etchings consisted of graffiti related to body parts, body functions, and a variety of combinations thereof. I debated whether I should call Walter and tell him that his grandson had disappeared . . . *again*—this time under my watch. I knew that I should, but the thought of being fired from my first case blew away any sense of moral obligation. Still, my fingers couldn't resist inputting Walter's number—it was as though there was a direct conscience-to-fingertip link that bypassed the more practical and self-serving part of my brain.

I counted the number of times the phone rang. After the fifth ring, I gave up and began moving the receiver away from my head and toward the phone's switch-hook. That was when I heard Walter's voice on the line.

"Walter Tompkins here." His voice sounded weak and tired.

I paused, not knowing where to begin.

"Hello? Hello? Is anybody there?" he said.

"Mr. Tompkins, this is Hank Hammond. How—"

"*Walter. Walter. Walter.* Dispense with the *mister* nonsense. Now, I just have one question for you. Think it over carefully before answering, because if you give me the wrong answer, you're fired. Do you understand?"

163

I didn't feel like playing games, but since my income depended on it I had little choice. "I understand," I said.

"Fine. Now here it is: *Where is my grandson?*"

I took a deep breath, prepared myself for the inevitable, and answered him honestly. "I'm afraid I can't tell you that, Walter."

"Well *good.*"

Good? That certainly wasn't the response I'd expected.

"You have passed my test, young man and I am very proud of you for not buckling under pressure and telling me something that I must not know. It takes a lot of gumption for a person to defy his employer for a higher good. You, my young man, have gumption. That is precisely why I like you. No, it's more than that—I *respect* you. I am honored to have you working in my—and Richard's—best interests. Now, why is it that you called?"

After that accolade, I couldn't very well tell Walter the truth. I'd started to. Really, I had. But now it was too late. "I just wanted to check in with you. I called last night, but you were asleep. I spoke with Crystal."

"She told me that you'd called. Said that you wanted to make certain that my car remained hidden."

"And has it?"

"No. The police have it."

My heart stopped. "The police?"

"They came here last night, right after you called. Woke me up. Wanted to know if I could tell them where my grandson was."

"What did you tell them?"

"The truth. I always tell the truth, young man. You stick with the truth and you can never get yourself into trouble."

"Can you be a little more specific about what you said?"

"I told them that, in all honesty, I didn't have the slightest idea where Richard was. I told them that I hadn't seen him in nearly a week." Walter coughed, cleared his throat, then continued. "I have *you* to thank for that. If you had told me where you had hidden Richard, I would have had no choice except to tell the police."

"And the car?"

"They asked if I owned a Fiat station wagon. I told them that I did. They asked me if I knew where it was. I told them that I did. They asked me where it was. I told them it was parked right outside Tony's Import Auto Repair."

I couldn't believe what I was hearing. "Why was it there of all places?"

"It needed to be serviced. I told Crystal to drive it there and park it outside their lot and then slip the key into an envelope along with my written instructions on what needed to be done to the car, then to stick the envelope into their mail slot. That is exactly what she did and then she returned here by taxi-cab. That's how I always drop the car off when it's after their normal business hours."

"But I told you to keep it hidden."

"Sometimes the best place to hide something is in plain sight."

"So the police have your car."

"I suppose so. You could drive past Tony's and check on it if you'd like."

I groaned in frustration.

"What?"

"Nothing. Walter, is there anything else that you told the police? Anything else that could affect your grandson?"

"That was all there was to it. They were very polite and didn't take up much of my time. I must have looked like death-warmed-over because they kept apologizing for waking me. Damn, I hate getting old. Lately I've been feeling worse and worse. You young folks—"

"Walter, I don't mean to be rude, but what else happened with the police?"

"Happened? Well, nothing. Nothing at all. We only talked for a short while and I'm certain that they knew that I was telling them the truth. They simply thanked me and left."

"Did they speak with Crystal?"

"Certainly. She answered the door. That's one of her jobs . . . to answer the door and to answer the phone for me. Maybe you haven't noticed, but I'm not exactly a spring chicken."

I'd noticed. "Do you know what she said to the police?"

"You'd be better off asking her. She's running errands right now, but will be back within an hour to give me my insulin. If you like, I could tell her to call you when she returns."

"Do that, please. And Walter, one more thing. Why didn't you call me after the police had contacted you? Didn't you think I should know about something that important?"

"It was late and I was tired. As soon as the officers left, I went straight to bed and fell asleep. Now, before you go thinking that I'm an old fool, let me tell you that I *did* call you as soon as I woke up. I called your office and spoke to a lovely woman named Lori. Is she your wife?"

"No sir."

"Well, she should be. She is a most delightful woman. She took my message and told me that she'd give it to you as soon as you either called in or came back to the office."

Walter's comment about marriage triggered something in me—not a desire to propose to Lori, or anybody else for that matter. It reminded me of Terri's supposed phone call from Richard's wife. I asked Walter if Richard had ever been married.

The line remained silent for several moments. I began to worry. "Walter? Walter, are you there?" I asked.

"I'm here," he answered softly. "I think I need to lie down and go back to sleep."

"But my question. Has Richard ever been married?"

"Of course not. I wish he would and I know that he has had the chance many a time. Girls are silly over him—part of the Tompkins charm, I suppose. But he's not a one-woman-man. At least not at this stage in his life. I've been to his apartment and I've seen those pin-ups he has plastered up all over his walls. Oh that boy loves the girls." Walter coughed. "Now, if you don't mind, I do need to get to bed."

I said good-bye to Walter and called my office. Lori dutifully informed me of Walter's message. She also told me that six other telephone messages had come in for me while she was at lunch. She switched on the answering machine and played them back for me.

The first was from Lou wanting to know what in the name of God had happened to his Corvette. The second was from Armando at Tony's Import Auto Repair telling me that the cops had impounded Walter's Fiat and that, by the way, the price of the Metro's wheels and tires had just quadrupled. Oh, and if I objected to the new price he'd tell the police that I'd been asking around about Walter's Fiat. The third call was from the police wanting to ask me some questions about the Corvette that had been parked in my assigned parking space. The fourth was from Arturo, sounding quite anxious, saying that I needed to contact him right away. The fifth was from MCI wanting me to switch over to their long-distance service. That last message really annoyed me, but not nearly as much as the sixth one, which sent a chill up my spine with its electronically altered voice:

"Bombs away, big boy. Next time, you won't be so lucky . . . you'll be dead."

Lori had been listening to the messages along with me. "What did he mean by that?" she nearly shrieked. "Did somebody actually try to kill you?"

My mind replayed the explosion. Fiberglas panels bursting, glass windows shattering, flames reaching toward the power lines, and smoke filling my lungs. "It appears that way," I said weakly.

"Are you o?"

"I'm fine. Don't worry about me—"

"I'll worry about you if I want to," Lori reprimanded. "Have you contacted the police?"

At that precise moment, a pair of conspicuously plain Ford sedans careened around the corner—just a few feet from my phone booth—then slammed up the driveway into the Humpty Dumpty's parking lot. One car screeched to a stop in front of the office, the other pulled back to room eighteen.

"I've got to go," I said to Lori. I hung up the phone and ran—holding my pants up—to the most attention getting car on the block. Just as I climbed into my little rental, a black-and-white streaked past me and into the Hump. I don't know if it was fact or my imagination, but I could swear that the officer riding shotgun looked directly at me.

I stopped past a bank for some dollars, and past a Penney's for a cheap belt—depressed that my waist had increased by two sizes—then I drove over to VAST's headquarters.

"Get into my office and close the door behind you, my *amigo*." I could hear Arturo's voice, but couldn't see him. His cop wanna-be at the desk pointed me through an open door. I entered Arturo's office and shut the door as instructed.

"Your client's grandson has stepped right into it," Arturo said without inflection or emotion. "The police picked him up late last night at the Denny's coffee shop over on Bissell."

I slammed my fist on Arturo's desk. "I told him to stay put. What the hell was he doing there?"

"Well, try this for a theory: maybe he was hungry," Arturo said sarcastically. "But his motive isn't what particularly matters at this point. What matters is that he started singing to the police, because now they know where he was hiding last night."

"I know, I saw the cops arriving there not more than a half hour ago."

"At the Hump?"

"Right."

"I won't ask you how you happened to select *that* motel, Hank. I certainly hope that it didn't have anything to do with their frequent customer program."

"I've never been there before in my life," I protested.

"Thou doth protesteth too much, my *amigo*. I'm only surprised that you didn't just rent the room by the hour."

It suddenly dawned on me that if Richard had started spilling his guts to the police, that he'd probably already given them my name. If he hadn't, the *Geraldo* fan in the office was probably providing them with a pretty good description of a man calling himself Sam Branberry. I mentally congratulated myself for not telling him my real name, then I mentally kicked myself for giving it to Goldie. If the cops talked to her, I figured that I stood a fifty-fifty chance of being identified as Hank Hammond . . . or John Doe.

Beads of sweat burst onto my forehead. "How'd you learn all this?" I asked.

"Some from the scanners, some from connections in the department."

"Do they have my name?"

"I don't know."

"You learn anything else about Richard?"

"Sure did. They found the murder weapon."

"Let me guess, it's a thirty-eight."

"It certainly is, and it belongs to none other than your client's grandson."

"His prints on it?"

"Wiped clean."

"Where'd they find it?"

"In the Dumptser behind his apartment. The same Dumpster that contained the crate he used to transport the body. Blood stains match Mansell's."

"That's bad," I said, stating the obvious. "Anything else that you've learned?"

"Nothing more about Richard Tompkins, but I remembered something interesting about Danny . . . or at least about his business." Arturo opened a desk drawer, pulled out a file folder and perused its contents. "He used to have a business partner, back when the store was called Audio Emporium. The partner's name *was* Jerry Wingate." Arturo looked up from the document and directly at me, waiting expectantly.

"And?"

"That was a clue, Hank—do I have to spoon-feed everything to you? I said that his name was Jerry Wingate. And the reason that I said was is because he's dead. He died a couple of years ago. Shot in the head—"

"Just like Mansell," I blurted out.

"Maybe, maybe not. Officially, it was a suicide. Maybe it was, maybe it wasn't. But I think that it is rather interesting that Wingate used to be

Danny's partner and that Mansell seems to have had something to do with the robbery of Danny's store."

I raised a finger to the side of my head, pointed it toward my skull, shaped my hand into a gun, and cocked my thumb. "And Wingate and Mansell are both dead . . . each with a bullet in the brain."

"Precisely," Arturo said, nodding.

"Except that Scott Mansell definitely didn't kill himself."

"Perhaps Jerry Wingate didn't either."

"Then why the suicide ruling?" I asked.

"Two things—evidence and motive. Wingate died of a single gunshot at point-blank range to the left side of the head. Since he was left-handed, that indicates possible suicide. Plus there was gunpowder residue on his hand and he was drunk at the time of the shooting."

"And the motive?"

"It's always either women or money . . . or both. With Wingate it was money, or rather, the lack of it. He owed more than you and I'll ever earn in our lifetimes. He and Danny were half owners of the Audio Emporium and as soon as The Electrical Outlet opened up down the street from them, their customers abandoned them."

"The story of thousands of independent retailers all over the country, unable to compete with the super stores," I added.

"Precisely. And once that happened, it didn't take long before their creditors called in their chips and their vendors refused to ship their merchandise. Wingate's world was crashing around all over him."

"But what about Danny's world? Didn't it crash along with Wingate's?"

"That's the irony. Danny is sitting pretty right now. In fact, he's been doing fine ever since Wingate died."

"Insurance money from Wingate's death?" I asked.

"Not at all. Neither of them even had key-man insurance. Danny didn't receive so much as a dime from Wingate's death. But about the time that Wingate died, Danny came up with a gimmick. He'd seen this store in New York where the owner claimed that he was so crazy that he was selling merchandise at a loss just for the fun of it. Customers absolutely ate it up."

"Crazy Eddie's." I knew it well, not because I'd ever been there, but because it had caused such a sensation in the retail world . . . until the owner skipped the country just a few steps ahead of the law.

"That's the one. Well, Danny closed down the Audio Emporium one day and reopened it as Discount Danny's the next. Great gimmick: catchy advertising, premium merchandise, and low prices."

"Maybe a little too low," I said almost to myself. I glanced at my watch and winced. The day was disappearing too fast. "What else do you have for me?"

"Like?"

"Like anything that positively ties Danny Murphy to the murder of Scott Mansell, or that links him to Treet, or explains who it is that wants me dead?"

Arturo shot me a dirty look. "You want me to do all of your work for you? You're the one getting paid for this, not me."

I took that as my cue to leave.

As I walked to my little pink car, I glanced at a newspaper rack on the sidewalk. The headline stopped my heart. The Norville brothers, and the rest of the drug smugglers I'd busted at W-L's, had just been released from prison on a technicality. Too bad I didn't have a couple of quarters so I could read all about it.

FOURTEEN

Things were spiraling out of control. Just when I'd resolved in my mind that Mansell's murderer was the same person who had just tried to blow me to kingdom-come, now I could just as easily be convinced that Ray and Roy Norville—or one of their partners in their drug trafficking gang—had tried to erase me from the planet. Of course, maybe neither of these conclusions were correct. Maybe the car bomb was strictly related to what I'd witnessed at W-L's receiving dock last night and it had nothing to do with Mansell's murder *or* with the druggies. Or maybe I'd been the victim of a random act of violence. Or maybe pigs can fly.

I drove fast along Pacific Coast Highway, dispersing a flock of sea gulls that had been pecking at a load of french fries some sloppy motorist had tossed onto the road. The birds flew into the air like an explosion, squawking their profanities at me as I passed underneath. One bird had been so busy concentrating on his catch-of-the-day that he hadn't noticed my Metro wobbling toward him. He saw me too late—or maybe it was that I saw him too late—and as he belatedly flapped skyward, I slammed into him. He somersaulted up the grille and hood of my little car until he finally hooked himself onto the windshield wiper and flapped in the rushing wind. My first reaction was to turn on the wipers and hope that the damn bird would fall off onto the road. Somehow, I couldn't bring myself to be so heartless. I jerked the car to the side of the blacktop, climbed out and gently removed the bird from the windshield.

His head was bloodied and his body was broken. I carried him to the side of the road, dug a hole in the sand with my hands, and buried him. Then I drove away with my windshield wipers smearing his blood and feathers across my view. The more I thought about the blood, the madder I became. *That bird had no business being in such a dangerous place and not paying attention . . . he should have had better sense.*

I forced my concentration back to my own situation. The more I thought about how I'd narrowly escaped being killed by the exploding Vette; the death threat I'd received on my answering machine; the way I'd broken into Richard's apartment and Mansell's boat, not knowing what was on the other side of the door; the fact that I'd discovered Mansell dead—twice; the way that I'd hidden in a flimsy box at W-L's, watching two guys stealing hundreds of thousands of dollars worth of merchandise while one waved a gun in my direction; the way I'd clung to a Dumpster while a man unloaded his pistol toward me, nearly neutering me . . . or worse; and the fact that Danny's old partner Jerry Wingate had ended up with a bullet in his head, I couldn't help but think that I was just like the bird . . . *in danger and not paying enough attention.* Well, at least I wasn't dead. Yet.

I pulled into my office parking lot. My office? My parking lot? I didn't own the office. I didn't own the lot. In fact, I didn't own much of anything except a Vette that isn't drivable, some stereo gear, and a few changes of clothes that Lori says clash with one other. I jumped out of the Metro and slammed its tiny door shut with such force that I thought it would fall off its hinges. I loathed that car and the sooner I got back into my Vette, the better. I needed something powerful to control.

"You hung up on me," Lori said as I stormed through the reception area and into my closet of an office. "Are you okay?"

"No," I shouted as I picked up my phone and called the garage where my car had spent the last month of its life. Lori stepped gingerly across my threshold and listened as I told off the owner of the Corvette shop. I looked up at Lori and smiled weakly to show her that I wasn't a complete jerk. Then I slammed down the phone.

"Sometimes you just have to be a jackass," I said.

Lori didn't respond.

"My Vette," I explained. "Somehow, miraculously, now that I've blown my cork, the owner of the shop says that it'll be ready within the next half hour.

"But that doesn't answer my question." Lori stepped into my office and pressed the front of her skirt up against the front of my desk. "Are you all right? I've been worried sick about you. Cars blowing up, threatening messages, the way you hung up on me the moment I asked you if you'd gone to the police. Not to mention the fact that your face looks like Mike Tyson used it for a punching bag." She wagged her finger at me. "What in the world is going on?"

I invited her to sit on the metal folding chair across from me and I filled her in on everything I'd learned since we'd last spoken. As I ran through the case, not editing even so much as one detail, I couldn't help but think how my opinion of her had changed. Originally, I'd thought of Lori as just someone to answer my phone and do some filing. Now, I reluctantly had to recognize that she had a lot on the ball . . . maybe more than I did. Hell, the way I'd handled this case so far, she definitely had more on the ball than I did. When I finished with my exposition, she shot questions at me like a reporter for the Associated Press.

"Did Danny kill his partner?" she asked.

"Could have."

"What about Scott Mansell? Do you think that Danny killed him?"

"Might have."

"Who blew up your friend's car and almost blew you away with it?"

"Not sure."

Lori scowled. "Do you think it was Treet, Metzger, or Danny—or some combination thereof?"

"Any one of them could've done it."

A roll of her eyes to the ceiling. "And what about the drug smugglers who've just been released? Do you think they could be the ones who tried to blow you up and then threatened you when they failed?"

"Wouldn't surprise me in the least."

Lori shook her head in an exasperated frenzy. "You don't know a damn thing! Hank, you've got to find out the answers."

Her words hit me like a Mack truck. What did she think I was . . . stupid? Of course I had to find out the answers.   "I'm working on it," I said as positively as I could.

"What can I do to help?" Lori said with a tone that told me that she really meant it.

I glanced at my watch. "Let's take a ride."

Lori grabbed some files, tossed them into her attaché case, locked up the office and we climbed into my pink-mobile. "Great set of wheels," she said with a smirk.

I ignored her comment. I didn't even want to think about the damn car.

"Where are we going in such a hurry?" she complained as we bumped awkwardly along the road, the speedometer straining for fifty.

I ignored her again. I knew she wouldn't like the answer.

She tried again, her irritation bubbling up. "Hank, where are we going?"

"We'll be there soon enough." I glanced over and gave her a patronizing smile. "And believe me, it's going to be a big help to me and to the case."

"You're not going to tell me are you?" she seethed. "I do have a right to know. After all, you could be putting my life in danger."

"It's not in any danger."

"Then tell me where we're going."

At that precise moment, I rounded the corner and Lori saw the bright yellow Corvette Country sign over a garage filled with the most unsubtle sports cars in the world. She exploded. "With all that you've got on your plate, this is what your priority is . . . your stupid car? I can't believe that you'd waste my time and yours on this. You've got a murderer to catch, for God's sake. He's already killed at least once and maybe even twice if Wingate's death wasn't a suicide. And you almost got blown to kingdom come.

"*But I need my Vette*," I protested lamely. Some women just don't understand this stuff.

"The only reason you *think* you need that Corvette is that you feel inadequate without it. You know what Freud would say about that long hood and that oversized engine don't you?"

I knew what Lori was getting at, and I knew what I wanted . . . logic, and psychology, be damned. "Don't give me any of that psycho-babble, Lori. The reason I need—yes need—my Vette is that I can't even get this piece of junk to go more than about fifty-five."

"So?"

"*So?*" I thought for a moment until I had a response to justify my actions. "What would happen if I had to get across town fast to keep somebody else from being killed. If I'm driving this junker, the victim would be dead and the perp would be long gone way before I even showed up. Now, if I were driving my Vette, I'd have plenty of time to save the victim's life and catch the perp."

"So you need the speed to save lives, is that what you're trying to tell me?"

"Exactly."

"Like an ambulance needs speed to save lives?"

"Precisely." I bumped up the driveway and parked the Kaopectate-mobile next to my glistening red Vette that positively glowed in a prime spot in front of one of the garage bays. My heart beat faster just looking at my car. I unsnapped my seat belt and grabbed the door handle, ready to hop out—Lori reached across and stopped me.

"UCLA conducted an interesting study about the speeds at which ambulances drive and their relationship to saving lives. Are you familiar with the study?"

"No," I said with a sigh. "But I'll bet that I'm about to."

"What they did was to select ten locations throughout Los Angeles and position an ambulance at each of them. Then they timed the ambulances as they drove to a predetermined hospital at or under the speed limits, *without* their lights flashing and their sirens blaring, and *obeying* all of the traffic laws—"

176

"Great. Fascinating. Now, if you don't mind—"

"The following week," Lori continued without missing a beat, "on the same day of the week and at the same precise time of day, they repeated the exercise. Only this time, the ambulance drivers used their lights and sirens and horns. They also drove as fast as they possibly could, going across the median into opposing traffic, hopping curbs and exceeding the speed limits. Do you know how much time they saved, on average?"

I tossed out a number. "Forty-five minutes."

"Seventeen seconds," Lori shot at me. "*Seventeen seconds.* That's it, almost nothing, nada, zilch, zero, zip. And they drove like absolute maniacs, putting themselves and everyone around them in danger. So don't tell me that you're going to save any lives or solve any crimes simply by virtue of driving that overgrown Hot Wheels toy of yours. Face it, the only reason you want your Corvette is because you want your Corvette. There's no logic, no reason. You just want your damn car. And you dragged me away from my work on the pretext of my being able to help you on your case. Well, I wanted to help you. I thought that I could do you some good. And what's the thanks I get? You drag me to this meat-head, muscle car, monkey wrench place—"

"Can I go now?" I interjected.

"Not until I'm done! If you have any intention of asking me to drive this rental car any place for you, you can just forget it. You can pick up your precious Corvette and then you can drive me back to the office. Do you understand me?"

I nodded, opened the door and extricated myself. Dave, the owner of Corvette Country, met me in the doorway to his office.

"Ain't marriage grand," he said as he walked over to his computer and punched some keys.

"We're not married."

"Could'a fooled me," Dave said as his dot matrix printer hammered out the repair bill. Once the printer stopped, he ripped the paper off and then proceeded to rip me off . . . or so I felt. The funny thing was that after the tongue-lashing I'd just received from Lori, I did feel kind of guilty about picking up the Vette. I simply wrote Dave a check for the balance of my bill, took my keys and walked to my car. Lori was already sitting in it. I fired up the V8 without saying a word. She didn't say anything either. We drove all the way back to the office that way. It was excruciating . . . but the engine sure sounded great.

When we pulled up to our building I saw something that was very, very wrong. Parked in the lot, directly next to Lori's Karmann Ghia, was a black Suburban. I'd already begun to turn into the lot, but made a quick correction and continued driving down the street.

"What's the matter?" Lori asked, breaking our self-imposed silence.

"That black truck next to your car, it looks like the one I saw at W-L's last night."

"Really?" Lori asked excitedly.

"And like the one that practically ran me off of PCH on Monday night."

"Yikes."

"And like the one whose driver shot at me while I was climbing around on that Dumpster on Monday morning."

Lori's eyes opened wide. "What's he doing *here*?"

"I don't have any idea."

"I should've kno—" Lori didn't finish her sentence. "What are you going to do about it?"

"I'm going to circle around and park across the street. Then we can watch and see what's going on."

"Real inconspicuous, Hank. A bright red Corvette isn't exactly a stealth machine, or did you buy some kind of cloaking device from that spy catalogue?"

I wrenched my Vette to the curb, a half block away from the office and shut it off. "I'll park over here where we're less likely to be seen. You're right—"

"Hallelujah, I finally get to be right."

I started to object, but before I could open my mouth, I saw Metzger walk away from the office and climb into the Suburban. I twisted the ignition key and pulled back onto the street as Metzger rolled out of the parking lot. Moments later, we were tailing him from a distance of about half a block.

"This is exciting," Lori said. "Want me to take down his license number."

"Thanks, but I already know it."

"Well, what can I do?"

"Just hold on, in case he spots us and tries to make a run for it." I glanced over at Lori. "See why I need my Vette?"

"Let's not get into that again, Hank."

Metzger drove straight for several blocks, then made a right, a left, and another right. It didn't take long for me to figure out where he was headed—Discount Danny's. I took another route so that he wouldn't spot us and ended up near the front of the store just as the Suburban rolled to a stop by the entrance.

"Don't let him out of your sight," I said to Lori as I drove past the truck, part way down the block, circled around, and then parked across the road. "Is he still in the truck?" I asked.

"Ten Four."

I looked over at her and crossed my eyes.

"Sorry, I was just getting into the spirit of the moment."

I watched as Metzger climbed out of the Suburban and walked into Danny's. I figured he hadn't spotted the Vette, otherwise he wouldn't have been able to resist the temptation to glance back at us.

"What are you going to do?" Lori asked.

"Nothing. I can't very well go into the store and pretend to be a customer. Not after all that's happened. I wouldn't last a minute in there."

Lori poked at her seat belt until it unfastened. "But I can. They don't know me from Adam . . . make that Eve. See you in five minutes."

Before I had a chance to object, she was out of the car and walking quickly to the entrance of Discount Danny's. *Nice walk*, I thought. Then I mentally slapped myself for being so easily distracted.

Five minutes turned to ten and ten into fifteen. It took all of my willpower to keep me from sprinting to the store and tearing it apart, searching for Lori. I imagined her tied up in the back room with a handkerchief stuffed into her mouth. But if I stormed the store, what could I realistically expect to accomplish? The second that Metzger or Danny saw me, they'd put two-and-two together and Lori and I could both have bullets in our skulls When fifteen minutes turned into twenty, I couldn't resist any longer and sprinted to the store. Just as I reached for the glass door, Lori exited. We collided and she dropped a large cardboard box.

She reached down for the box and then looked up at me with a blank expression. "You should look where you're going, sir," she said flatly.

I turned around so that my back was to the store. "I'm sorry," I said. "I—"

"You don't know me," Lori whispered with incredible intensity. She walked away from the store, carrying the box in the opposite direction from where we'd parked. I walked quickly to my car, glancing over my shoulder from time-to-time to see if Metzger or Danny had stepped outside to see what had happened, and to keep tabs on where Lori was heading. I jumped into my Vette, drove past her, rounded the corner and parked. Moments later, she slid into the passenger's seat with the box on her lap.

She tapped the box with her perfectly manicured fingernail. "I think I've got some evidence for you."

What she said went right past me. "What took you so long?" I bellowed. "I was worried sick." I couldn't believe that such words were popping out of my mouth.

"I told you. I picked up some evidence. For your case. Now drive me over to your apartment and let's see if it will do us any good."

I didn't like the way Lori was bossing me around, but ever since I'd seen Metzger's truck in front of my office, I'd wondered if he'd first been to my apartment. And if he had, I wondered what kind of shape he'd left it in. "Okay," I said. Then I floored the accelerator just to make sure Lori knew that I was still in charge.

I studiously avoided parking in my assigned place and was very happy, not only to find that the cops weren't hanging around, but that my apartment was fine. Well, fine isn't really the right word. The place was an absolute mess, as usual. But, at least it hadn't been broken into by Metzger . . . or anybody else. I carried Lori's *evidence* into the living room and set it down on the coffee table. Lori dropped off her attaché case on my dinette table, then marched over to me.

"Here's what I did," she said as she sat on the sofa and leaned toward the box. "I told the salesman that I wanted to buy a new VCR. He walked me over to a wall with about a hundred different models of VCRs and began explaining how each one was better than the one he'd just finished explaining to me. Finally, after listening to all this boring technical stuff about five different VCRs, I just told him that I wanted one like I'd seen at W-L's. He asked me what brand and model it was and I told him I didn't know, but that it was one that would look really great with my new drapes. Then he asked me about my drapes and I—"

"Can't we just cut to the chase?"

Lori's body sagged. "Oh all right. He showed me three models that he knew were carried at W-L's, I picked one and bought it. Here it is." She pointed to the box.

"What makes this evidence?"

"I don't know. That's for you to figure out . . . you're the detective."

I examined the box from the top and from all sides, picked it up and looked on the bottom. I didn't want to appear stupid, but I didn't see anything unusual about it; certainly nothing that would constitute calling it evidence. I slit the seal with my Vette key and opened the carton. Everything inside looked normal, just the usual preformed Styrofoam packing, a plastic bag around the VCR, the VCR itself, various electrical cords, the instruction manual, and the product registration card with its envelope. Nothing any different from what I'd found inside the cartons of every piece of electronic equipment I'd ever purchased in my entire life . . . including the CD changer that I'd bought at Danny's the night before last. "I hope you didn't just waste your money," I said as I pulled the VCR out of its plastic bag and examined it.

"Can't you tell if that's a stolen machine?" Lori asked with a voice already deflating.

"Well, each model has its own model number." I flipped the VCR around so I could see the engraved plate on the back. "See, the model you bought is DJP102750. But that doesn't do us any good because every VCR just like this one has the same model number."

"Oh."

"But each individual machine has its own particular serial number. This one is 12515ETBTAZ49."

"Does that help? Does W-L's record the serial numbers of all of the stereo equipment that their vendors deliver to them?"

I shook my head. "Unfortunately they don't. It would be too time consuming and time is money. At least that's what W-L's corporate geniuses say. They've automated and streamlined everything so much that the company just doesn't have the checks-and-balances that you'd expect them to have. Sorry, the serial number doesn't do us any good whatsoever."

Lori slouched into the sofa. "Me and my evidence. Big deal. Two hundred dollars down the tubes . . . the *boob tube* at that. How humiliating."

I kept looking at the serial number, trying to think of some way that it could prove that the VCR had been stolen from W-L's . . . if it had been stolen from W-L's. Then I set the machine on the coffee table and reached over to the product registration card and read it:

Thank you for purchasing an ElectroPro Video Cassette Recorder. You will find the serial number and model number on the back of your VCR. Please enter both of the numbers in the spaces below, along with the name of the store where you purchased your VCR and the date of your purchase. Once you have completed filling in this information, place this card in the envelope provided and immediately mail to the ElectroPro Company. Failure to do so will invalidate your warrantee."

As I read the card, my eyes must have lit up because Lori leaned forward and yelled into my ear with excitement. "Have you discovered something?"

"Maybe," I said as I recoiled from the sound of her voice. "People are required to fill out these registration cards and mail them in to ElectroPro, otherwise they void the warrantee."

"Yes?"

"Well, ElectroPro knows the serial numbers of all the merchandise they sold to W-L's."

"And—"

"We could contact ElectroPro and ask them to go through all of the registration cards they've received in the past, say six months, and see if any of the cards for machines they'd shipped to W-L's show that the customers actually purchased them from Discount Danny's."

Lori hopped out of the sofa and circled around the coffee table. "See? I told you that I had some evidence. This could break the case wide open." She practically danced a jig she was so pleased with herself.

"But that wouldn't make any sense," I continued after thinking more about the registration cards. Lori stopped her gyrations. "Treet wouldn't have done something as clever as deceiving the scanners at the distribution center to throw off the inventory only to blow it by having customers tell ElectroPro that the merchandise had been purchased at Discount Danny's. That would be too stupid."

"Maybe he *is* stupid," Lori protested. "Maybe he didn't think about the cards."

"Believe me, if Treet hadn't thought of it, Danny would have." I picked the card up again and flipped it over and over in my hands. "There's got to be some way that they've circumvented the customers from sending these cards to ElectroPro."

Lori pointed to my CD changer. "And SoundScan too."

The second she said that, I ran across the room, picked up the box my CD changer had come in, turned it upside down and shook it. The product registration card and envelope fluttered down to the floor. I picked them up, returned to the sofa and compared the CD changer's card and envelope to the ones that had come with Lori's VCR. The language was different on the cards, which made sense since they were from two different manufacturers. And, of course, the envelopes were different as well—one had the name ElectroPro on the address, while the other had the name SoundScan on it. But there was something exactly the same on the envelopes: the mailing addresses. Which didn't make any sense unless Danny, Treet and Company had printed up dummy envelopes and were having the customers mail the cards to a dummy address. The customers would never know that they hadn't actually mailed their cards to the manufacturers until their machine broke down and they tried to use their warrantee. Then ElectroPro and SoundScan and whatever other manufacturers that Danny, Treet, Metzger, and Mansell were ripping off would probably give the complaining customers what would seem like the typical run-around until either the customer or the manufacturer gave up or gave in.

"*Bingo*," I said, and handed the cards to Lori. I could tell from her expression that she'd figured it out without my having to utter a word of explanation.

"Do you think that Richard or Metzger printed these up at Mansell's cousin's print shop?" she asked.

"I don't have any doubt about it. Richard told me that he was pretty sure that he'd printed up some envelopes for Mansell . . . these have to be them."

"But there's no proof," Lori said. "Metzger certainly won't tell you, and you can't even talk to Richard."

I stood up. "Oh, that's okay. Proof shouldn't be too hard to get." I walked into the kitchen and dug around until I found the phone book. I opened it to the yellow pages and thumbed back to the mailing services section. "What's the address on the envelopes again?" Lori read it aloud to me as I scanned the display ads. *Bingo*. The address on the cards matched that of a Postal Plus store not more than a few blocks from Discount Danny's. I picked up my phone and punched in the number. A man answered. I identified myself as Danny Murphy and asked if I had any mail in my post box. The man put me on hold for a few minutes. When he came back he told me that my partner had already picked up my mail.

"Metzger or Treet?" I asked.

"I think it was Metzger this time," he answered.

I thanked him and hung up. My phone rang the very moment that I let go of it, startling me so much that I practically jumped out of my skin. I answered the call with my heart pounding at about a thousand beats a second.

The message from Arturo was short and simple: "Hank, the police are on their way to your place right now and you better get the hell out of there. Somehow, they've linked you to the Mansell murder and to hiding Richard Tompkins. If they catch up to you, they're going arrest you for obstructing a criminal investigation, hindering prosecution, tampering with physical evidence, conspiracy, and—better make a note of this one my *amigo*—murder in the first degree."

I stood paralyzed until Arturo's message soaked in. Then I simply uttered the word "thanks" to him, slammed down the phone, and told Lori to immediately grab her stuff so we could get out of my apartment. She could tell by my demeanor that I meant business, and she threw the registration cards and envelopes into her attaché case as I grabbed the front door knob. I wrenched open my door at the precise moment that a man on the other side of the door thumbed my door bell. I recognized him in an instant—Ray Norville, one of the druggies I'd busted at W-L's. I decided to act now and ask questions later and threw a punch to his jaw so hard it sent shock waves though my knuckles.

Norville staggered backwards about a foot, then regained his balance and jabbed me several times in the face with both fists. He drew his knee up fast between my legs and I doubled over, my mind sparkling like the Fourth of July. I felt his hands on my head holding me down as he kneed me over-and-over again on my left arm and the left side of my chest. I fell over to the right as he pulled out a gun that looked about as big as all of Florida. Somehow I managed the strength to lunge at him, pushing the gun skyward as he fired off a couple of rounds. I heard Lori scream from inside the apartment. Her scream was all the distraction that I needed. As Norville looked toward the apartment door, I jumped on him and brought him to the ground. The gun flew out of his hand and skittered along the sidewalk just out of my reach. I straddled his body and slammed my fist into his face, bloodying his nose and mouth. His right hand slithered toward his boot as his leg moved up. He grabbed inside his boot and pulled out a knife as long as a ruler. I'd anticipated his move, picked up a brick from the edge of the sidewalk and smashed it across the back of his hand. He dropped the knife and I grabbed it. I held it to his throat, ready to slit it at the slightest provocation. Then I heard them. Sirens in the distance that were growing closer. I called out for Lori to pick up the gun and aim it at Norville's head. She hesitated at first, then did as instructed. Then I demanded that Norville tell me if he'd just planted another bomb in my Vette. When he didn't answer, I drew the blade of the knife gently along his throat, blood staining his T-shirt and dripping onto the concrete.

"We already did your Vette," he said at last. "Then we found you were drivin' some sissy little car." That was all the information I needed. Besides, the sirens were growing closer. I jumped off of Norville while Lori continued to aim his gun at him. I ran for my Vette, closed my eyes and prayed as I wrenched open the door. No explosion. So far, so good. I inserted the key and twisted it. The Vette roared to life, drowning out the sounds of the sirens. When Lori heard the rumble of the V8, she actually shouted a threat to Norville and then fired a couple of shots into the ground. He froze in fright as she ran to join me in my car while keeping the gun aimed in Norville's direction. Lori tossed her attaché onto my lap and kept the gun trained on Norville. We raced out the back of the parking lot—rear tires spinning for grip—just as four black-and-whites raced in the front of the lot and screeched to a collective stop right in front of my apartment—and a baffled and battered Ray Norville, with a bloody knife at his feet.

FIFTEEN

I turned to Lori after we'd hustled down the road a couple of miles. "A little more exciting than filing Green's briefs, isn't it? Hope it didn't scare you too much."

"I'm more frightened by your driving than anything that happened back there." Lori finally realized she still held the gun in her hands. She opened her attaché and dropped it in with a loud *clunk*. "But for the life of me, I can't understand why you didn't stay for the police."

"Because they're after me."

Lori rolled her eyes. "Yeah, right. *Now* they are, after you beat the living heck out of that guy."

"I'm serious. The cops think that I obstructed a criminal investigation by hiding Richard in that motel. That call I got, just before we were so rudely interrupted, was from Arturo Garcia telling me that the cops were on their way to arrest me."

"Well, you probably did obstruct their investigation by hiding him."

"He's innocent. I didn't obstruct anything."

"So just tell the cops that he didn't do it. Tell them that Danny, Treet and Metzger killed their partner Scott Mansell." She pulled the registration cards and envelopes out of her case and waved them at me. "We've got the proof right here."

"We only have proof that they're ripping off W-L's. We've got nothing to prove that any one of them killed Mansell." I finally slowed to a reasonable speed; no sense attracting a traffic cop. "Besides, the cops are convinced that Richard did it, with my help."

"You didn't kill him. You didn't even know who Mansell was when you found him . . . the first time anyway."

"The cops won't see it that way. They don't just want me for obstructing justice, they've got a warrant out in my name for tampering with physical evidence, conspiracy, and murder in the first degree."

All the color drained out of Lori's face. Even I can see someone turning pale.

"What in the world are you going to do?" she asked, looking over her shoulder and out the back window with a sudden concern.

"Well, I sure as hell can't go back to my apartment or to the office. I've got to find a place where nobody will look for me."

Lori gave me a look that I couldn't interpret. "You could stay at my place."

I liked the sound of her invitation, but knew that the police would be checking the homes of anyone even remotely associated with me. "Thanks, but I need a place where nobody can find me. Not the police; not Treet, Metzger, or Danny; and especially not any of Ray and Roy Norville's friends."

"The man at your front door? Who was he?"

"Ray Norville, one of the guys I busted for drug trafficking."

Lori swallowed hard. "How many guys are there?"

"Counting the ones I never even met, but who were arrested because of my part in the investigation?"

"Yes."

"Twenty-five . . . give or take a few."

Lori turned even paler, so white she was almost translucent. "You're in big trouble, Hank."

"I hate to tell you this Lori, but we're in big trouble. You're in this as thick as I am. Who knows what my neighbors saw out of their windows and reported to the cops. We're probably considered the reincarnation of Bonnie and Clyde by now."

"So where are we going?"

I looked to the right of the road. The ocean was filled with white caps and brown surfers. "Well, since the water is to our right, we must be going south. If you want more details than that, I don't have any."

Lori shook her head. "We can't just keep driving like this. We need to get out of this car before we're spotted. Let's just go check into a hotel." Lori finally noticed that her skirt had hiked up a bit too much when she'd entered my Vette. She tugged at it while wriggling in the bucket seat. "Any hotel other than the Humpty Dumpty, if you don't mind. I do have a reputation to maintain."

I continued driving south out of Kingston Beach and into La Camino until we both spotted a twenty-story, high rise hotel rising above the surf. Lori tugged at my arm and pointed to the entrance. "There," she said.

The Edgewater Inn looked pretty pricey. I didn't have much cash and I definitely didn't want to broadcast my name to the desk clerk or anybody else by using my credit card. "We'll have to go someplace a little less expensive. I'm flat broke."

Lori grabbed the top of my steering wheel and pulled it toward her. My Vette jerked to the right and nearly hopped the curb before I had the chance to hit the brakes. We screeched to a stop in the circular driveway that led to the hotel's entrance. "What the hell are you doing?" I gasped once my blood pressure dropped back to normal.

"I told you. We need to check into a hotel."

"But I can't afford this place," I objected.

"Consider it my treat," Lori said just as I was about to reprimand her for nearly wrecking my Vette. I decided that in this instance, her generosity outweighed her impertinence and I kept my mouth shut.

"Just park this thing quick," Lori continued. "I feel a nervous breakdown coming on." She flashed a smile at me to let me know that she was kidding. "And you've got to tend to that ugly mug of yours."

I looked at myself in the rearview mirror and winced. I looked even worse than I felt. My cheeks were puffed out and my nose was battered in. My lips looked like a folded-over Frisbee and my right eye socket was turning such a strange hue that it made me grateful I couldn't see colors properly. I pulled my Vette underneath the hotel's canopy and waited as Lori checked us in under the name of Mr. and Mrs. Sam Branberry.

She returned with a self satisfied expression on her face unlike any I'd ever seen. "What's that look all about?" I asked her through my open window.

Lori wouldn't answer me. Instead, she just stood with her hands on her hips and tapped her toe. I climbed out of the car and followed her as she walked with her attaché through the lobby to the elevator—a glass one with a stupendous view of the ocean—which we rode to the top floor in complete silence. The elevator stopped on the twentieth floor, the doors parted and Lori led me along a glistening marble floor to a door which she unlocked and swung open with great flourish.

I couldn't believe my eyes. The room was three times the size of my entire apartment, with a crystal chandelier right in the center that could have lit up an entire town. To the right was a gigantic circular bed, setting atop a two-foot-high platform. To the left was a wet bar lined with cut crystal glasses and bottles of every type of liquor imaginable. A pair of overstuffed chairs and a decadent looking chaise rested toward the middle of the room, surrounding a glass topped table that held a huge bouquet of exotic flowers. The entire back wall was glass, with an uninterrupted view of the Pacific.

I walked across the room and began opening doors. The first were a pair of mahogany ones inset into one of the side walls. Behind the doors was a television screen as large as a roadside billboard. The next door opened into the bathroom. It was nearly as big as the bedroom and came complete with a two person spa nestled up into a bay window, a bottle of champagne in an ice bucket, two crystal champagne glasses, and a pair of luxurious white robes

I stumbled out of the bathroom in disbelief. "Lori, what's the deal with this room?"

Lori turned away from the ocean view to face me. "It's the honeymoon suite. Do you like it?"

I inhaled too quickly and choked on the air. "Honeymoon suite?" I finally gasped. "Is there something that we need to talk about?"

Lori laughed. "Don't start getting any wild ideas Hank. I just went a little over the top when I told the desk clerk about Sam and Samantha Branberry. I embellished the reason for our visit just a bit. By the way, you and I are from DeMoines and we just flew in for our honeymoon. We were married this morning."

"Cool," I said as I eyed the circular bed. It had a panel of buttons and knobs attached to the headboard that I couldn't resist. I walked over and turned one of them—the bed rotated to face the ocean. I turned it the opposite direction and the bed spun slowly toward the TV. I hopped onto the bed and pushed more buttons. The first one I pushed dimmed the chandelier. Another switch closed the drapes. The next one filled the room with Ravel's Bolero. The final one caused the mattress to vibrate like a prolonged aftershock from California's next big one.

"Come over here and try this out . . . *Samantha*," I said, beckoning her with open arms.

Lori walked over to the bed and flipped yet another switch on the headboard. The mattress abruptly jackknifed itself into an approximation of a hospital bed and forced me to sit bolt upright. Lori walked away from me and sat at a small desk. "In your dreams, Hank." She pointed to the chaise. "That's where you'll be sleeping tonight."

I pouted like a kid as I electronically reopened the drapes, shut off the music, reclined the mattress, and brightened the lights. I kept the magic fingers going though; the motorized mattress felt pretty darn good on my aches and pains. After all my fights and mishaps, my body hurt from my neck down to my toes. Suddenly, every muscle seemed to have gone on strike and my nerve endings were picketing in protest.

I turned the TV on with the remote and watched the news through my swollen eyelids as Lori opened her attaché and pulled out a dozen file folders and a notebook computer. I couldn't believe she was so dedicated to her job—*and to Barry Green who never ever even bothers to show up at his office*—that she'd be working at a time like this. But there she was, firing up her computer, plugging something into something into another something, setting up her files, and making her own miniature version of her office command post. I had to admire her and detest her

191

at the same time. I rolled over so I didn't have to look at her diligently tapping at the keyboard, and watched the TV. There, right before my very eyes—and those of everyone else watching the *Four O'clock News with Morgan Harrison*—was a picture the police must have removed from my apartment. There I appeared—bigger than life on the big screen TV—grinning like some kind of a dimwit while wearing a lime green tuxedo and a yellow ruffled shirt. *Why, of all the pictures to choose from, had they picked one from my brother's wedding?* Harrison's voice described me as a twice divorced, unemployed security guard in his mid-forties. Then my picture was replaced by one of Richard Tompkins, then one of Scott Mansell, then a shot of Walter's mansion in La Camino, and finally one of Lou's exploded Corvette. Morgan Harrison said that Richard Tompkins and I were the only suspects in the murder of Scott Mansell and—in a perfect example of error-prone reporting—that one of my two identical sports cars had been bombed, probably during a drug deal gone bad. I was depicted as being armed-and-dangerous and traveling with an unidentified woman who had nearly killed Ray Norville, a man suspected of being my former partner in a drug ring. The anchorman reappeared on the screen and shook his head in a shocked and troubled way, then made a comment about how people like Hank Hammond and his gun-toting moll were examples of what is wrong with America today and how we ought to be locked up and the keys thrown away.

"You see that?" I yelled across the room to Lori.

"I heard," she said unbothered, clicking away at her computer. "But I'm much more interested in what I'm seeing on *my* screen." She paused and looked at me. "Come look at this."

I turned my head in her direction and groaned. "Lori, I'm very impressed that you can be so productive away from the office, and I'm sure that Green really appreciates all that you do for him, but I'm just too beat to get out of bed. Every bone in my body aches and—"

"Get over here!" Lori commanded with such urgency that it almost made my tired muscles respond. "What I'm working on might very well have something to do with your case. It could be really important. Didn't you say that Walter Tompkins's nurse's was named Crystal?"

"Yes," I said, rolling over to face her.

"Well, your client just made her his sole beneficiary."

"He what?" I shut off the TV, and hobbled over to Lori at her makeshift command post.

"I was catching up on some of Barry's work. According to this, Walter Tompkins contacted Barry early this morning and asked him to alter his will."

"I didn't know that Green was Walter's attorney."

"He wasn't. But apparently when Barry was a CPA, he used to do Mr. Tompkins's taxes. Then when he became a tax attorney, Mr. Tompkins must have balked at Barry's new rates and hired someone else to figure out what he owed Uncle Sam."

"Tompkins is loaded, he could've still afforded to use Green."

"That's beside the point." Lori tapped her computer with her finger. "According to the information I have on my screen, Walter Tompkins's will was prepared by an attorney named Patterson."

"What's that have to do with anything?"

"Well, Mr. Patterson died about six months ago—"

"And you think that has something to do with Mansell's murder?"

"No, but it explains why Mr. Tompkins contacted Barry when he wanted his will revised. His attorney had died and Tompkins knew Barry from when he was his CPA. It made sense for him to call Barry and ask him to be the one to modify the will." Lori flipped the computer around so I could read the screen. "See, your client just wrote Richard *out* and wrote Crystal *in*. When Walter Tompkins dies, she gets *everything*."

"And Richard gets nothing?"

"That's right."

I shook my head in disbelief. Writing Richard out of his will simply didn't make sense to me. "But you haven't heard how Walter talks about his grandson, that boy is like a son to him. And Richard absolutely worships his grandfather. I can't believe that Walter would do this."

"Well, believe it. It's been done."

Since I'd never owned anything worth leaving to anybody—except my Vette—I didn't know too much about wills, but I did know that they probably had to be signed by all parties and notarized up the ying-yang. "It can't happen that fast. Walter would have to meet with Green and drafts would have to be made and signatures obtained and all kinds of stuff."

"All done." Lori pushed the cursor key and the text scrolled up the screen. "Here's the revised portion of the will, and those," she pointed to some squiggles, "are all the required signatures."

"But this is just a computer screen it's not a—"

"Barry fed the documents into the fax machine he has at his home. What you see on this screen is the copy of the fax. We do business like this all the time." Lori raised her eyebrows. "You have noticed that Barry is hardly ever in the office, haven't you?"

I picked up the computer and shook it. "But this isn't an official document, it's just a damn computer."

"He'll FedEx the originals to me and I'll file them. He always faxes documents like this to me as they occur so that I can anticipate my workload." She rested her hand on my forearm. "Now, if you don't mind, would you please return my computer to the table?"

I did as directed and stared at the screen in disbelief. My eyes focused on Walter's signature. It sure looked like the one on the check he'd written me. "What about a witness? What about a notary?"

Lori pointed to a pair of signatures and a stamped image. "Done and done," she said.

"Well I just don't know what to think. This just isn't fair to Richard."

"Maybe Mr. Tompkins is convinced that his grandson is a murderer and he doesn't want any of his money to go to him. Maybe he believes that this Crystal woman is the only person left in his life who he can trust."

"Trust? I don't see that trust enters into it. She's just an employee."

"Not according to the notes that Barry included in his fax." Lori scrolled to another screen. "According to this, Crystal was almost a part of his family."

"What do you mean by that, that he thought of her as a daughter?"

"No, I mean that she was actually almost a part of his family. She was engaged to his grandson. Didn't Walter ever tell you that?"

"It never came up. The only thing I knew about a relationship between Crystal and Richard was that Richard found her for Walter. I had no idea that they'd been engaged. Walter had told me that Richard loved the ladies, but the only girl I knew for certain that he'd gone out with was the one he'd just spent a few days with in Mexico . . . and his one-night-stand with Terri."

"The girl who said she'd been threatened?"

I nodded.

"Well Hank, I don't know what to make of any of this." Lori shrugged, then walked over to the TV and switched it back on. "I thought that his revised will might be of some help, but all it does is confuse things."

Morgan Harrison's generic anchorman face appeared on the giant screen along with a recap of the day's most important events. The picture of me grinning like a drunken nincompoop flashed across the screen along with a special hot-line number. I looked at the picture, hating that any photo of me was on the air, hating that they'd chosen that particular one to display, and hating that the police had violated my privacy by taking it from my apartment. I imagined the cops walking through every square inch of my home, commenting on my taste in music and on my housekeeping standards. I could see them rifling through my drawers and peeking under my bed. A photographer had probably shot pictures of everything in my place as they tried to figure out what kind of a person lived there. Then I remembered that I'd done exactly the same thing in Richard's apartment, right down to photographing the closet and the entire living area.

"Damn," I shouted.

"What's the matter?" Lori asked.

"I feel like we're onto something. I feel like we've got all the pieces, but we just haven't put them all together."

Lori cocked her head. "I don't see how anything fits together."

"I just thought of something. That stupid picture of me in that lounge lizard tuxedo kind of jogged me. You know those pictures I took of Richard's apartment? Well, maybe there's something we missed when we looked at them. Damn, I wish I had them right now."

"You do."

I looked at Lori and wrinkled my brow. I couldn't figure out what she was talking about. I knew that I didn't have the pictures and I knew that she didn't have them either. They were securely locked up in my desk drawer back at the office.

Lori shut off the TV and returned to her computer. She sat down and manipulated the keyboard like a concert pianist. Soon she had a satisfied smile on her face. She turned the computer around so I could see the screen. "*Voila*," she said. "The first of your pictures, in living color."

I couldn't believe my eyes. There was a picture of Scott Mansell's body, half spilled out of Richard's closet.

Lori tapped the screen. "I scanned all of the pictures into my desktop computer system back at the office. We're retrieving them from it via the modem right now. She reached over and pushed a button on the lap top. Now we were looking at a picture of the closed closet door, showing bullet holes pierced through the poster of a swimsuit model. Another push of the button and we could see one entire wall of Richard's apartment, including two more posters of scantily clad women. The next picture showed another wall, also decorated with his favorite subject matter. I leaned toward the screen and examined one of the posters.

"You don't have to leer at her," Lori protested.

"I'm looking for bullet holes. There," I pointed at a spot on the model's forehead, "don't you think that could be a bullet hole?"

Lori performed some magic with the computer and the swimsuit model's head suddenly filled the screen. The spot was definitely a bullet hole.

"Let's look at the other posters," I said. Lori zoomed in on the heads of the other beauties. Each model had at least one bullet hole in her forehead. "Go back to the one on the closet door."

Lori gave me a dirty look.

"Please," I said.

We both stared at the screen, there were two holes in the poster girl's head, and they appeared to be one inch apart—*exactly* as I remembered the bullet holes in Mansell's forehead.

"What's this mean?" Lori asked.

"Judging from how tall Mansell was and where those bullet holes are in the model's head, I think that whoever killed him was actually shooting at the image of the girl. Mansell just happened to be at the wrong place at the wrong time. I think he was hiding in the closet and that those shots were never even intended for him."

Lori stared at the screen, pressed a couple of keys and returned to the image of Scott Mansell. "I think you're right," she said. "The bullet holes probably lined up perfectly when he was standing." Lori returned to the image of the poster girl. "Let me get this straight, Hank. You think whoever did the shooting was actually aiming at the pictures of these girls."

"Right."

"And that whoever it was didn't even know that Mansell was inside the closet?

"Also right."

"But what would he have been doing in Richard Tompkins's closet?"

I took a deep breath and explained my theory. "Well, Richard told me that he'd found his grandfather's Fiat in the garage near his apartment. So that must mean that Mansell had returned the car while Richard was in Mexico. Later, when I took the Fiat keys away from Richard, I noticed that his apartment keys were on the same ring as the keys for the Fiat. Maybe when Mansell returned the car, he used Richard's keys to get into the apartment to see if there was anything worth stealing. And maybe while he was there, he heard someone unlocking the front door and he panicked and hid in the closet."

Lori made a face that told me she wasn't buying my story. "That assumes that the person who came in the front door was some kind of lunatic who just went in and started shooting at Richard's posters. That doesn't make any sense. And even if it did, why would a lunatic have keys to Richard's apartment. Unless, of course, *Richard* is the lunatic."

"Every picture tells a story," I said. "Look at those pictures I took at Richard's apartment. There are at least eight or nine bullet holes in the walls and the closet door, and every one if them is right smack dab in the middle of a beautiful poster girl's forehead. I think whoever shot up the place was angry about Richard's attraction to beautiful women. I think whoever it was had let herself into his apartment and then discovered that he had gone to Mexico with a woman and was due back that very day."

"How would she find that out?"

"It was on his calendar."

Lori motioned me to continue.

"I think that when she realized this, she went into a frenzy and shot at every one of those girls on the posters."

"In effect, symbolically killing every beautiful girl that Richard was attracted to." Lori said, her head nodding almost imperceptibly.

"Precisely."

"But aren't you forgetting that the gun that killed Mansell belonged to Richard? That blows your theory right there."

"Not if the killer knew where Richard kept his gun."

"But the key. The killer would have needed a key to Richard's front door."

I nodded. "That's right, she would."

"But who?"

"Didn't you just tell me that Crystal and Richard had been engaged?"

Lori's eyes opened as wide as saucers. "You think *she* killed Mansell?"

"It makes sense to me. For certain, she would have known that Richard kept his gun in his nightstand, and she would have had a key to his apartment."

"How do you know she had a key?"

"One of two ways. Richard probably gave Crystal a key to his place just like any guy would give a key to the woman he was engaged to marry."

"But the engagement was off. Wouldn't he have taken the key back?"

"Maybe. Maybe not. But even if Richard had taken it back, Crystal still had access to a key . . . the one he'd given to Walter. The very key that Walter instructed Crystal to give to me."

Lori thought for a moment. "But you said that the key didn't work when you went to Richard's apartment. You said that you had to pick his lock."

"Maybe that's because Crystal had substituted the wrong key. Perhaps because she hadn't yet returned the key to Walter's ring, or perhaps because she didn't want me to be able to get into Richard's apartment."

Lori shook her head in astonishment. "Okay, so Crystal went into Richard's apartment and saw the notes on his calendar. She went into a rage—"

"And we know that someone had been furious with Terri, even threatening to kill her," I interrupted.

Lori nodded and continued. "She went into a rage, went into his bedroom, took his gun from his nightstand and then shot all the pictures of the sexy models. Two of the shots went right through the closet door and killed Mansell who was hiding inside."

I nodded. "And when she heard the body fall to the floor, inside the closet, Crystal assumed that she'd shot Richard."

"He would have had good reason to hide from her if she had such a temper," Lori added. "I have to admit that it does sort of make sense, in a convoluted sort of way."

I nodded again. "It also explains why Crystal reacted the way she did when I told Walter and her that I'd found Richard. It didn't really register much to me at the time, but she expressed too much surprise when I told her that Richard was okay. And her reaction was also rather odd when she learned that a man named Scott Mansell had turned up dead in Richard's closet."

Lori thought for a moment, then spoke. "Don't you think that she would have opened the closet to take a look at who she'd killed?"

"Would you?"

Lori twisted her mouth in agony. "No," she said emphatically.

"I rest my case."

Lori stood and walked directly to the wet bar. She removed a couple of cubes from the icemaker with a pair of silver tongs and plopped the cubes into a crystal goblet. Then she poured from a bottle of imported water, waited for a moment as the cubes cooled the water, and gulped the contents down. "I wonder how it feels to kill somebody," she said across the room to me. "Especially when you didn't even intend to do it."

"I hope I never find out," I said. "Who knows what would have happened if Richard had actually been at his apartment when Crystal arrived. Maybe they would have just talked it out, or maybe she would have killed him."

"Or think what might have happened if she'd walked into his apartment and found Richard with that woman he'd taken to Mexico. She might have killed them both." Lori jerked almost imperceptibly. "What did you say her name was?"

I thought for a moment. "Rita something. He told me she lived not too far from his grandfather's home in La Camino."

Lori cocked her head. "I'll be right back." She grabbed some change out of her attaché case and walked out of the room. Moments later she returned with a newspaper. She paged through the paper until she found what she was looking for, folded the paper back and handed it to me. "Rita Sandoval," she said as she pointed to a photo of a beautiful brunette woman. "She died last night. Cardiac arrest. Not what you'd expect of someone so young."

I scanned the article quickly.   "Crystal killed her," I blurted out. "She overdosed her on insulin."

"I don't follow you," Lori said. "Where did you come up with this insulin thing?"

"Simple. Walter is a diabetic and Crystal injects him with insulin. So I know that she has access to insulin and to a syringe."

"So?"

"So. An insulin overdose causes cardiac arrest. I saw it on an old *Magnum PI* not more than two weeks ago. What better way to kill someone than to make it look like natural causes? It's perfect. There probably won't even be an autopsy. And even if one is performed and insulin is detected, there very likely won't be any evidence to point toward Crystal."

Lori sat, processing my theory without reacting.

"Crystal killed Rita Sandoval," I said. "I'd bet my life on it. And you know what else? She's going to overdose Walter too. She's going to kill him and inherit everything he owns. That's even better for her than when she was going to share the inheritance with Richard as his wife." I grabbed my Vette keys off of the table. "And she has to kill Walter right away, before Walter has a chance to change his mind about his will."

I ran to the door.

"Where are you going?" Lori asked.

"To Walter's before it's too late."

"Why don't you just call the police?"

"*Me?*" I asked incredulously. "You think they'd listen to me? They'd just slap a pair of cuffs around my wrists and cart me away. It'd be the last anybody'd ever see or hear of me." I started turning the knob. "No, I don't have any choice. I have to drive over to Walter's."

"You don't even know if he's home. He could be anywhere. *She* could be anywhere."

I had to agree with Lori, but I knew how to find out the answer. I let go of the door knob, walked to the room phone, and punched in Walter's number. Crystal answered. I didn't know what to say. A look of panic must have crossed my face, because Lori grabbed the phone from my hand.

"Is Mr. Walter Tompkins in please?" Lori said. "Oh, that's too bad. I'm calling from the law office of Barry Green and this is about the revisions to his will. Would you please have him call me when he wakes up? The number is," Lori motioned frantically at me but I couldn't figure out what she wanted. Finally I realized she wanted the number from her cell phone. I read it aloud to her from across the room and she repeated the number to Crystal. "Thank you very much."

Lori turned to face me. "He's asleep, but she will be waking him in about fifteen minutes to give him his medication."

"Then I don't have a minute to spare." I walked back to the door. "I'm on my way."

"What about me? What do you want me to do?"

"Just stay here. I'll call you when I'm done."

"But what exactly is it that you're going to do?"

I reached for the door knob. "I'll figure that out while I'm doing it. Right now, I don't have time to think . . . I have to move."

Lori ran over to the desk, pulled Ray Norville's automatic out of her attaché and handed it to me. "Well then, take this. And be careful, I think I may have used the last bullet."

I tucked the gun into my Dockers and pulled my shirt tail out to cover it. "Thanks. I guess."

SIXTEEN

I ran to my Vette with my chin pushed down into my chest; partly because I didn't want anyone to recognize me from TV, but also because I knew that my smashed up face would attract unwanted attention. Fortunately, my car looked a whole lot better than I did; it actually seemed to be beckoning me, telling me to get in and drive the hell out of it. I opened the door, slid in and did just that.

I screeched out of the parking stall, angled the front wheels toward the street and slammed my foot to the floorboard. The nose of the Vette raised up like a speedboat's prow and the rear tires squealed black lines for thirty feet. We *whumped* down the drive and onto the street, momentarily losing traction as we fishtailed perpendicular to the hotel and toward Walter's house. I pushed the small button to the right of my digital dash clock, transforming it into an electronic stop watch. I pressed the button a few more times to program it to begin counting down the seconds from eight minutes—the length of time I figured that were left before Crystal administered Walter's fatal dose.

Traffic enveloped us—my Vette and me—and we were soon boxed in between commuters who'd just hit the roads to get home from work. Everyone, it seemed, was going the same direction we were; away from the business district and toward the suburbs. I made a decision—not a smart one, but a decision nevertheless. My inspiration was Lori's story about the speeding ambulances driving on the wrong side of the road, lights and sirens blaring and only getting to the hospital seventeen seconds faster. I needed the seventeen seconds—Walter needed the seventeen seconds. I switched my headlights onto high beam, flipped on the emergency flashers, and jerked the Vette across the median and into the center lane of the opposing side of the road—then I floored the accelerator and jetted past the commuters to my right. I glanced at my dash clock: seven minutes, twenty-one seconds. When I looked back up through my windshield, I saw two cars—one in each of the two lanes—rapidly approaching me head-on. I kept my foot on the accelerator, buried the heel of my hand into the horn button and steered between the cars. They parted like the Red Sea and I said my first prayer in at least fifteen years. Another car approached. When he saw me, moments before it was too late, he slammed up onto the median. My speedometer said one hundred and six miles-per-hour. My clock said five minutes, four seconds. I said "Sweet Jesus."

I needed to turn right. Not an easy thing to do when you're on the wrong side of the road—unless you're in England, which I definitely was not. I spotted a minuscule break in traffic to my right and pointed the Vette into the hole. It was a delicate maneuver like threading a needle, except that a five hundred horsepower Vette isn't some wimpy little piece of thread. Brakes locked and tires squealed around me as I wrenched the Vette over, across, and around the traffic and onto the new street. I floored the car again. Three minutes, sixteen seconds.

I was now on a one-way street. The good news was that the traffic was going *my* way. The bad news was that it wasn't moving very fast—in fact, it wasn't moving at all because of a red light just ahead. I slammed on the brakes and the Vette's nose dropped drown trying desperately to grab the road—but there wasn't enough road to grab. The brake lights of four generic family sedans loomed large ahead of me and I knew that if I kept heading east I'd smash right into them. The solution? Head south. I tossed the Vette to the right, we hopped the curb and rocketed over the city's finest landscaping effort in the past decade. I pulled the wheel back to the left and tore up more politically correct xeroscape as I passed the sedans and approached the intersection. The light turned green and I floored the Vette again, hopping off the curb and bouncing back onto the roadway. Two minutes, thirty eight seconds.

One more turn, this time to the left, and I was into Walter's neighborhood. The traffic of the city was replaced by birds nesting in the trees and rich retired people walking their pure-bred dogs in expensive Ralph Lauren casual wear—the rich people, not the dogs. The roar of the Vette's engine shattered the neighborhood like an air raid siren. Shocked fuddy-duddies stared in disbelief and disdain—I rather enjoyed it. One minute, six seconds.

The suburb darkened as the sun set behind giant palm trees. Streetlights popped on, one-by-one, each triggered by its own electric eye. My headlights raked across the fronts of mansions as I turned onto Walter's street. At the end of the cul-de-sac, gray and imposing, Walter's manor stood looking disturbingly like a mausoleum.

I flew up the street, shot up his circular driveway and slid to a stop. I didn't have a key to his door. My lock gun had been stolen. All I could do was to ring the door bell and wait. I looked at the dash clock: *seventeen seconds*. No time for bells. No time for anything. I jumped from the Vette and ran toward the leaded glass window in the library. When I was four feet from the window, I tucked my head into my shoulder and assumed the position I'd used thousands of times during my glory days in high school football. I slammed into the window so hard it shattered in a thousand directions. The leaded panes broke apart and cut at my clothing. I fell head first into the library, picked myself up and ran through the house desperate to find Walter.

I threw open every door I encountered. The house had more bathrooms and bedrooms than the Edgewater Inn . . . or the Hump. I ran through the kitchen, the dining room, past a study and then entered a long, dark hallway with an impressively large hand carved door at the end . . . it *had* to be Walter's bedroom. I sprinted down the hall. When I reached the half-way point, the door opened and Crystal appeared like a back-lighted apparition, holding a syringe.

"Stop," I yelled, still scrambling down the hall.

She quickly stepped back into the room and slammed the door between us. I lunged for the door knob and twisted it, but it wouldn't open. I beat on the carved panels with both hands, yelling at Walter through the door to not let Crystal near him. I had to get through the door, but as I pounded on it I could tell that it was so solid it might as well have been made of steel. *Nothing ventured, nothing gained*, I thought. I stepped a few feet back into the hall and assumed my best football tackling stance. At the count of three, I thrust myself into the door . . . it didn't give, but my body did.

I yelled in frustration through the door: "Walter, this is Hank Hammond. Don't let her near you with that needle. She's going to kill you." Just as I thought that getting into the room was impossible, I noticed the hinges. The door was hinged toward me and the pins were on my side. If I could knock the pins out, I could pull the door off of its hinges. I needed a hammer; all I had was a gun. It would have to do. I snatched Ray Norville's automatic out of my Dockers, held it by the barrel and bashed the butt against the bottom of the top pin. Old paint flaked off the pin as I pounded. Finally, the head of the pin popped up far enough that I could reach up and pull it out of the hinge. I repeated the process on the other two hinges, then I pulled back on the door and it fell off of its hinges and dropped diagonally across the doorway . . . the locked latch keeping it from falling all the way to the floor. I climbed over the door and saw Walter crouched in a fetal position in the corner of the dimly lit room. He must have heard my warning and the only way he could think of to escape was to curl up into a ball and roll into a corner. Crystal stood over him with the syringe, but her startled gaze was on me. She turned to face me, holding the syringe out toward me like a knife.

"Get out of here," she screamed. "I'll kill you. So help me god, I'll kill you."

I aimed Norville's gun at her. "Not if I kill you first," I said. "I'll shoot you right between the eyes, just like you did to all of those pictures of beautiful women in Richard's apartment . . . and just like you did to Scott Mansell."

Crystal stepped toward me, the syringe aimed at my chest. "I didn't mean to kill him. I didn't even know he was in that closet. You can't blame his death on me."

"But it wouldn't have happened if you hadn't gone into a jealous rage and started shooting up the place."

"*Jealous rage?*" Crystal laughed. "Jealousy didn't even enter into it. I only wanted Richard for his grandfather's money. I couldn't care less about that little creep. Oh, I was in rage all right, but it wasn't from jealousy, it was from knowing that another female had come between me and what I wanted. I didn't mean to kill Scott Mansell, he was just in the wrong place at the wrong time."

"But you meant to kill Rita Sandoval, didn't you?"

Crystal's face flushed and her eyes seemed almost to glow from within. A thin smile twisted across her face like a snake slithering on a pathway. "Yes, I killed her. She was after Richard's inheritance too. Well, I fixed her *and* I fixed Richard. Thanks to you, I knew that Richard was safely hidden away. And, knowing Richard the way I do, I knew that it would be easy to draw him out and lead him right to the cops."

"But I never told you where I'd hidden him."

"You didn't have to. All I had to do was call him on the beeper he keeps stuffed in his pocket and leave him Walter's phone number. I knew that he'd call his precious grandfather back within a couple of minutes, and I was absolutely right. He called from a pay phone, I answered it, and told him that he had to meet his grandfather. I asked him where he was and he gave me the cross streets. I knew there was a Denny's coffee shop nearby, so I told him to go there as soon as possible. He never even thought to ask why, he just did it. Then I made an anonymous call to the police and told them where they could pick up their murderer. The rest is history."

Crystal spun around abruptly, then kneeled halfway to the floor, crouching next to Walter. "Well, I may have lost Richard to Rita Sandoval, or to Terri at the country club, or whoever else caught his eye, but there is no way I'm going to lose out on Walter's money." Crystal pressed the tip of the needle against Walter's arm. "Drop the gun or I inject him," she yelled at me as Walter winced.

I had a choice to make. I could do as she said, but she'd probably inject Walter anyway. Or I could shoot her. I'd never killed anybody in my life. I'd never wanted to. I'd never contemplated it. I'd never thought myself capable. Now it seemed that I had no choice. My heart pounded so fast and hard that I could feel it in my ears. I took a quick, deep breath and pulled the trigger. Nothing. The gun was empty.

I lunged at her and Walter somehow summoned the strength to pull his arm away just as she was about to stick him. The needle missed his arm but she still held onto the syringe as I jumped onto her. I pinned her shoulders to the floor and held one of her arms down with my knee. But her hand that held the syringe was still free and I could feel it coming toward me . . . and in my position I couldn't stop it. I rolled off of her, repositioned myself into a crouch, then slammed the back of my hand against the syringe so hard that it flew across the room.

Crystal jumped up and I expected her to scramble toward the syringe. I stretched out my body, arm, and fingers toward the hypodermic, crawling across the floor to get to it first. But she didn't go for the syringe, she went for me; jumping onto my back, riding me like she was some kind of demented rodeo star. Her feet kicked wildly at my legs. One of her arms locked around my throat and squeezed it so tightly I couldn't breathe. A set of long fingernails raked their way across my face toward my eyes. I shut my eyelids tight, trying to compact my brow and cheekbones together to protect my pupils. She screamed obscenities into my ear and then bit it hard and twisted it. I could feel the warm blood as it dripped into my ear and down my neck. I tried to shake her off, but she seemed to have more extremities than an octopus, each one thrashing and beating and squeezing and scratching.

As I physically wrestled with her, I mentally wrestled with my own aversion to striking a woman. Something deep inside of me—inbred or learned, I couldn't be sure which and it didn't really matter—was keeping me from doing what had to be done to stop this woman. In spite of the fact that Crystal was doing all in her power to kill me, I just couldn't bring myself to hit her.

She must have sensed my weakness, because she grabbed an iron doorstop from the floor and banged it against the side of my head with a sickening thud. My world suddenly went cloudy and gray. My mind spun like an amusement park ride. Tiny bits of light exploded in my head like a Disneyland celebration. I was going down for the count, I knew it. I had to do something quick or I'd be dead . . . with Walter by my side.

I concentrated what thoughts and energy I had left, and—applying the proper lifting techniques drummed into me as a stock boy at W-L's—raised myself up by my legs. Crystal screamed more obscenities at me and dug her nails into my face. Her wild side-to-side motions nearly toppled us both as I struggled to stand upright. Finally I stood, Crystal clinging to me like some kind of obscene back-pack. She wrapped her legs around my torso and kicked at my groin. She pulled my hair. I staggered backward and we fell back to the floor. She scrambled onto her knees. I did the same, but I was too slow and felt barely conscious. She crawled across the floor, picked up the hypodermic syringe and leaped on top of Walter.

"It's over," she said, looking at me with wild eyes and holding the needle against Walter's neck. "This is his final dose. It's just exactly enough to kill him and no one will ever know that he didn't die of natural causes."

Walter moved for only the second time since I'd entered the room. He opened his eyes and pulled his head away from Crystal. "Don't do it," he said in a voice so frail I hardly recognized it. Tears streamed down his cheeks.

Crystal slapped him across the face. "Shut up, old man. Die with some dignity, won't you?"

Walter grimaced, but I wasn't certain which hurt more; the slap or the knowledge that this woman had turned on him in the ugliest of ways. "You used me," he said. "And you used my grandson. All you wanted was my money."

Crystal smiled. "You got that right," she scanned the room, "*and* your house *and* your furniture *and* your dead wife's jewelry."

I started slipping out of consciousness. I inhaled deeply and held in the oxygen. I felt marginally better, and took a couple more breaths.

Walter shook his head slowly. "You told me that Richard was no good. You said that he killed that man in his apartment. You made me believe that you were the only person left on earth who cared about me." More tears dropped from his eyes. "I cared about you. I wrote you into my will, for heaven's sake. Doesn't that mean anything to you?"

"It means a lot to me Walter; about fifteen million dollars, by my last estimate."

Crystal pushed the needle against Walter's neck. He cringed with fright. She moved her thumb to the hypodermic's plunger. There wasn't any time left. I was too far away from her to wrestle the syringe out of her hand. I looked desperately around the room for something to throw at her, but there wasn't anything near enough to me. The only thing close to me was a wall, but on that wall—just within my reach—was an electrical outlet. I scanned the floor, the loose change that had dropped out from our pockets was mingled with a couple of paper clips, some rubber bands, and a chewed up number two pencil. I picked up one of the paper clips, unfolded it partly, and jammed the straight end into the pencil's eraser. Then, holding the pencil as an insulator, I reached over and thrust the curved end of the paper clip into the socket. A spark spit from the outlet. The lights flickered momentarily. The room went black.

I heard a scuffling sound and I scrambled across the floor toward Crystal and Walter, my eyes unable to adjust to the darkness of the room. I reached out wildly and grabbed what had to be Crystal's arm and wrestled it to the floor. I heard the syringe drop out of her hand and wondered if she'd already injected the poison into Walter's body. She thrashed at me with her free arm and I pinned it to the floor, then rolled over on top of her to keep her from escaping. I called out for Walter, but he didn't answer me and I didn't hear any movement. I prayed that Crystal hadn't killed him.

I shifted my body, attempting to put my knees across her arms to hold them to the floor. Just as I let go of her hands, she raised herself up and bit me hard on my chest. I'd had about enough of this woman. I jammed my left knee on top of her right arm, let go of her hand, and reached out wildly to where I thought I'd remembered a floor lamp had been standing. She swore at me, calling me every filthy word ever created and putting them into combinations never uttered before. I shifted my right knee over her left arm as I continued to grope for the lamp. Finally my fingers touched it and I pulled the lamp down across her throat. As she lay there, afraid to resist for fear that I'd strangle her, I ripped out the electrical cord and tied her hands together. Then I tied her feet to her hands. Then, just so that I wouldn't have to listen to her cursing any more, I pulled off one of her shoes, removed her sock, and stuffed it into her mouth.

Suddenly I heard a man's voice call out. "Hammond, are you in here?"

The voice sounded familiar, but in my condition I couldn't quite place it. My first thought was that Lori had told Arturo Garcia where I'd gone and he'd come to help out. I stood up and walked toward the voice. "Thanks man, but you're a little too late," I said.

"Not too late at all, big boy," came the voice. Wild gunshots rang out, shattering the windows and ricocheting off the brick walls. I instinctively dropped to the floor. *Big boy?* That's what the person who'd left the threat on my answering machine had called me—the person who'd nearly killed me when he blew up Lou's Corvette.

"You think you're quite the hero for getting me and my brother busted back at W-L's don't you? Well, thanks to that news report on TV today, I was able to find you right here at your client's mansion. And now you're going to pay for ruining our lives." More shots filled the room. I heard Crystal whimpering and thought I heard a moan from Walter.

My eyes were finally adjusting to the darkness, which gave me an advantage over Roy Norville. I assumed my best pre-tackle stance, and charged at him. He fell backward onto the partially attached bedroom door. It splintered apart with our combined weight as we fell together to the floor. He dropped his gun and I grabbed for it, just barely touching it with my fingertips. I reached for it again, but instead of grabbing it, I inadvertently knocked it across the room . . . right next to Ray Norville's identical automatic that Lori had given to me.

Norville and I both got up and scrambled for the guns, his younger eyes able to compensate for the darkness more quickly than mine. The two guns were identical and I didn't know which was which. I mentally counted the number of shots that Norville had fired in the room. Seven shots. There should be two shots left in his gun, and there would be none left in his brother's. We each snatched a gun at the same precise moment and scrambled to opposite sides of the room. Norville reached his side first and turned his barrel toward me. Moments later, I turned mine toward him.

"I'm going to kill you Hammond," Norville said, then he aimed the gun directly at my forehead.

I aimed my gun at Norville's forehead, then watched as he squeezed his trigger moments before I could fire my gun. I said a quick prayer, thought about Lori in the honeymoon suite, and closed my eyes . . . all in a fraction of a second.

Click.

Norville had picked up his brother's gun. I had the one with the bullets. I now had the power to kill the man who'd nearly blown my body into a million pieces and who had provided the drugs with the power to kill desperate people across the country. Then I looked over at Crystal and I thought about how she'd killed Rita Sandoval, Scott Mansell and—possibly—Walter Tompkins. I had two bullets in the gun. I could rid the earth of two evil predators with two quick pulls on the trigger. I could call it self defense and nobody could say otherwise.

I held the gun with the barrel aimed squarely at Norville's forehead, then repositioned it toward Crystal's. I began counting to three.

Then I heard a voice. "Hank, don't do it."

At first I thought it was my conscience speaking, but then I recognized it as Lori's voice. I glanced toward the door and saw Lori with Arturo and four uniformed police officers. The lights in the house suddenly came back on.

"You did well my *amigo*," Arturo said. "And your lovely Lori did well too. You make quite a team."

I lowered the gun as the police cuffed Norville and untied Crystal so that they could cuff her. A pair of paramedics rushed past me and tended to Walter. The first one looked back at me and gave me the thumbs up. I scanned the floor and spotted the syringe . . . still filled with the deadly dose that Crystal had intended for my client.

Lori and I rushed toward each other, embraced and kissed passionately until we simultaneously realized what we were doing and stopped. I blushed profusely, and Lori gave me her patented smirk.

EPILOGUE

I don't know what I would have done if Lori and Arturo hadn't arrived at the very moment that I was contemplating taking the law into my own hands. Perhaps I would have pulled the trigger and dispensed some instant justice. Perhaps I would have simply walked over to the phone and dialed 911.

What I do know is that Richard was cleared of all charges and has moved in with his grandfather so that he can take care of him . . . or vice versa. Walter was so ecstatic about having Richard back that he wrote me a bonus check.

Both of the Norville brothers are back in prison, although their accomplices in the drug smuggling ring are still out on some technicality that protects criminals and endangers innocent people. When I heard the rumor that the Norville's have put a price on my head, I joked that it had already been marked down to $1.97 and wouldn't be worth anybody's effort. But I still look over my shoulder every so often.

I'd gathered more than enough evidence for the police to book Treet, Metzger and Danny Murphy for various permutations of theft, trafficking in stolen property, committing fraud using the US Postal Service, as well as insurance fraud. I also learned that Jerry Wingate, Danny's former business partner, had killed himself because he couldn't live with his business's new practice of selling merchandise stolen from the La Jolla W-L's store.

In a sense, I suppose that I had inadvertently caused the so-called robbery at Danny's Discount. I'd noticed—but hadn't really thought much about it—that the robbery had occurred shortly after I'd resigned from my position at the Kingston Beach store. Treet had been providing Danny with merchandise from the La Jolla W-L's where he'd been the security manager. When I quit and Treet was transferred over to my position, it instantly dried up his merchandise supply . . . no wonder Treet had tried to turn down the transfer. During Danny's dry spell—before Treet could begin diverting merchandise to the Kingston Beach store—Danny became seriously short of merchandise, sales volume and profits. That was when he, Mansell and Metzger had faked a robbery so that he could collect enough money from his insurance policy to tide his business over until the Kingston Beach merchandise began arriving.

That whole situation with the robbery had puzzled me, but no more than why Walter had clipped out the article about it and placed it into the leather box. I had assumed that Walter thought his grandson had been one of the robbers. The truth was that Walter had cut it out because he'd been concerned about Richard working alone at the print shop with all the cash in the cash register—Walter had clipped the article to give to Richard as an example of why he needed to be careful at work. Walter had forgotten to give it to Richard, and had forgotten that it was in the box when he'd given it to me.

Two other outcomes came from my case. One being that I owe the discount rental company for a highly abused Geo Metro—my bonus from Walter only making up about half of the tab. The other being that a potential client heard about my bar-code investigation and just contacted me about a very confidential undercover assignment. Lori already has some ideas—communicated with a smirk—on how I might actually be able to make a profit on my next case.

AUTHOR'S NOTE

Thank you for reading **DOUBLE TAKE.**

Writers can only survive and flourish with the help of readers. If you like what you've read, please consider reviewing **DOUBLE TAKE** on Amazon and on your favorite readers' websites. Just three or four short sentences are all it takes to make a huge difference! Thank you.

Stay in touch at j-p-david.com

Please visit my website j-p-david.com where you can learn more about my writing. While you're there, please visit the CONTACT page where you are invited to write any thoughts to me that you may have. My readers know that my books are heavily researched, edited, proofed and professionally formatted. If you find errors, please let me know by writing me through the CONTACT page.

On j-p-david.com, you can sign up for my infrequent email updates about upcoming books, appearances, and other information. You have my promise that your email address will remain private and you will not receive any form of spam.

Once again, thank you for reading **DOUBLE TAKE.** I look forward to sharing Hank and Lori's next adventure with you!

ABOUT THE AUTHOR

J.P. David, a speaker at the 2016 Left Coast Crime mystery convention, is a member of Sisters in Crime and former coordinator of a Mystery Writers of America satellite. His first book, Double Take, was a Kindle Top-Ten seller in the detective category. He has a degree in creative writing from the California State University at Long Beach.

Before writing novels, J.P. likes to say that he wrote memos and company policies that nobody paid any attention to. Before climbing to (and jumping from) the top of the corporate ladder, J.P. supervised a team of store detectives, an experience that provided the inspiration for his private detective character, Hank Hammond.

MIND GAME
Coming early 2017

J.P.'s second book, **MIND GAME**, will be released in early 2017. For updates, please visit j-p-david.com.

Printed in Great Britain
by Amazon

47782733R00126